IS A WINNER!

"A rich ciminal lawyer announces he is going to give $5 million to an art museum. What could be safer than that? Unfortunately, the lawyer is found dead in the newspaper's parking lot, shot in the head. Fletch is pulled off the story, which is given to a veteran crime reporter. You think Fletch is going to leave it alone? Do hungry tigers like red meat? Fletch perseveres, breaking every rule in the journalistic book..."
—*Newgate Callendar*,
New York Times Book Review

"**Fletch Won** *is the eighth and one of the best in the series by former* Boston Globe *reporter Greg Mcdonald. Fletch's style is like no other. When he goes into a liquor store, the clerks hold him up. He ends up swimming naked in the victim's pool, is arrested for armed robbery and is offered a job as a male prostitute. Despite all these diversions, he solves the crime. Of course.*"

more . . .

About the Author

GREGORY MCDONALD is the author of sixteen books, including eight Fletch mystery novels and three Flynn mysteries. He has twice won the Mystery Writers of America's prestigious Edgar Award for "Best Mystery of the Year" for his Fletch novels—the only mystery author ever to have been so honored. A former reporter for the *Boston Globe*, he has published a collection of his writings from the 1960's, *The Education of Gregory Mcdonald*. Gregory Mcdonald lives near Boston and was recently elected President of the Mystery Writers of America.

GREGORY MCDONALD

Fletch Won

WARNER BOOKS

A Warner Communications Company

To Edward (Ned) Leavitt,
scholar, agent and friend.

WARNER BOOKS EDITION

Copyright © 1985 by Gregory Mcdonald
All rights reserved.

Book design by H. Roberts Design

Warner Books, Inc.
666 Fifth Avenue
New York, N.Y. 10103

A Warner Communications Company

Printed in the United States of America

This book was originally published in hardcover by
Warner Books, Inc.
First Printed in Paperback: April, 1986

10 9 8 7 6 5 4 3 2 1

1

"Did I ask to see you?"

"No, Frank, I—"

"I want to see you anyway." Frank Jaffe, The Editor, refolded the competing newspaper, the *Chronicle-Gazette*, and put it under his elbow on the desk. "I have some tough things to say to you."

"Little ol' me?"

"How would you like lifting a shovel eight hours a day, every day, five days a week, maybe half-days Saturdays?"

Fletch looked at his sneakers on the rug of Frank's office. Through the top of his left sneaker he saw the knuckles of three toes. Only the smallest toe showed through the top of his right sneaker. "It's not what I see for myself in the parade of life, Frank."

"That's what I see for you. In the parade of life, what do you see yourself suited for?"

"Journalism."

"And what's journalism, young Fletcher?"

"Developing the skill of ending sentences with prepositions? Especially questions?"

"Did I just do that?" Behind his thick lenses, Frank's watery eyes moved across the top of his messy desk. "I just did that."

"Frank, what I wanted to see you about—"

Frank opened a folder on his desk. "I've dug out your personnel file." The folder was not thick. "You're suited for journalism, or pick-and-shovel work. I wonder which it will be?"

"Why are you looking at my personnel file? You hired me months ago."

"Three months ago. Do you remember why? I don't."

"Because I can be really good, Frank. I—"

"I think I had the idea this newspaper needed a breath of fresh air, young maverick who would shake things up a bit, see things differently, maybe, jerk people out of their ruts."

"How can I do that, Frank, if you won't give me a job?"

"I've given you a job. Lots of jobs."

"Not a real job."

"First, I put you on the copy desk."

"Writing headlines is for poets, Frank."

"And kept you there, over the growing protests of your co-workers, I might add—"

"I spilled orange soda on somebody's terminal keyboard."

"That's not all you did."

"I made it up to him. I bought him a pair of surgical gloves."

"—until you wrote the headline GOVERNOR JOKES ON PURPOSE."

"I thought that was news."

"And somehow the headline appeared in two editions before being killed."

"Sheer poetry, Frank. Not long-lived poetry, I admit, not deathless poetry, but—"

"So then I assigned you to writing obituaries."

"You know I want to write sports, Frank. That's why I came in to see you this morning."

"Not the toughest job in the world, writing obituaries. You answer the phone, listen politely, sometimes you have to check a few facts."

"I'm very good at checking facts."

Frank held up a piece of paper. His hand quivered and his eyes shook as he read the first paragraph from it. " 'Ruth Mulholland died peacefully today, having accomplished nothing in her fifty-six years.' Did you write that?"

"It was a fact, Frank. I checked."

"Fletcher, one of the points in your writing obituaries is in our being able to print them."

"I kept asking her sister, *What did she ever do!* The sister kept talking. But I was listening, you see. This person, Ruth Mulholland, never graduated from anywhere, never got married, never had a baby, never held a job, never even supported herself. I mean, in fifty-six years she never accomplished a damned thing. Finally, I asked the sister, Did she ever make anybody a sweater? Cook a pan of brownies for anybody? Or even for herself? The sister kept saying, No, no, in fact Ruthie never did a damned thing in her life. I said, Well, is that what I should print? And the sister said, Well, yes, I guess that's the truth about Ruthie. I checked the facts, Frank. Ruthie never applied for Social Security, or a driver's license; she didn't even support her local beauty shop!"

"Fletcher—"

"What, there's not supposed to be any truth in obituaries? When someone has won the Nobel Prize we print that in an obituary. When someone accomplishes exactly nothing in life, why don't we print that? Doing absolutely nothing is a statement, Frank, a response to life. It's news, it's interesting."

"Ruthie didn't get her obituary printed, either." Frank held up another shaking piece of paper. "So you were assigned to

writing wedding announcements. That's just a job of taking
dictation. You don't even have to be responsible for the main
fact, the wedding, because it hasn't taken place yet. Your
very first announcement read, 'Sarah and Roland Jameson,
first cousins, are to be married Wednesday in a ceremony
restricted to family.''

"Crisp."

"Crisp," Frank agreed.

"Concise."

"Concise."

"To the point."

"Absolutely to the point."

"And," Fletch said, "factual."

"Took talent, to dig that story out."

"Not much. When the mother of the bride called, I simply
asked her why both the bride and groom had the same last
name."

"And she answered you without hesitation?"

"She hesitated."

"She said they were first cousins?"

"She said their fathers were brothers."

"And neither the bride nor the groom was adopted, right?"

"Frank, I checked. What do you think I am?"

"I think you're an inexperienced journalist."

"If the rules of journalism apply on political and crime and
sports pages, why don't they apply on obituaries and wedding-
announcement pages? Newspapers are supposed to tell both
sides of a story, right? Pah! Sundays we devote pages and
pages to wedding announcements. Why don't we give equal
space to divorce announcements?"

"Fletcher—"

"News is news, Frank."

"You think that by writing obituaries and wedding announcements in this heavy-handed, factual way is how you're
going to get yourself assigned to the sports pages, is that it?"

"Truth is truth, Frank."

"Someday, Fletcher, may you be a victim of someone like yourself." Through his pupils dipped in clam juice, Frank looked at Fletcher. "You're getting married Saturday?"

"Yes. Next Saturday."

"Why?"

"Barbara has the day open."

"Unless the purpose is to have children," Frank said slowly, "marriage is a legal institution guaranteeing only that you get screwed by lawyers."

"You don't believe in true love "

"True Love ran at Saratoga Saturday. Made a strong start, faded fast, and ended at the back of the pack. I suppose you expect time off, for a honeymoon?"

"Barbara's rather counting on it. That's another thing I wanted to see you about."

"You haven't worked here a year yet. In fact, some say you haven't worked here at all yet!"

"Yeah, but, Frank, how many times in life do you have a honeymoon?"

"Don't ask. Why are you so sunburned?"

"I ran in the Sardinal Race yesterday."

"Your hair looks like it hasn't crossed the finish line yet." Fletch smiled. "There's a story there."

"In your hair? I'd believe anything is in your hair."

"In the race. Do you know about the Ben Franklyn Friend Service?"

"Guess I don't."

"Basically, it's a company specializing in health and prostitution."

"What?"

"You call them and this sultry voice answers, saying, 'Ben Franklyn Friend Service. You want a friend?' Only sometimes she slurs a little, and it sounds more like, 'You want to, friend?' "

"You call them often?"

"The guys on the desk played a joke on me one night. They told me to phone out for pizzas and that was the number they gave me. The girl on the phone was trying to set up an appointment for me, and I kept asking if she had anchovies and pepperoni. I guess she thought I was a pervert. You ought to call them sometime."

"I need a friend."

"So I looked into 'em. Big business. Beautiful girls. All of 'em in great physical condition. They're made to work out, you know?"

"What's the story?"

"They were running yesterday. In the race. All of 'em. A flotilla of call girls. About twelve of them, all together. Running through the city streets. Downtown. Wearing T-shirts that read in front, YOU WANT A FRIEND?, and in back, BEN FRANKLYN. They all made it to the finish, too."

"So what's the story? Don't tell me. I've got it." Frank put his hands to his forehead. "STREETWALKERS JOG—"

"Joggle."

"CALL GIRLS COME RUNNING?"

"Consider their leg muscles, Frank."

"I'm all excited."

"They were advertising their business, Frank."

"So where did you finish in this race?"

"Right behind them. I was following a story, you might say."

"Faithful to the last."

"You're not getting the point."

"I'm not?"

"These call girls were using a city-run health and sports event to advertise their service."

"So a few prostitutes ran in the city footrace yesterday. Why shouldn't they? Not against the law. They wore T-shirts advertising their services. Gave thrills to a few dirty old men leg-watchers standing on the curbs. So where's the story?"

"You ran pictures of them today. On your sports pages. Coming and going. Front and back."

Frank paled. "We did?"

"*You* did."

"Jeez!" Frank grabbed the *News-Tribune* off the floor and turned to the sports pages. "We did."

"There's the story."

"You mean, we're the story."

"Gave a call-girl service a nice big spread. Lots of free publicity. Have you heard from the archbishop yet? How about the district attorney? Any of your advertisers object?"

"Damn. Someone did this on purpose."

"You need me on the sports pages, Frank."

"Look at the caption. Oh, my God. *Physical beauty and stamina exemplified by employees of the Ben Franklyn Service Company who ran together yesterday in the city's Sardinal Race. Group finished near end of race* . . . I can't stand it."

"They weren't in any hurry."

"Neither were you, apparently."

"You were just telling me never to get ahead of my story."

"Get up and come into the office early Monday morning . . ." Frank was tearing through the competing newspaper, the *Chronicle-Gazette*, on his desk, trying to find the sports pages. ". . . Have to waste the damned day firing people . . ."

"The *Gazette* didn't run pictures of the call girls, Frank. Front or back. They just ran pictures of the winners. Jeez, they practice tired old journalism over there."

Frank sat back in his chair. He looked like a boxer between rounds. "Why did I have to start off the week by seeing you?"

"Bring a little freshness to your life. A few laughs. Shake

you up a bit. Make you see a few things differently, like a couple of photos on your sports page.''

"You own a necktie?''

"Sure.''

"I've never seen it.''

"It's holding one end of my surfboard off the floor.''

"I suppose you're serious. What's holding up the other end?''

Fletch looked down at the top of his jeans. "A belt someone gave me.''

"I decided over the weekend to give you one more chance.'' Frank looked at his watch.

"You're going to try me out as a sportswriter!''

"No. After all, what companies do is expect youth, energy, and experience all from the same person. That's not fair.''

"The police beat? Fine!''

"Thought we might try knocking a few of the rough edges off you.''

"City Hall? I can do it. Just give me a score card.''

"So I figure it's experience, polish, you need. You do own a suit, don't you?''

"The courts! Damn, you want me to cover the courts. I know how the courts work, Frank. Remarkable how little they have to do with the law, you know? I—''

"Society.''

"Society?''

"Society. Seeing you're so quick to identify deceased people who never accomplished a damned thing in their lives, and point out to the public first cousins who intend to marry each other, I think you might have a little talent for covering society.''

"You mean society, like in high society?''

"High society, low society, you know, lifestyles: all those features that cater to the anxieties of our middle-class readers.''

"Frank, I don't believe in society.''

"That's okay, Fletch. Society doesn't believe in you, either."

"I'd be no good at it."

"You might be attractive, if you combed your hair."

"Little old ladies slipping vodka into their tea?"

"Habeck. Donald Edwin Habeck."

"Didn't he once try out as goalie for the Red Wings?"

"If you read anything other than the sports pages, Fletcher, you'd know Donald Edwin Habeck is one of this neighborhood's more sensational attorneys."

"Is he on an exciting case?"

"Habeck called me last night and said he and his wife have decided, after much discussion, to give five million dollars to the art museum. You're interested in art, aren't you?"

"Not as poker chips."

"He wants the story treated right, you know? With dignity. No invasion of their privacy, no intrusion into their personal lives."

"Frank, would you mind if I sit down?"

"Help yourself. I forgot you ran slowly in a footrace yesterday."

Fletch sat on the rug.

"Sit anywhere."

"Thanks. La-di-da philanthropy."

"Finish the verse and you may have a hit song."

"Frank, you want me, I.M. Fletcher, to do an arm's length, hands off, veddy, veddy polite story about some for-God's-sake society couple who are giving five million pieces of tissue paper to the art museum?"

"Polite, yes. Why not polite? Here are a couple of people doing something nice for the world, sharing their wealth. Curb your need to report Mrs. Habeck slips vodka into her tea. Time you learned how to be polite. By the way, I can't see you over the edge of the desk."

"I disappeared."

"Well, you'd better reappear. You're meeting with Habeck in the publisher's office at ten o'clock. Pity your necktie and belt are holding up your surfboard."

"God! Any story which starts with the reporter meeting the subject in the publisher's office isn't worth getting up for."

"See? You're improving as a journalist already. You just ended a sentence with a preposition."

"I won't do it."

"Fletch, I'm pretty sure you'd be just as attractive working a pick and shovel in the city streets. You wouldn't have to wear a necktie, belt, or comb your hair. I can arrange to have you leave here Friday and you and Lucy can take as long a honeymoon as you can afford."

"Might make a nice weekend. And her name's Barbara."

"I thought so. Sunday bliss with Barbara. Tuesday with blisters."

"Frank, why don't you let Habeck write the story himself? He's paying five million dollars for the privilege."

Hamm Starbuck stuck his head around the office door. He looked at Fletch sitting cross-legged on the rug. "It's that kind of morning, is it?"

"So far," Frank answered. "Floored one. After glancing at certain photos on the sports page, I see I have a few more to floor today."

"Frank, were you expecting Donald Habeck?"

"Not me. John's expecting him. He should be sent to the publisher's office."

"He'll never make it."

"He telephoned?"

"No. He's dead in the parking lot."

Frank asked, "What do you mean?"

"In a dark blue Cadillac Seville. Bullet hole in his temple."

Fletch sprang off the floor without using his hands. "My story!"

"Guess we should call the police."

"Get the photographers down there first," Frank said.

"Already done that."

"Also Biff Wilson. Has he reported in yet?"

"I radioed him. He's on the freeway."

"Biff Wilson!" Fletch said. "Frank, you gave this story to me."

"I haven't given you anything, Fletcher."

'Habeck, Donald Edwin. Was I supposed to interview him at ten o'clock?"

"Fletcher, do me a favor."

"Anything, Frank."

"Get lost. Report to Ann McGarrahan in Society."

"Maybe there's a necktie in my car."

"I just made a career decision," Frank said to his desk.

"What's that, Frank?"

"I'm not coming into the office early Monday mornings anymore."

2

"Habeck, Harrison and Haller. Good morning."

"Hello, H cubed?"

"Habeck, Harrison and Haller. May I help you?"

"Mr. Chambers, please."

"I'm sorry, sir. Would you repeat that name?"

"Mr. Chambers." Looking across the city room of the *News-Tribune*, no one could guess that someone had just been shot to death in the parking lot of that building, and that everyone there knew it. Did everyone know it? Absolutely. In a newspaper office, unlike most other companies, the process of rumor becoming gossip becoming fact becoming substantiated, reliable news was professionally accelerated. It happened with the speed of a rocket. Assimilation of news happened just as fast. Journalists are interested in the stories they are working on; some have a mental filing cabinet, some a wastebasket into which they drop all other news. "Alston Chambers, please. He's somewhere down in your stacks, I expect. An intern lawyer, a trainee, whatever you call him. A veteran and a gentleman.''

"Oh, yes, sir. A. Chambers.''

"Probably drifting around your corridors, without a place to wrinkle his trousers.''

"One moment, sir.'' A line was ringing. The telephone operator had to add, "Excuse me, sir, for not recognizing the name. Mr. Chambers does not have clients.''

"Chambers speaking.''

"Sounds sepulchral.''

"Must be Fletcher.''

"Must be.''

"Hope you've called me for lunch. I gotta get out of this place.''

"In fact, I have. One o'clock at Manolo's?''

"You want to discuss your wedding. You want my advice as to how to get out of it. Does Barbara still have it scheduled for Saturday?''

"No, no, yes. Can't talk right now, Alston. Just want to give you the news.''

"Barbara's told you she's pregnant?''

"Habeck, Harrison and Haller. That the law firm you work for?''

"You know it. Bad pay and all the shit I can take.''

"Donald Edwin Habeck?''

"One of the senior partners in this den of legal inequity.''

"Donald Edwin Habeck won't be in today. Thought I'd call in for him.''

"I don't get it. Why not? What's the joke?''

"He's been shot to death.''

"This is a joke?''

"Not from his point of view.''

"Where, when?''

"At the *News-Tribune*. A few minutes ago. I gotta go.''

"I wonder if he left a will.''

"Why do you say that?''

"Lawyers are famous for not writing wills for themselves."

"Alston, I'd appreciate it at lunch if you'd talk to me about Habeck. Tell me what you know."

"You on the story?"

"I think so."

"Does anyone else think so?"

"I'm on it until I'm ordered off it."

"Fletch, you're getting married Saturday. This is no time to flirt with unemployment."

"See you at one o'clock at Manolo's."

3

"Did he do himself?" Fletch was looking over Biff's shoulder into the front seat of the Cadillac.

A man in his sixties was slumped over the armrest. His left leg hung out of the car. His shoe almost touched the ground.

Biff turned his head slowly to look at Fletch. His look said that plebeians were not supposed to initiate conversations with royalty.

"Or was he shot?"

Not answering, Biff Wilson stood up and turned. He waited for Fletch to move out of the way. Despite the heat, the strong sun in the parking lot, Biff wore a suit jacket and tie, although his shirt collar was loosened. Hair grew out of his ears.

Biff walked the few steps to the three policemen standing by the black-and-white police car. Only two of the police were in uniform.

"Do we know who found him yet?" Biff asked.

"Do *we?*" Fletch said to himself.

The younger uniformed officer was staring at Fletch.

Three cars were parked at odd angles around the blue Cadillac. One was the plainclothesman's unmarked green sedan. The second was the black-and-white sedan, front door open, police radio crackling, red and blue roof lights rotating.

The third said NEWS-TRIBUNE on the sides and back. This was the car Biff Wilson used. Its front door was open, too. Radios crackled from its interior. And a blue light flashed from its roof as well.

The older man in uniform looked at his notebook. "Female employee of the *News-Tribune* named Pilar O'Brien."

Biff let spit drop on the sidewalk between his shoes. "Never heard of her."

"Suppose she's a secretary."

"And she called the cops?"

"She told the security guard at the gate."

"And he called the cops?"

"No," said the plainclothesman. "He called the news desk."

Biff's smile glinted. "Everybody's buckin' for promotion."

"Your photographers have already come and gone," said the older uniform.

"They didn't touch anything," the youngest cop said. "I saw to that. Photographed him from the side and through the windshield. Took a few long shots. Didn't touch the car or the victim."

"Gun been found?" Biff asked.

"Not visible. Might have slipped under the seat," said the plainclothesman. "Where's forensics? I want my coffee."

"Donald E. Habeck," the older uniform read from his notebook. "Anyone know what he was doing here?"

"Yeah," Biff answered. "He was here to see John Winters, the publisher. Ten-o'clock appointment. They were going to set up the announcement that Habeck and his wife are going to, *were* going to, give five million bucks to the art museum."

"How do you know that, Biff?" the plainclothesman asked.

"How do I know everything, Gomez?" Again Biff spat on the sidewalk.

"I know you're the greatest, Biff. I spent all last night tellin' my wife that."

Biff shrugged. "Car telephone, jerk. Hamm Starbuck said Donald Habeck was dead in the parking lot. I asked him, What's he doin' at the *News-Tribune?* Wouldn't you say that's a natural question?"

"That's why I just asked it, Biff." At least Gomez had taken off his coat and rolled up his sleeves.

There was no shade in the parking lot.

The younger uniformed policeman kept giving Fletch long, hard looks.

"Five million dollars. Jeez." The older uniformed policeman rubbed his forehead with his sleeve. "Think of bein' able to give away five million dollars."

"You've never been able to do that?" Biff asked.

"Saturday I gave my niece and her new husband an old couch we had in the den. Slob didn't even come for it. I had to truck it over myself."

"Nice of you," Biff said.

"Didn't get no story about myself in the newspaper for it, though."

"Maybe Biff will write you up a story," Gomez said.

"Sure," Biff said. "Friday night I gave my kid a welt under his left eye. I'm generous, too."

"Here comes your competition, Biff." Gomez nodded toward the security gate.

There were two cars there from the *Chronicle-Gazette*.

"Sunday I realized how much I missed that couch. I had to sit up during the ball game. And my back was sore from movin' the damned thing the day before."

The younger uniformed cop touched Biff's sleeve and then pointed to Fletch. He spoke quietly. "He with you?"

Biff considered Fletch from his throne as *News-Tribune* crime writer. "Naw."

"Does he work for the *News-Tribune?*"

"I dunno." Biff was not keeping his voice low. "Maybe I've seen him around. Emptying wastebaskets."

"Didn't know the *News-Tribune* had any wastebaskets," Gomez said. "Just delivery trucks."

At the gate the security guard was delaying the arrival of the *Chronicle-Gazette*'s reporter and photographer at the scene of the crime.

"Haven't you had any coffee yet this morning?" Biff asked Gomez.

"Only two cups," Gomez said. "Anglo."

"You act like you haven't had any."

"El mismo," Gomez said.

"Because I've seen something about that guy," the younger officer said. "Recently. A picture, or something."

Biff fixed Fletch with his distant gaze again. "Maybe on the funnies page."

Finally the two cars from the *Chronicle-Gazette* reached the scene of the crime. Neither had lights flashing nor radios crackling.

"Don't you guys touch anything," the younger uniformed officer shouted at them.

The reporter said, "Shut up." He looked into the car.

The photographer was bending around taking pictures without the reporter in them.

"Who is he?" the reporter asked.

"Not confirmed," Biff answered.

"Employee of the *News-Tribune?*"

"Probably," Biff answered. "Most of us have Caddy Sevilles. I let my kid take mine to school."

"Security guard must know who he is," the reporter said. "He must have given a name when he came in."

"Go ask him," Biff said.

"This is your story, uh, Biff?" the reporter asked.

"It happened in his backyard," Gomez said.

"Yeah," the reporter said. "Expect I can make something of that. Murder in the parking lot of a family newspaper. Tsk, tsk."

"That's Habeck," said the photographer. "Donald Habeck, the attorney. Rich guy. Lives over in The Heights."

"Yeah?" said the reporter. "What's he doin' here?"

"Natural question," said Biff.

"Yet to be determined," said Gomez.

"How long you been workin' for the *News-Tribune*, Gomez?" the reporter asked.

"Nothing's going to be said until the medical examiner and forensics team have come and gone," Gomez answered.

"Not by you." The reporter went to his car and began talking into his telephone.

"Here they come." Gomez nodded at the station wagons coming through the security gate into the parking lot. "Want to get some coffee inside, Biff?"

Biff looked at the side of the *News-Tribune* building. "Coffee's no good in there, either."

"I'll get Maria to make some special."

"Oh, yeah," Biff said. "I forgot your sister-in-law works in the cafeteria."

"You did like hell. You got her the job."

Fletch began moving out of the area into which the forensics team was moving.

The younger uniformed policeman said to Fletch, "You work here?"

"Naw," said Fletch. "Just makin' a delivery. Just bringin' Mr. Wilson his uppers."

The young cop looked alert. "His uppers?"

"Yeah," said Fletch. "He really messed 'em up last night with taffy apple. Took the dental lab an hour to get 'em clean this morning."

"Oh."

The older uniformed policeman was looking inside the car at Donald Edwin Habeck. "I'll bet my giving away that old couch," he said slowly, "meant more to me than this guy's givin' away five million bucks."

4

"*News-Tribune* resource desk. Code and name, please."

"Seventeen ninety dash nine," Fletch answered into the car phone. He was driving toward The Heights. "Fletcher."

"I haven't had a call from you before."

"They don't let me out much."

"We have some messages for you."

"I want the address for Mr. and Mrs. Donald Edwin Habeck. I believe that's H-A-B-E-C-K, somewhere in The Heights."

"That's 12339 Palmiera Drive."

"Mapping?"

"It's a little road northwest of Washington Boulevard. There are lots of little roads in there. Winding roads. Your best bet would be to stop at intersection of Washington and Twenty-third and get exact directions. You'll be turning onto Twenty-third there."

"Okay."

"Messages are, call Barbara Ralton. She wants lunch with you. Says she has things to discuss."

"Like how many babies we're gonna have?"

"My, my. This old mother suggests you have lunch before you pick up on that heavy topic."

"Thank you."

"See how much it costs to feed just two mouths."

"It doesn't cost much to feed a kid. Just squirt orange juice into him a few times a day. Peanut butter."

"Ha."

"Beg pardon?"

"Ha."

"How much does peanut butter cost?"

The bumper sticker on the car in front of Fletch read: NASTINESS WILL GET YOU EVERYWHERE.

"Should have taken my own advice and stayed in bed. One more message for you, Fletcher. From Ann McGarrahan, society-page editor. She said if you phoned in to tell you to report to her immediately. Your assignment has been changed."

"Oh."

"So it looks like you don't need that address in The Heights after all."

"One more question: Who is Pilar O'Brien?"

"Why do you want to know?"

"What kind of answer is that?"

"A personal answer. Why do you want to know?"

"Just heard of her. Does she work for the *News-Tribune?*"

A hesitation slightly longer than normal before the *News-Tribune* resource-desk person said, "You're talking to her."

"Ah! Then you're the lady who found Habeck this morning."

"Who?"

"The guy dead in the parking lot."

"Is that his name? I thought you just asked for the address of—"

"Forget about that, will you?"

"How can I? How can a reporter I never heard of before be asking for the address of—"

"I said, please forget about that. I never asked."

"Mrs. McGarrahan—"

"I'll call her. Tell me about finding Habeck."

"I'm not permitted to talk to any reporters until after the police question me. Then I may only report what I told the police."

"Jeez, you know the rules."

"That's what Mr. Starbuck said."

"When you found him, was the car door opened or closed?"

"I can't answer you."

"It's important."

"Maybe that's why I can't answer you."

"Did you see a gun?"

"What's-your-name...Fletcher. Shall I tell Mrs. McGarrahan you're returning to the office?"

"Sure," Fletch said. "Tell her that."

"Would you please give me directions to Palmiera Drive?"

The eyes of the man behind the counter of the liquor store at the intersection of Washington Boulevard and Twenty-third Street shifted from Fletch through the store window to Fletch's Datsun 300 ZX outside the front door, motor running, and back to Fletch. There was a hole in the car's muffler. The engine was noisy.

"I'm looking for the twelve-thousand block of Palmiera Drive, if there is such a thing."

Looking Fletch full in the face, the man behind the counter whistled the first few bars of "Colonel Bogey's March."

"Do I turn right on Twenty-third Street?"

The man raised a .45 automatic pistol from beneath the counter. He pointed it at Fletch's heart.

"Jeez," Fletch said. "I'm being held up by a liquor store!"

Fletch was grabbed from behind. Muscular brown arms, fingers clasped just under Fletch's rib cage, pinned Fletch's own arms to his side.

"Hey!" Fletch yelled. "I asked politely!"

The gun kept Fletch's heart as its target.

The man holding the gun called toward the back of the store, "Rosa! Call the cops!"

"I'll get the muffler fixed!" Fletch said. "I promise!"

"Report a robbery in progress!" the man behind the counter shouted.

"All I did was ask for directions! I didn't even ask for change for a parking meter!"

"He ain't got no gun," the voice behind Fletch's ear rumbled.

The man behind the counter looked at Fletch's hands and then the pockets of his jeans.

"Let me point out to you," Fletch said with great sincerity, "you can't shoot me with that cannon without blowing away the guy behind me."

The gun wavered. The steel bands clamping Fletch's arms to his sides slackened just slightly.

"Workmen's Compensation won't cover!" Fletch yelled as he ran backward, pushing the guy holding him.

Within a meter, they crashed into a tall, wire bottle rack.

Instantly, as bottles smashed, there was the reek of bourbon.

The guy's hands disappeared from in front of Fletch. "I'm gettin' cut," he yelled.

Sitting on the guy's lap, Fletch bounced up and down once or twice, then he leaned back against his chest.

"Ow!" the guy yelled.

Bottles were raining down on them. One landed on Fletch's left knee, causing more pain than Fletch thought possible.

The bottles that hit the floor smashed and splashed bourbon over both of them.

The guy with the gun was moving along the counter trying to get a bead on Fletch that did not include the guy Fletch was sitting on.

Fletch rolled through broken glass and bourbon puddles to the door. "Last time I'll ask you guys for directions!"

As he stood up he grabbed the door open.

Halfway through the door the gun banged. The breakproof glass in the door shattered.

Opening his car door, Fletch shouted back at the store, "If you don't know where Palmiera Drive is, why don't you just say so?"

At a sedate pace, he turned right off Washington onto Twenty-third.

Sirens filled the air.

5

"Mrs. Habeck?"

The lady with blued hair, flower-patterned dress, and green sneakers sat in a straight chair alone by the swimming pool. There was a red purse near her feet.

"Yes, I'm Mrs. Habeck."

Looking up at Fletch in the sunlight, her nose twitched like a rabbit's.

"I.M. Fletcher. *News-Tribune*. I was to meet your husband at ten o'clock."

"He's not here."

Fletch had spent a moment ringing the front doorbell of 12339 Palmiera Drive. It was a nice property, a brick house floating on rhododendrons, but not, to Fletch's mind, the home of someone who could or would give away five million dollars without taking deep breaths.

And there was no one in the house to open the door to him on a Monday morning.

Fletch had explored through the rhododendrons until he

found the blued-haired lady contemplating the clear, unruffled swimming pool.

"One never knows where he is," Mrs. Habeck said. "Donald wanders away. That's the only thing, for certain, that can be said for Donald. He wanders away." She reached out her hand and closed her fingers as if grabbing something that wasn't there. She said, "He wanders."

"Maybe I can talk to you."

Again her nose twitched. "Young man, are you very, very drunk?"

"No, ma'am. Do I seem drunk?"

"You smell drunk."

Fletch held a section of his T-shirt up to his nose and sniffed it. "That's my new deodorant. Do you like it?"

"It's an odorant."

"It's called Bamn-o."

"It's called bourbon." Mrs. Habeck averted her nose. "You reek of bourbon."

Fletch sniffed his T-shirt again. "It is pretty bad, isn't it."

"I know bourbon when I smell it," said Mrs. Habeck. "You're not wearing a very good brand."

"It was on special sale, I think."

"Friday that bourbon did not exist." Mrs. Habeck spoke slowly, and there was sadness in her small, gray eyes. "I've heard of you newspapermen. Donald once told me about a journalist he knew who filled his waterbed with bourbon. He told his friends he had refined the art of being sloshed. Lying there, he could nip from the waterbed's valve. He said he could get the motion of his bourbonbed to match exactly the swing and sway of the world as he got drunk. Well, he sank lower and lower. Within three months he was back sleeping flat on the floor." Mrs. Habeck resettled her hands in her lap. "It was a double bed, too."

Fletch took a deep breath and held it. He sensed that Mrs. Habeck would be offended by laughter.

Tightening his stomach muscles to restrain himself, he looked away across the pool. Down a grassy slope, a gardener wearing a sombrero was weeding a flower bed.

"Oh, my," he finally said, sighing. "Truth is, I had an accident."

"You people always have an excuse for drinking. Good news. Bad news. No news."

"No," Fletch said. "A real accident. I stopped at the liquor store at the intersection of Washington and Twenty-third, and while I was there, a rack of bourbon got tipped over. It splashed all over an employee and me."

Her pale, sad eyes studied Fletch.

"I haven't been drinking. Honest. May I sit down?"

Reluctantly, she said, "All right."

He sat in another wrought-iron straight chair. She was in the shade of the table's umbrella, but he was not.

"About this five million dollars, Mrs. Habeck . . ."

"Five million dollars," she repeated.

". . . you and your husband decided to give to the art museum?"

Slowly, she said, "Yussss," in the hiss of a deflating tire. "Tell me about it."

"What?"

"What about it?" she asked.

Fletch hesitated. "I was hoping you'd tell me about it."

Mrs. Habeck drew herself up slightly in the chair. "Yes, well, my husband and I decided to give five million dollars to the art museum."

"I know that much. Your husband is a lawyer?"

"My husband," said Mrs. Habeck, "wanders off. Away, away. He always has, you know. That's something that can be said about him."

"I see," Fletch said politely. He was beginning to wonder how much vodka Mrs. Habeck had slipped into her morning coffee. "He's senior partner in the firm of Habeck, Harrison and Haller?"

"I told him he shouldn't do that," Mrs. Habeck said, frowning. "Three different *H* sounds. In fact, three different *Ha* sounds." Still frowning, she looked at Fletch. "Don't you agree?"

"Of course," said Fletch. "Disconcerting."

"Gives the impression of inconsistency," she said. "As if, you know, the partners couldn't be counted on to get together on anything. To agree."

"Yes," said Fletch.

"To say nothing of the fact that when people say 'Habeck, Harrison and Haller,' what they actually hear themselves saying, underneath everything, you know? is *Ha Ha Ha.*"

"Ah," said Fletch.

"Except the actual sound is *Hay Ha Haw.* Which is worse."

"Much worse," agreed Fletch. His fingers wiped the perspiration off his forehead.

"I wanted him to take on a fourth partner," said Mrs. Habeck. "Named Burke."

"Umm. Didn't Mr. Burke wish to join the firm?"

Mrs. Habeck looked at Fletch resentfully. "Donald said he didn't know anyone named Burke."

"Oh. I see."

"At least not any lawyer named Burke. Not any lawyer named Burke who was free to join the firm."

"Did you know a lawyer named Burke free to join the firm?"

"No."

Sweating in bourbon-soaked clothes in the sunlight, Fletch's head was beginning to reel. He felt like he was on a bourbonbed. "Does your husband do any corporate-law work?"

"No," she said. "He was never a bit cooperative. He was always arguing in court."

There was still no humor in her sad eyes.

"I know his reputation is as a criminal lawyer." Then Fletch cringed, awaiting what Mrs. Habeck would make of *criminal lawyer*.

She said, "Yussss."

Fletch blew air. "Mrs. Habeck, did you or your husband have any income other than that derived from his practice of criminal law, and from his partnership in Habeck, Harrison and Haller?"

"Hay, Ha, Haw," she said.

"I mean, were either of you personally wealthy, had you inherited . . . ?"

Mrs. Habeck said, "My husband is most apt to wear black shoes. You don't see black shoes too often in The Heights. He doesn't like to dress flamboyantly, as many criminal lawyers do."

Fletch waited a moment.

She asked, "You wouldn't think a man who wears black shoes would be so apt to wander away, would you?"

He waited another moment. "It isn't that I'm trying to invade your privacy, Mrs. Habeck."

"I don't have any privacy." She looked at her green sneakers.

"It's just that I'm trying to assess what donating five million dollars to the museum means to you and your husband. I mean, is he almost giving away the proceeds of his life's work?"

"Mister, you're making me sick."

"Beg pardon?"

"The smell of you. You seem sober enough, for a newspaperman, for a young man, but you reek of bourbon. It's beginning to affect my stomach, and my head."

"I'm sorry," Fletch said. "Truth be known, me, too."

"Well? What are we going to do about it?"

Fletch looked at the back of the house. "Maybe I could go take a shower."

"If you said bourbon got splashed all over your clothes, your taking a shower and putting the same clothes back on won't do any good."

"Right," said Fletch. "That's very sensible." He nodded. "Very sensible."

"Why don't you jump in the pool? It's right there."

"I could do that." Fletch began taking things out of his pockets. "With my clothes on."

"Why would you jump into the pool with your clothes on?"

"To get the smell of bourbon off them?"

"But then your clothes would be wet. You want to go around the rest of the day in wet clothes?"

"It's a hot day."

"Hotness has nothing to do with wetness."

"Hotness?"

"My daughter used to say that. When she was a little girl. *Hotness*. No wonder she ended up married to a poet. What's his name?"

"I don't know."

"Tom Farliegh."

"Okay. I was going to ask you about your children."

"They're fine, thank you. Obviously, you take your clothes off before you jump in the pool."

"Then I won't have any clothes on."

"I mind? I'm a mother and a grandmother. I don't mind. This is a private pool." She looked down the slope at the gardener. "That's Pedro. He doesn't mind. If he minds seeing a naked man, he shouldn't be a gardener."

"Clearly."

Mrs. Habeck stood up. "Take off your clothes. I'll avert my eyes so you can tell your girl friend no woman has seen you naked since your mother last changed your diapers. Last week, was it?''

Fletch was taking off his sneakers. ''Really, I don't mind.''

''Leave your clothes on the chair. After you get in the pool, say *Hallooo*, and I'll pick up your clothes, take them inside, and put them in the washer and then the dryer.''

''This is very nice of you.'' Standing, Fletch peeled off his stinking T-shirt.

''Hallooo!'' Mrs. Habeck called loudly. She was waving at the gardener.

He raised his head and looked at her from under his sombrero. He did not speak or wave back.

Fletch averted his eyes. He took off his jeans and underpants and dived into the pool.

Enjoying the cool water and getting away from the stink of his clothes, he drifted underwater across the pool, turned, and swam back to the nearer edge.

He stuck his nose above the edge of the pool.

''Hallooo,'' he said.

Mrs. Habeck was already headed for the house with his clothes and sneakers.

She was also carrying her red pocketbook.

6

"Hey!"

It was the third time Fletch had heard someone yell that, but this time, just as he was about to make his turn between laps, the shout was distinct. There could be no doubt it was he who was being hailed. He put his hand on the pool ledge and raised his head.

As water cleared from his opened eyes, he saw Biff Wilson, fully dressed, including suit coat and tie, standing on the pool edge.

"Hallooo," Fletch said.

"God," Biff said. "It's you."

"No, it's not," said Fletch. "It's Fletcher."

Two meters behind Biff stood Lieutenant Gomez.

"That your name? Fletcher?"

"Yes, sir."

"You were just in the parking lot of the *News-Tribune*."

"Yes, sir."

"How did you get here so fast?"

"I didn't stop for coffee."

"Are you the reason that young cop asked me if I have false teeth?"

"False what?"

Biff stuck his thumb under his upper front teeth and demonstrated how solid they were. "False feeph!"

"Gee, Biff, that gum cement you use must be pretty good."

Biff gave Gomez a tired look, then turned to Fletch. "Are you or are you not an employee of the *News-Tribune*?"

"I am. Sir."

Biff spoke distinctly. "What is your assignment?"

"I am newly assigned to Society."

"Society." Biff's face expressed the contempt he had for society writers. "What are you doing here?"

"Here?"

"Here. At the home of Donald Edwin Habeck."

"Swimming, sir."

Biff exploded at Gomez. "He's swimming bare-assed!"

Fletch said, "I was assigned to interview Donald Habeck at ten o'clock this morning regarding the five million dollars he and his wife had decided to donate to the art museum."

"But you knew Donald Habeck was dead! I saw you in the parking lot!"

Fletch shrugged. "Obstacles are encountered in doing any story."

As if personally offended, Biff shouted at the sky, "He's swimming bare-assed in the murder victim's pool!"

Lieutenant Gomez stepped closer to the pool edge. "What have you done since you've been here?"

"I interviewed, I tried to interview, Mrs. Habeck."

The eyes of both men widened.

"Did you see Mrs. Habeck?" Gomez asked.

"Yes."

"Tell us about Mrs. Habeck," Biff said. "What does she look like?"

"About sixty. Blue hair. Green sneakers. A sort of weird lady."

Biff and Gomez looked at each other.

"Son," Biff said with heavy patience, "what are you doing swimming bare-assed in Habeck's pool two hours after Habeck was murdered?"

"I didn't smell so good, my clothes—"

"What?" said Gomez.

"Yeah, see, I got held up by this liquor store on my way here, I got bourbon splashed all over me, I was really reeking of the stuff—"

Biff stepped on Fletch's hand on the pool ledge.

"Ow." Fletch went entirely underwater a moment and rubbed his hand.

When he resurfaced, Biff and Gomez were still there, staring down at him.

Fletch placed his left hand in a pool drain.

He asked, "What's the matter with you guys?"

"Oh, nothing," Biff answered. "We should have expected to find a reporter from the *News-Tribune* swimming bare-assed in the murder victim's pool two hours after his death."

Fletch asked, "Isn't that what society writers do?"

"Probably," answered Biff. "I wouldn't know."

"Where are your clothes?" Gomez asked.

"Mrs. Habeck took them."

" 'Mrs. Habeck took them.' " Biff repeated. He sighed.

"Where is she?" Fletch asked. "Didn't she let you in the house?"

"The cook let us into the house," Gomez said. He added, "She had just returned that moment from grocery shopping."

"You haven't talked to Mrs. Habeck?"

"Mrs. Habeck isn't here," Gomez said.

"She isn't? Where are my clothes?"

"I think that's something we'd all like to know," Gomez answered.

"She couldn't have left with my clothes," Fletch said.

"Maybe this Mrs. Habeck wanted to make another donation to a museum." Biff chuckled. "An example of late-twentieth-century bummery costumery."

Gomez laughed.

"I didn't get much out of her anyway," Fletch said.

"Oh, you didn't," said Biff. "She got your clothes off you."

"Frankly, she seemed a little off-the-wall. Weird, you know what I mean?"

"Weird, uh? She got your clothes off you and disappeared with them, and you say *she's* weird?"

"Come on, Biff," Fletch said.

Down the grassy slope Fletch saw the gardener's sombrero rise, move a few meters, and lower from sight again.

Biff said, "You're not supposed to be here, and you know it."

"There's still the story of the donation, Biff. What happens to it now?"

"Your name is Fletcher?" Biff confirmed.

"Spelled with an *F*."

"Get out of my face, Fletcher. Get out of it, and stay out of it."

Dripping and naked, Fletch stood over the gardener.

"Any idea where I can get a towel?"

The gardener looked up at him. His face was younger than Fletch had expected.

Slowly the gardener stood up. He took off his denim shirt and handed it to Fletch.

"Gee, thanks. I really mean it. Those guys just said the cook is in the house." He wrapped the shirt around him. "I'll get it back to you as soon as I find some clothes. Nice guy. Give someone his shirt right off his back.''

The gardener knelt down and resumed weeding the flower bed.

"You have any idea where Mrs. Habeck went?"

"La señora no es la señora."

"What?"

"La señora no es la mujer, la esposa."

"What? 'The lady is not the wife.' You speak English better than I do. What are you saying?"

"You mean that broad you were talking to, right?" the gardener asked.

"Right."

"She's not Mrs. Habeck."

"She's not?"

"Mrs. Habeck is young and pretty." The gardener sketched a shapely form in the soil with his finger. "Like that. Blond."

"She said she was Mrs. Habeck."

"She's not."

"She's the cook?"

"The cook is Hispanic. Forty years old. She lives two blocks from me."

"Then who was she?"

"I dunno," the gardener said. "Never saw her before."

As Fletch was going through the Habecks' kitchen, the cook shrieked at the sight of a strange man naked except for a denim shirt hanging from his waist.

As Fletch was going up the stairs, Biff Wilson came out of the living room and said, "I've just talked to Frank Jaffe. He says you're a dumb kid who misunderstood your assignment. You're to get your ass back to the office and report to Ann McGarrahan in Society double quick time."

"Right," said Fletch. "Double quick."

He began taking the stairs two at a time.

"Why are you going upstairs?" Biff yelled.

Fletch yelled back, "I parked my car up here."

As Fletch handed the denim shirt back to the gardener, Fletch said, "Sorry I can't give it back to you washed, dried, and pressed, but that's how I lost my last clothes. They were headed for a wash."

As the gardener stood up and put back on his shirt, his eyes crinkled at the sight of the clothes Fletch was wearing.

Fletch shrugged. "Found this suit in Habeck's closet. He'll never miss it."

"The suit is short and fat."

"I got a belt. Nice tie. The necktie should distract the eye from the rest of the ensemble, right?"

"You're ready to boogie, man."

"Thanks again. The cook yelled at me."

"I heard. I thought it was the noon whistle."

"What would she have done if you hadn't lent me your shirt?"

"Scrambled eggs while they were still in the refrigerator."

"Where did you learn your Spanish?" Fletch asked.

"BHHS."

"BHHS?"

"Yeah," the gardener said, stooping to his work. "Beverly Hills High School."

7

"Cecilia's Boutique. Cecilia speaking. Have you considered jodhpurs?"

"I'm thinking very seriously about jodhpurs," Fletch said into his car phone.

"They're just coming in, sir. In another month they'll be all the rage. I'm sure your wife would be really impressed if you bought her jodhpurs now. Impressed by your prescience."

"So should the jodhpurs be impressed. I haven't got a wife." Waiting at the red light at the intersection of Washington and Twenty-third, Fletch saw that all was peaceful at the liquor store. Plywood had been nailed over the shattered breakproof glass of the door. They were ready for their next attack. "May I speak with Barbara Ralton, please?"

Cecilia hesitated. "Sales personnel are not to take personal phone calls. May I take a message for her?"

"Sure. This is Fletcher. Tell her I can't see her for lunch today. Please also tell her I look forward to buying her a pair of jodhpurs, at Saks."

*   *   *

"Here I am," Fletch said.

"Here who is?" Ann McGarrahan, society editor of the *News-Tribune*, was a tall broad-shouldered woman in her forties. She sat behind a desk that was too small for her in an office that was distinctly too small for her.

"I thought you people in Society knew everyone."

"Everyone who is anyone," Ann said softly. The corners of her mouth twinged with a smile. "Which obliges me to repeat: Who are you?"

"I.M. Fletcher." Fletch looked at the dead, brown fern on Ann's windowsill. "A nobody. Beneath your attention. May I go now?"

"Where have you been?"

"Oh, I changed clothes." Fletch held out the skirts of Donald Habeck's suit coat. "Frank said something about my needing a suit and tie for this job."

Ann studied him over her half-lenses. "And that's the suit? That's the tie?"

"Good material in it."

"I daresay. Clearly you made your investment in the material, and not the tailoring."

"I've lost weight."

"Gotten taller, too. Your trouser cuffs are a half-foot above your ankles."

"Have you heard that in another month jodhpurs will be all the rage? Lord, what I bring to this department."

"I see. Your sleeves are modified knickers, too, are they? They stop halfway down your forearms."

"I'm ready to cover the social scene."

"The young women around here call you Fletch, don't they?"

"When they call me at all." Fletch sat in a curved-back wooden chair.

"Why don't they use your first name?"

"Irwin?"

"What's wrong with Irwin?"

"Sounds like a hesitant cheer."

"Your middle name then. Don't you have a middle name?"

"Maurice."

"I know lots of nice people called Maury."

"I'm not one of 'em."

"Okay. You're a Fletch. It just sounds so much like a verb."

"To fletch, or not to fletch: that is the copulative."

"Guess I'll have to fletch. Well, Fletch. Not only has Frank Jaffe sent me you, with warnings regarding your appearance which, however dire, were still insufficient, he also sent me a strong suggestion as to what your first assignment might be."

"I know what it is."

"You do?"

"Yeah. Stay on this story concerning the five million dollars Donald Habeck and his wife decided to donate to the art museum. To stay right on it until I get to the bottom of it and everything else concerning the Habecks. Right?"

"Wrong. Of course."

"That was my assignment, for about a minute and a half this morning."

"Wasn't Donald Habeck the man murdered in our parking lot this morning?"

Fletch shrugged. "Just makes the story more interesting."

"Oh, we have an interesting story for you to work on, Fletch. It was Frank's suggestion. In fact, he mentioned the suggestion originally came from you."

"From me? A story for the society pages?"

"We don't really think of this section as being society anymore, Fletch. Although, of course, there's always the social aspect of it. We think of it more as human interest, with the emphasis on women's interests."

"That's why I brought up the latest scoop on jodhpurs."

"It's not just fashion anymore, it's more lifestyle. It's not just beauty, it's health."

"Right: women's healthy lifestyles."

"You'd be surprised at some of the topics some of our younger women writers want to discuss these days." Ann picked up some copy off her desk. "Here's an article comparing the relative merits of manufactured dildos. With pictures, supplied by the manufacturers, I expect. Do you think we should run an article comparing dildos, Fletch?"

"Uh . . ."

"Which do you think is the best dildo in the world today?"

"I can't tell you."

"Why not?"

"I couldn't be disinterested. I'm attached to it. It would be a subjective opinion."

"I see." Again Ann McGarrahan struggled to keep the corners of her mouth straight. She dropped the copy onto her desk. "Ah, the woes of being an editor. Needless to say, I've had that story on my desk for some time."

"Dildo?"

"Yes."

"I'm sure you'll find space for it."

"So, you see, we're into all sorts of areas of interest to you. We are not just concerned with little old ladies who slip vodka into their tea."

"Big-mouth Frank."

"So you haven't yet figured out what your assignment is? I was hoping it would come to you, on your own."

"Something about sexual aids? I know: you want me to do a report on what sexual aids do two out of three gynecologists recommend."

"You ran in the Sardinal Race yesterday."

"Oh, no."

"Didn't you?"

"Yes."

"Frank told me you ran behind a group of about a dozen women you couldn't bring yourself to pass."

"Oh, no."

"These same women received rather wide publicity, it seems, on this morning's sports pages of the *News-Tribune*." As she was saying this, Ann McGarrahan opened the *News-Tribune* to the sports section and looked at the two large photographs, on facing pages, of this group of women, coming, and going. "My, they are attractive, healthy young women, aren't they?"

"Not too shabby."

"For some reason, Frank takes this spread on his sports pages as some sort of personal affront. Also, I suspect he is in his office right now getting considerable flak for it, from the usual groups."

"Oh, boy."

"'Ben Franklyn Friend Service. A service company,'" Ann appeared to read from the newspaper. "What sort of service do you suppose they provide, Fletch, to have Frank so upset?"

"You're kidding."

Ann jutted her large face across the desk and asked, "Does it have something to do with men?"

"I suspect so."

"Tell me what."

Fletch felt the back of his chair pressing against his shoulder blades. "It's an escort service of the traveling-whorehouse variety, and I suspect you know that."

"Ah! Sounds like there's a story here."

"What? No story . . ."

"As I've outlined to you," Ann said, "on these pages we're concerned with women's interests, their health, how they make their livings—"

"This is a family newspaper!"

"Nice to hear you say so. Your investigation, of course, will be discreetly reported."

"You want me to investigate a whorehouse?"

"Who better?"

"I'm getting married, Saturday!"

"Have you already passed your blood test?"

Fletch took a deep breath.

Ann held up the flat of her hand to him. "This is a new thing, as I understand it: prostitutes who are obliged to stay in prime physical condition. Goes along with several articles we've run on organic gardening, I think. How does this Ben Franklyn Friend Service operate? What is the source of their discipline? How do they entertain men professionally without having to drink a lot themselves? If they are not dependent upon drugs themselves, why are they prostitutes? How much money do they make?" Ann continued to hold up her hand. "Of most importance, who owns Ben Franklyn Friend Service? Who derives the profit?"

Fletch let out his breath, and said nothing.

Ann said, "I think we could have a story here."

"Best way to do it," said Fletch, "might be to send one of your young women writers in to apply for a position with Ben Franklyn Friend Service."

"Ah, but it was your story idea, Fletch. Frank said so himself. It wouldn't be right for us to take it away from you. Of course, we may send a young woman in, too, for a preliminary investigation, that side of the story."

"I said I'm getting married Saturday."

"Doesn't give you much time, does it?"

"Ann—"

"Besides that," Ann said, refolding the newspaper on her desk, "I think Frank feels that such a story—well done, of course—would go a long way toward getting him off the hook for these unfortunate pictures that ran on the sports pages this morning." She folded her hands on the desk. "Not all is tea and biscuits on the lifestyle pages, Fletcher. Definitely, you're the man for the job.''

Fletch was looking out the window. "P.S., your fern is dead.''

"I happen to like brown fern," Ann said, without looking around. "I feel they make a statement: despair springs eternal.''

"Oh, boy.''

"Happy to have you in the department, young Mr. Fletcher. At least you won't have your purse snatched.''

"It's not my purse I'm worried about.'' He stood up.

"It will be interesting to see what you turn in.''

"You're asking me to 'turn in' under wicked circumstances.''

"Oh, and, Fletcher . . . ?''

"Yes, ma'am?''

"Be careful of Biff Wilson. Don't get in his way. You do, and he'll run over you like a fifty-car railroad train. He is a mean, vicious bastard. I ought to know. I was married to him, once.''

"Fletch, there's a call waiting for you.'' The young woman outside Ann McGarrahan's office jangled her bracelets at him. "Line 303. Nice suit. 'Fraid you're goin' to get raped 'round here?''

"Hello,'' Fletch said into the phone.

"Hello,'' said Barbara. "I'm furious.''

"I'd rather be Fletch.''

"What the hell do you mean by chewing out my employer?''

"Did I do that?''

"Cecilia's very serious about jodhpurs just now. She overbought.''

"I care. She wouldn't let you come to the phone.''

"Company policy. The phone's for the business, not for the employees.''

"But I'm the fiancé of her number-one salesperson.''

"And what do you mean you can't have lunch with me?''

"Things are a little confused here."

"This is Monday, Fletch. We're getting married Saturday. We have things to discuss, you know?"

"Anyway, I'd already agreed to have lunch with Alston. We want him as my best man, don't I?"

"That's the least of my worries. We don't have much time. You've got to get with it."

"I'm with it."

"I mean, really with it. Look at all you've got to do. Cindy says—"

"Barbara! Cool it! Don't chew me out now!"

"Why not?"

"Because I've just been chewed out by absolutely the best. Next to her, you sound tin-horn."

"Then why don't you marry her, whoever she is?"

"I would," answered Fletch, "except she has other ambitions for my proclivities."

8

"Good afternoon, Alston." Fletch slid into a chair at the café table.

"Good afternoon," Alston said. "I'm having a beer."

"Enjoy."

"Want a beer?" Fletch nodded. Alston signaled the waiter. "Two beers, please." With the back of his hand, Alston then brushed a speck of lint off the sleeve of his suit jacket. "Fletch, I couldn't help notice, as you scuffed along the sidewalk . . ."

"What?"

"Your suit."

"I've been assigned to the society pages."

Alston grinned. "Well, that's a real to-hell-with-society suit."

"It makes a statement, I think," Fletch said. "Like dead ferns. Despair springs eternal."

"I see you had a super morning, too. Did they finally get you for that headline you wrote?"

"Headline?"

"DOCTOR SAVES LIFE IN ACCIDENT?"

"They never noticed that one." The waiter brought the beers. "Sometimes I think I'm the only one at the *News-Tribune* with any news sense."

"I have that headline hanging on my wall."

"We must look at the bright side, Alston."

"Yeah," Alston said. "Barbara."

"Barbara just chewed me out."

"Oh."

"This morning I was chewed out by the managing editor, Frank Jaffe, the *News-Tribune*'s star crime writer, Biff Wilson, Ann McGarrahan, the society editor, and my fiancé, Barbara Ralton. And it's only Monday."

"In a suit like that—as much as you can be said to be *in* it—I'm surprised anyone takes you seriously."

"Oh, yeah." Fletch removed his coat and put it on the back of his chair. "I was also held up by a liquor store. Shot at."

"Lots of people have been held up in a liquor store. Once, my uncle was in a hurry; you know, before the rabbits started nibbling his toes? And—"

"And I interviewed a nice, kooky lady who said she was someone apparently she isn't."

"You interviewed an impostor?"

"I guess."

"Did you get anything interesting out of her?"

"I did have the feeling I was leading her, Alston."

"I would think you would have to feed answers to an impostor," Alston said. "To get any kind of a story."

"What's more, she got my clothes off me. Ran away with them."

"All this happened just this morning?"

"And those sneakers were just getting comfortable."

"Fletcher, are you sure you can make it outside the U.S. Marine Corps?"

"It's hard, Alston, getting a start in life."

Alston held up his beer. "To youth."

"No one takes us young people seriously."

"And we are serious."

"We are indeed. Seriously serious."

The waiter said, "Are you gentlemen ready to order now?"

"Yes," Fletch said. "The usual."

"Sir," the waiter said with poised pen, "it may be usual to you, but whatever it is, is not usual to me."

"You mean I have to tell you my order?"

"You could keep it to yourself, sir. That would cut down on my work."

"I had it here just last week."

"I'm pleased to see it was you who returned, sir, and not whatever it was you had for lunch."

"This is Manolo's, isn't it?"

The waiter glanced at the name on the awning. "That much we've established."

"A peanut-butter-and-sliced-banana sandwich with mayonnaise on pumpernickel," Fletch said.

"Ah," said the waiter. "That is memorable. How could we have forgotten?"

"You make it special for me."

"I would hope so. And you, sir?"

"Liederkranz-and-celery sandwich on light rye," Alston answered. "Just a soupçon of ketchup."

"I beseech Thee, O God, that's another special."

The waiter went away, hurriedly.

"Even the damned waiter doesn't take us seriously," Fletch said.

"No one takes youth seriously. Maturity is too precious to be wasted on the old."

"Aren't we mature? Veterans. You're a lawyer. I'm a journalist."

"People still plunk us in the to-be-seen-and-not-heard category, though."

"Could it be that we're pretty?"

"In that suit, Fletcher, you dim daffodils."

"I should think so."

"This morning I got called into Haller's office. Senior partner. Summoned. You see, I'm supposed to sit in on meetings, keeping my mouth shut, of course, and never, never laugh, let my jaw drop in shock, or stare too much."

"Those the conditions of your employment?"

"You got it. I'm supposed to just listen. Pretend I'm not there. That way, I get to learn how grown-up lawyers work up their fees to the exorbitant, pay the rent for us lesser souls, and maintain their Mercedes."

"Sounds edifyin'."

"Educational. Also, of course, peons such as I are to be present at meetings so we can understand what research, leg work, is to be done on the case underfoot."

"Don't you mean, under consideration, or under advisement, or something?"

"Underfoot. So here's a client, new to Habeck, Harrison and Haller—"

"Ha ha ha."

"Excuse me? I haven't finished yet."

"I should have said, *Hay, Ha, Haw.* Have I got that right?"

"Probably. Whatever it is you're saying."

The waiter put their sandwiches in front of them. He said, "Here's your fodder."

"Yeah," said Fletch. "Thanks, mudder."

"Anyway," continued Alston, while checking his ketchup and apparently finding it satisfactory. "This new client was interrupted Saturday night by the police while removing silver, stereo, and other glittery things from a home up at The

Heights. The scandal, and the reason for this gentleman coming to Habeck, Harrison and Haller, is, you see, that the home, silver, stereo, and other glittery objects did not belong to him.''

"A burglar."

"Well, someone in the front lines in the theft business."

"Why wasn't he in court this morning?"

"Came directly to us from court, having had the wisdom to ask for and get what will be, I'm sure, the first of many postponements."

"He was out on bail."

"Which modest amount he posted himself. His reason for doing so and rushing off, he told the court, was that he was obliged to take his fifteen-year-old dog to the dentist."

"Had he an appointment?"

"Unbreakable."

"A mission of mercy."

"Doubtlessly the court is now prejudiced in his favor."

"You're not about to tell me he was lying to the court?"

"Well, he told us, or, rather, he told Mr. Haller, that while he was in court, the dog, waiting to be brought to the dentist, was howling so in pain, a neighbor shot him."

Fletch shook his head. "He needn't have rushed." He salted his peanut butter-banana-and-mayonnaise sandwich. "Tell me, did he call up and cancel the dentist's appointment?"

"He didn't say."

"I'm trying to gauge the degree of this man's honesty, you see, his concern for the social contract."

"In meetings, I am not allowed to put forth such questions."

"I forgot. You're a hanging plant."

"That, or whatever is put at the base of plants to aid their growth."

"I'm surprised Mr. Haller, being senior partner in an important law firm, would be interviewing a simple burglar himself. Why would he be taking on a burglar as a client?"

"Ah, Fletch, you are innocent as to how law firms, and thus the law, works."

"I thought I knew a few things."

"I'll bet you thought law firms practice law."

"They don't?"

"That's not their primary function."

"It isn't?"

"No. What they actually practice is something called cooling the client."

"Do they teach that in law school?"

"No. Which is why starters, such as myself, work in law firms a few years at just enough above the minimum wage to keep in clean collars. Because it is not being taught in law schools, we must learn this technique essential to keeping the law firm afloat."

"So what's 'cooling the client'?"

"When a client first knocks on the door of a law firm as ambitious as Habeck, Harrison and Haller, the law firm's first job is to discover how much the client—the client, not the case—is worth. It takes experience and wisdom to make such an assessment."

"I don't see how what the client is worth has to do with what the case is worth."

"Suppose it's a simple, straightforward case. But the senior partner, who conducts the first interview, discovers the client is rich. Under the circumstances, what would you do?"

"Practice law."

"How little you know. You cool the client. The senior partner, having made an assessment of the client's worth, decides how much of his wealth the law firm will take from him in fees, regardless of how simple or complicated the case is. It would amaze you to know how a talented law firm can complicate the most simple case by creating setbacks, other delays, filing wrong or useless motions, petitions, initiating incorrect lines of argument, et cetera. The object, you see, is to keep the case going as long as possible, all the while milking the client for nearly every penny he or she may be worth. If, despite the law firm's best efforts, the case is ever brought to a conclusion, and if the law firm has done a masterful job of cooling the client consistently throughout his ordeal, the client ends up impoverished and very, very grateful.''

"Pardon me, Counselor, but isn't that called robbery?"

"In the law, it's called building a solid reputation."

"Supposing, Counselor, in the initial interview, the senior partner discovers this particular client isn't rich enough to be worth robbing?"

"One of three things happens. First, the client could be persuaded that his case could be handled just as well, and more cheaply, by a smaller, less prestigious law firm. Which law firm, incidentally, is expected to kick back to the recommending law firm a percentage of whatever fees the poor client is able to pay."

"The rich get richer."

"And the poor get screwed. Or, second, if the case has any value to the partners socially, or if it might generate beneficial publicity, or whatever, even if the client doesn't have sufficient wherewithal to be worth robbing, the case is taken. It is then handled with such dazzling speed and efficiency the world is breathless as it watches. The old-boy network is used. Private deals are struck. A settlement is arrived at swiftly, and cheaply, not always to the client's complete benefit."

"And the law firm's reputation becomes even more solid."

"I'm giving you the internal workings of your average, greedy law firm. At least of Habeck, Harrison and Haller. How some lawyers look at the law, you might say."

"You're robbing me of my innocence."

"The third thing that might happen is that which happened this morning, which is what I'm trying to tell you about."

"If a person who engages himself as a lawyer is a fool, what's a person who engages Habeck, Harrison and Haller?"

"You can see why violence is not always an illogical solution."

"A solution discovered by an increasing percentage of our population," Fletch said. "Have you heard the complaint, 'The courts don't work'?"

"Once or twice," Alston admitted. "The third thing that can happen with an impecunious client is what I saw happen this morning. A burglar rushes from the court and finds himself being interviewed by Mr. Haller."

"The presumption can be made that if the burglar had enough money to afford Habeck, Harrison and Haller, he wouldn't be a burglar."

"A lot of burglars do afford Habeck, Harrison and Haller. There's a system to everything, you see."

"The legal system."

"Burglars, obviously, must be represented."

"They have their rights."

"They are in a hazardous profession. No telling when their presence might be requested in a court of law."

"That's the breaks. And entering."

"So Mr. Haller, this morning, after pretending to listen to the bare bones of our new burglar-client's difficulty, explains to the burglar that many of his colleagues in the burglary business retain Habeck, Harrison and Haller on an annual basis. A kind of occupational insurance, you see. Just in case their earning a living is threatened by an arrest, conviction, and jail sentence. For example, Mr. Haller explains, if our burglar this morning had already paid such a retainer to Habeck, Harrison and Haller, a Habeck, Harrison and Haller lawyer, such as myself, would have been waiting for him at the police station when he was arrested Saturday night, to do the proper and necessary. He wouldn't have even had to set bail for himself."

"How much of a retainer?"

"Ten thousand dollars. Not much, really, when you consider that a burglar in prison is no good to anyone. Not to his family, not to his friends, not to the economy, and not to Habeck, Harrison and Haller. In jail, he can't make a living."

"Alston, if this guy had ten thousand dollars Saturday, who would he go burglarizing Saturday night?"

"That's not the idea. He wouldn't have ten thousand dollars. The law firm would have ten thousand dollars. So the man can go earn his living without fret. Peace of mind, Fletcher, is worth almost any price."

"I've heard."

"So our burglar-client is told this morning by Mr. Haller that if he comes up with ten thousand dollars within ten days—that is, before his next court appearance—he may look forward to the full services, support, and talents of Habeck, Harrison and Haller. If not, Mr. Haller can recommend to the burglar a smaller, cheaper, less prestigious firm which can be counted on to represent the burglar to the best of their limited resources."

"How the hell is a two-bit burglar supposed to come up with ten thousand dollars within ten days?"

"Guess."

"You're kidding."

"I'm not kidding."

"You mean, a senior partner, in a major law firm, is sending a burglar out to burgle?"

"Really, we only want professionals among our clientele."

"Isn't Mr. Haller technically a member of the court?"

"He's a half-decent golfer, and a doting grandparent."

"Did the burglar accept this deal?"

"Of course. Where would his family be if he went to jail? Lock your doors tonight."

"In other words, the burglar is now burglarizing on behalf of Habeck, Harrison and Haller."

"If he's going to be in this profession, obviously his professional fees and expenses have to be guaranteed."

"Supposing he gets arrested again?"

"All the more work, and all the more fees, for Habeck, Harrison and Haller."

"Alston, you're making me sick."

"I'm sure it's not the sandwich you just ate affecting you. What could be more soothing to the stomach than peanut butter, banana, and mayonnaise? I must try it someday."

"Frankly, I'm shocked. In the first place, that your man, Haller, who must have just heard that his partner had been shot dead in a parking lot, would sit down and have a serious discussion with any client, burglar or not."

"It only took fifteen minutes. After the client is hooked by the senior partner, he is spun off to one of the lesser lawyers in the firm. The rent must be paid. The Mercedes must be maintained."

"Alston, do you want a Mercedes?"

"My ambition for one is dimming."

9

The waiter stood over them. "Would you gentlemen like some coffee, tea, or would you prefer sludge?"

"What kind of sludge do you have?" Fletch asked.

"Chocolate, vanilla."

"No strawberry?" Alston said. "I wanted strawberry sludge."

"No strawberry," sighed the waiter.

"Guess I'll have coffee," said Fletch.

"I'll have another beer," said Alston. "Put a cherry in it this time, will you?"

"One coffee," said the waiter. "One beer with a cherry."

"Alston," Fletch said, "I'd like to know anything you can find out about Donald Habeck. Anything you can tell me."

"Only actually shook hands with him the day I was hired. A short, pudgy man—"

"I know," Fletch said, adjusting his belt.

"Considered one of the most brilliant criminal trial lawyers in the country."

"That's the point. It can't be too surprising a man with

57

such a wide acquaintance among criminals ends up shot in a parking lot."

"It is surprising," Alston countered. "He's the one person you'd think would be safe from that sort of thing. I should think all the villains around here would consider themselves indebted to him."

"One coffee," said the waiter. "One beer with a cherry in it."

Fletch looked at Alston's beer. "He actually put a cherry in it."

"I wanted a cherry in it."

"Are you going to eat it?"

"You're eyeing my cherry."

"Sorry."

"I mean, just suppose this were a contract murder. A contract were put out to murder Habeck. Who'd accept it? Habeck's defended most of the murderers worthy of the name."

"Hey, a job's a job."

"From what I hear, professional hit men do not like to murder anyone they know, even people toward whom they have nothing but good feelings. Always afraid a connection might be made."

"Someone who isn't grateful to Habeck. Someone Habeck failed, defended improperly, lost the case. For example, I'd look for an ex-client of Habeck who got out of prison lately. Spent time nursing the grudge."

"I doubt there is anyone like that."

"There must be. Habeck can't be successful every time he goes to court."

"Successful in one way or another. Mr. Harrison, the other senior partner, once said to me, 'You can commit mass murder in front of witnesses, including police witnesses, and we can guarantee you'll never go to prison for it. The police or district attorney can always be counted on to make some technical mistake, in the arresting process, indictment, in the gathering and presenting of evidence.' ''

"He actually said that?''

"He actually said that.''

"That's terrible.''

Alston shrugged. "The average policeman in this country has something like six weeks of formal training. The average defense lawyer has more like six years, if you add his internship in a law firm. And district attorneys are hopelessly overworked and understaffed.''

"How do people ever succeed in getting to jail?''

"They don't hire Habeck, Harrison and Haller.''

"Alston, Habeck could not have won one hundred percent of the cases he brought to trial.''

"Pretty near, I'll bet. He gets to choose his own cases. Thanks to plea bargaining, I'll bet even those of his clients who are or have been in jail have been happy to go. On reduced charges, you know?'' Alston quaffed his beer. "But, I'll look.''

"Was Habeck a rich man?''

"Pretty rich. He knew where his next Bang and Olufsen was coming from.''

"Rich enough to give away five million dollars?''

"Is anybody that rich?''

"That's how I first heard of him, this morning. He was coming in to see the publisher, John Winters. Habeck wanted to announce that he and his wife were giving five million dollars to the museum but he wanted it announced discreetly, whatever that means, so their privacy wouldn't be invaded.''

"He's never been the most flamboyant lawyer, this coast, but he's never shunned publicity before.''

"I suspect he's never given away five million dollars before.''

"That's an awful lot of money.'' Alston munched on his beer-soaked cherry.

"What does it mean when someone gives away five million dollars?"

"It means he ought to get lunch. At the minimum."

"No, seriously."

"It means he's a philanthropist. Kindly. Generous. Has the well-being of the world in his heart."

"Is that how you'd describe Donald Habeck?"

"No. As I say, I only met the man once. But that's not how I'd describe him."

"He was a partner in a law firm which keeps murderers out of jail and sends burglars out to burgle."

"In this country, Fletch, everyone has the right to the best defense."

"Come on, Alston. Not all law firms operate the way you describe Habeck, Harrison and Haller."

"Not all. Many do."

"Is it possible for Habeck to have earned so much money simply by being a lawyer?"

"Oh, yes. Over a lifetime. That and more."

"Much more?"

"I'm not sure."

"Why was he giving away five million dollars?"

"Didn't have anything else to do with it, I suppose. A man in his sixties . . ."

Fletch wrinkled his nose in the sunlight. "He had children, I think. Grown, of course. Grandchildren. The impostor I interviewed this morning, the weird lady who said she was Mrs. Habeck and wasn't, mentioned children and grandchildren. The gardener at the Habeck house said the real Mrs. Habeck is young. I don't get it."

"Expiate guilt. Maybe Habeck was trying to rid himself of his own guilt."

"He sounds like a man who spent his life rationalizing away guilt. Professionally. His own and others'."

"Yeah, but he was getting older."

"With a young wife. I don't get it. His home just doesn't look like the home of someone who can give away five million dollars. I mean, if you've got one hundred million dollars, giving away five can be a casual experience. It needn't interrupt the flow of one's life, the rhythm of one's coming and going. But giving away five million when maybe you have six million, a young wife, probably grandchildren..."

"Which of you gentlemen would like the bill?" the waiter asked.

"He would," Alston said solemnly.

"No," Fletch said. "Give it to him."

"You invited me to lunch," Alston said.

"You asked me to."

"Shall I pay it?" asked the waiter. "I had the pleasure of serving you."

"He's got a point," Fletch said.

"It would be the ultimate service," agreed Alston. "I mean, it would indicate this waiter did everything possible for us."

"It is the one possibility you haven't considered," concurred the waiter.

"But what about the tip?" Fletch asked. "That presents a moral dilemma. Also practical confusion."

The waiter looked around the outdoor café. "Oh, to work in a grown-up restaurant," he sighed. "One with walls."

"I'll pay the bill," Alston said to Fletch, "if you answer me a question."

"Anything." Fletch watched Alston pay the bill.

"Gee," Alston said after the waiter went away. "Over lunch we talked about philanthropy, murder, and the law, and we didn't get any respect even from the waiter."

"No one respects the young," mourned Fletch. "Not managing editors, crime writers, society editors, liquor-store-counter help—"

"Fiancées."

"Fiancées."

"Waiters."

"Now that you've paid the bill," Fletch said, "I've got a question for you."

"Then why didn't you pay the bill?"

"Will you be my best man?"

"You mean, better man? How many of us do you expect there to be?"

"Saturday morning. Whenever you wake up."

"Did you get that suit for your wedding?"

"Don't you like this suit?"

"Gray doesn't suit you."

"Barbara said something about our getting married naked."

"Stark naked?"

Fletch nodded. "She said it would be honest of us. Fitting. She says a marriage is the coming together of two bodies, male and female...."

"You sure you want to marry Barbara?"

"No."

"Wearing anything, or wearing nothing, would be better than wearing that dumb-looking suit."

"So, will you be my best man?"

"My question is: Where did you get that suit? I want to never go there."

"I thought you'd recognize it."

"Why should I recognize it?"

"I thought you might have seen it before."

"Fire hydrants don't usually wear suits."

"Walking along the corridors at Habeck, Harrison and Haller."

Alston's eyes widened. "Habeck? That's Habeck's suit?"

"Now you'll have respect for this suit. Habeck wasn't screwing jurisprudence to get his suits from Goodwill."

"You stole a dead man's suit?"

"I guess you could say that. If you insist."

"I don't know, Fletch. I worry about you."

"So, will you be my best man?"

"Fletch, ol' buddy: you shouldn't go anywhere without a lawyer. Especially to your own wedding."

10

"Frank?" Fletch said.

At the urinal, the managing editor jumped. He did not turn around. "Who wants me?"

"That's a different question."

"Different from what?"

In the men's room, empty except for them, Fletch stepped to his own urinal three away from Frank Jaffe's. "Matters in hand," Fletch said.

"Oh, it's you. Nice suit." Frank flushed. "Didn't know the tide came in already this morning."

"Have I invited you to my wedding yet?" Fletch asked.

"God, no."

"It's Saturday, you know."

"Which day is Saturday?" Frank was washing his hands.

"End of the week. Day between Friday and Sunday."

"Yeah: that's the day I try to get away from employees."

Fletch followed Frank to the washbasin. "I'm pleading a case, Mr. Jaffe."

"A case of what? Have you confessed yet to what's-her-name you have a case of something-or-other?"

"That's my point, Frank. Don't want a case. Don't want a nose. Don't want to go near that place."

"What place is that?"

"Frank." Fletch shook his wet hands over the basin and then held them in front of him. "I'm getting married Saturday. And you've got me investigating a whorehouse!"

"Every nook and cranny." Frank dried his hands on a paper towel.

"Is this some kind of an office joke?"

"Not yet," Frank said. "But I'm sure it will be."

"Dump on the kid, is that it?"

"Fletch, you need the experience. Don't you?"

"Not that kind, I don't. Not to get married, I don't."

"Come on. You asked for a job, a real job, so I gave you one."

"A whorehouse the week before I'm married?"

"Gives you a chance to show your stuff. Let us see what you can do."

"Very funny."

"We want you to give it your all, kid. Get to the bottom of things. Really get into the crux of the matter. What we want is a penetrating report. We want everybody to get your point."

"You forgot something."

"What did I forget now?" Frank looked at his fly.

"My expense account."

"We expect there to be expenses."

"Yeah, but I'm going to write my expense account with accuracy painful to you."

"That will be a novelty."

"In detail. I'm going to write down exactly what money I'm spending on the Ben Franklyn Friend Service, and for what services."

"Expense accounts are never questioned, if the story' worth the expense."

"Frank, I'm gonna file a pornographic expense account.'

Frank opened the door to the corridor. "Maybe we'll prin that, too."

"What will the publisher say about that?"

Leaving the men's room, Frank said, "Give it your bes shot, kid."

11

"As I live and breathe," said the Beauty in the Broad-rimmed Hat. "You must be Fletcher."

Standing in the door of her small office, Fletch frowned. "What makes you say that?"

"Your suit, darling. Your suit." Sitting corsetless at her console, Amelia Shurcliffe, society columnist for the *News-Tribune,* perpetually wore the facial expression of someone who had just been invited to a party. Perpetually she had just been invited to a party. Everyone wanted dear Amelia at his or her party. For some, giving parties makes life worthwhile. For everybody, a sentence or two in Amelia's column made giving parties worthwhile. What Amelia did not know about people on the party circuit was not worth knowing. "I've heard so much about you, and your exciting style of dress."

Fletch looked down at Donald Habeck's suit. "Exciting?"

"You don't mean to tell me you don't know what you're doing! At fashion, you're just an unconscious genius!"

"I'm unconscious, all right."

"Look how you're dressed, Fletcher darling." Althoug
Amelia was staring at Fletch, head to toe and back again, sh
nevertheless kept glancing at her telephone. "That gra
businessman's suit is miles too small for you. Surely yo
know that?"

"One or two have mentioned it."

"Your trousers are up to your shins, your sleeves nearly u
to your elbows, and you have yards of extra material aroun
your waist."

"Pretty cool, uh?"

"I'll say. The point of fashion, my dear, if you'll listen t
old Amelia, not that you need to, clearly, is to wear clothe
which make other people want to get them off you."

"Have I succeeded at that?"

"Brilliantly. You look lost and uncomfortable in that suit.'

"I am."

"Anyone, seeing you, would want to tear those clothes o'
you."

"Would they turn down the air-conditioning first?"

"And you encourage that impulse, you see. The jacket an'
shirt are much too narrow across your chest and shoulders
Your shirt buttons are straining. Why, you're just ready t'
burst out of those clothes."

"I'm a fashion plate, am I?"

"So original. What do you call that style?"

Fletch shrugged. "Borrowed."

"'Borrowed,'" Amelia said with great satisfaction. Sh'
typed a few words on her console. "I'll use that."

"Have you heard about jodhpurs?"

"What about jodhpurs?"

"They're going to be all the rage in a month. Cecilia'
Boutique is fully stocked with them."

"Jodhpurs, darling, were all the rage months ago."

"Oops."

Amelia glanced at her telephone. "Now, darling, othe'

than your presenting me with a vision of brilliant, new, young fashions, to what do I owe the honor of this visit?''

''Habeck, Donald Edwin. Haven't done my homework on him yet, but I was hoping you'd point me in the right direction.''

Amelia's eyelids lowered. ''You mean that sleazy criminal lawyer who was shot in our parking lot this morning?''

''The same.''

''Not Society, darling. A creature like Donald Edwin Habeck could be shot just anywhere. And was.''

''But supposedly he was giving five million dollars to the art museum.''

Slowly, Amelia Shurcliffe said, ''I should think Biff Wilson would have the exclusive on that story for this newspaper.''

''Oh, right,'' said Fletch. ''I'm just tracing down the social aspects of it.''

''The social aspects of murder? Are there any other?''

''You know, the five million dollars.''

''Did he actually give the five million dollars to the museum?''

''I believe he was just about to announce it.''

''Well,'' Amelia sighed. ''People do give money to charities.''

''You say Habeck was not socially prominent?''

''People like Habeck exist in a very peculiar way,'' Amelia said. ''One knows them, of course, but, at best at the other end of a telephone. You know, if one shoots one's husband in the middle of the night, having once mistaken him as one's lover and now wanting to have mistaken him as a burglar, one must have someone to call, mustn't one?''

''I guess.''

''One must know people of that sort well enough to be able to call them, but have them to dinner as a regular thing? No. Their presence might give one's husbands ideas.''

''I guess you're serious about all this.''

''The Habecks of this world are not to be trusted. After all,

when we hire someone like Habeck we're hiring someone t
lie for us. Isn't that what we're doing? That's what peopl
like Habeck do for a living. They're professional liars. W
don't mind hiring them to lie for us. But do we want them t
lie to us, at our own dinner tables? Of far more importance
do we want them lying to other people about what happene
and what was said at our dinner tables?''

"Generally, aren't lawyers trained to follow rules o
evidence?''

Amelia Shurcliffe stared at Fletch a long moment. "Law
yers, my dear, are trained to follow rules of gullibility.''

"Okay. How rich was Habeck? Was he rich enough to giv
away five million dollars?''

"I have no idea. Probably. He's always in the news ove
some sensational case or other. Although how crimina
lawyers get criminals to pay their law bills has always been
puzzle to me. There must be some trick to it.''

"I think there is.''

"His partner, Harrison, does all the divorces worth doing
These chaps aren't in the law business to serve justice or jus
make a living, you know.''

"What about Mrs. Habeck? I'm a bit puzzled—''

"Have no idea. Don't even know if there is a Mrs
Habeck. I'll have to read Biff Wilson in the morning. As
said, the Habecks of this world do not shine socially.''

"Amelia, I was in Habeck's house this morning, ver
briefly, I admit, but I didn't notice any paintings or other ar
works that caused me to pause.''

"Do you know about paintings?''

"A little bit.''

"Of course you do. Foolish of me to ask. Look at the
clever way you've dressed yourself.''

"Why would a person, especially, as you say, not socially
prominent, and who does not have an immediately obviou

interest in art, be giving five million dollars to an art museum?''

''I find the generous impulse generally inexplicable.''

''What was he buying?''

''Respectability? That's as good an answer as any I can give, in this case. Here's this man, Habeck, whom society has been using like a tissue, employed only when one has sneezed, or, to mix metaphors, like a high-priced prostitute, picked up, used, and dropped off, without ever an invitation to visit hearth and home. He's getting older. Or, he was, when his aging was concluded this morning. Wouldn't such a person, at the age of sixty, have the instinct to do something that says, 'Eh! I'm as good as you are! I can give away five million bucks, too!''

''Would society then accept him?''

''No. Especially if society knows there isn't another five million bucks to be gotten from him. But it might make him feel better.''

''That's very interesting.''

''I'm always very interesting. That's my job, you see.'' Amelia glanced at her phone again. Clearly, Amelia's phone not ringing made her nervous.

''So.'' Fletch took a step backward toward the door. ''Ann McGarrahan and Biff Wilson were married once.''

''I forgot that,'' Amelia answered. ''Yes. Years ago. One of the greater mismatches in my experience. They were married for about three weeks perhaps as many as twenty years ago. Why do you ask?''

''What happened?''

''Who ever knows what happens in someone else's marriage, let alone one's own? My opinion would be, if I were rudely asked, that Ann is a strong, intelligent, good, and decent woman who found herself married to a violent, nasty scumbag.''

''Phew! I'm glad I didn't ask.''

"But you did. You and I are in a rude business, Mr. Fletcher."

"Did Ann ever marry again?"

"To someone who died. She's not now married. If you're interested in Ann McGarrahan, who's old enough to be your mother, dare I cherish hope for me?"

"And Biff Wilson?"

"I shudder to think. Somewhere in Biff's background there lurks a succubus he calls wife. Named Aurora, or some such dim thing. Now, unless you have more social notes regarding sleazy lawyers, or fashion notes regarding jodhpurs—"

"I do, in fact."

"Out with it."

"I'm getting married Saturday."

"To whom?"

"Barbara Ralton."

"I never heard of her."

"She sells jodhpurs. At Cecilia's."

"I should have figured that. Now, darling, the Stanwyks are giving their annual bash for Symphony next week, and I'm absolutely desperate to find out which colors Joan's using for her table settings. You wouldn't happen to know, would you?"

"Me? I don't even know what Stanwyks are."

12

"Hey, what are you doing at my desk?"

"All right if I use your computer terminal?"

"You're probably screwing it up." Clifton Wolf, religion editor, looked over Fletch's shoulder at the screen. "'Habeck,'" he read. "You doing research for Biff Wilson now?"

"We all work for the same newspaper."

"Like hell we do. I work for my inch of space, you work for your inch. Biff Wilson works for his foot and a half. If you're not on the story, buddy, you'd better get off it."

Fletch turned off the terminal. "Just curious."

"Curious will turn you into dog food. Also, get off my chair."

"I don't have a terminal of my own." Fletch stood up, picking up a sheaf of notes he had made.

"We always wondered why you were hired. Now we know: to cover whorehouses. I don't want anyone who spends his time in whorehouses sitting in my chair."

"Haven't gone to the whorehouse yet. Haven't got my mother's permission."

"No tellin' what you might be givin' out. Al!" Clifton Wolf yelled across the city room to the city editor. "Call the disinfectant guys! Fletcher's been using my stuff!"

"I bet you'd like this assignment," Fletch said. "Only place they send you is church."

"Scat!"

"Do you know of a poet named Tom Farliegh?" Fletch asked.

Fletch suspected that, without much deliberation, people who wrote for the various sections of the newspaper dressed like the people about whom they wrote. People in the business section wore business suits; in the society section they always seemed dressed for a lawn party; in the sports section, white socks and checkered jackets seemed to be the style.

Mentally they identified with their subjects, too. Business writers thought in terms of power, profit and loss; society writers cherished an incredible web of lines of the acceptable rudeness of old money versus the crudeness of new money, attractiveness versus beauty, style versus ostentation; sports-writers thought in terms of winners and losers, new talent versus has-beens, and the end-of-life standings.

Standing before him in the dark part of the corridor was Morton Rickmers, the book editor. He wore thick glasses, a chalet tie, tweed jacket, baggy trousers, and soft, tire-tread shoes. It was clear from his book reviews that he loved people and their stories honestly told, loved words and putting them together in their most magical, concise form, and considered the good book humans' most noble achievement, perhaps our only raison d'être.

Frequently his reviews were more interesting and better written than the books he was reviewing.

"Why, have you met Tom Farliegh?" Morton asked.

"No."

"I might like to meet him," Morton mused. "I'm not sure."

"Just heard of him."

"First," Morton said, "I might enjoy knowing why you're dressed that way."

His notepapers in hand, Fletch held his arms out to his sides. "I've been assigned to investigate an escort service. Is that an answer?"

"I see. Trying to disguise yourself as an out-of-town businessman? You look more like the victim of a raid, obliged to grab someone else's clothes."

"You're nearly right. I lost my clothes this morning, and had to borrow this rig."

Morton smiled. "I'm sure there's a story behind how you lost your clothes."

"Not much of a one."

"It's been years since I've lost my clothes. In fact, have I ever lost my clothes?"

"I don't know. It's easy to do."

"Make an interesting short story. *How I Lost My Clothes.* Something Ring Lardner might have done."

"Tom Farliegh lives locally, does he?"

"Oh, yes. Teaches something at the university. Being a poet in academia, he's probably wrongly assigned. You know, to teach English or something, instead of music, or math, or equestrian skills."

"Is he the son-in-law of Donald Habeck?"

"How interesting. I have no idea. You mean the man who was shot in the parking lot this morning?"

"Yes."

"That would be fascinating."

"Why?"

"You've never read him?"

"Not that I remember."

"Not many have. But, if you'd read him, you'd remember. He writes what we call a Poetry of Violence. His best-known poem is something called *The Knife, The Blood*. His publisher entitled his book of collected poems after that one poem. I think I have a copy of it in my office. Come with me."

In his bright, book-walled office, Morton took a slim volume from a shelf and handed it to Fletch. "Here's *Knife, Blood*. You can borrow it."

On the cover, bare skin was deeply slashed by a knife. Blood poured from the skin, down the knife onto a satin sheet.

"This is a book of poetry?" Fletch asked. "Looks more like an old-fashioned mystery novel."

"It's unusual poetry. Rather thin on sentiment."

"Thank you."

"I do believe in reading about what you're doing," Morton said, almost apologetically. "Widens the base of your perception."

Skimming through the book, Fletch said, "I don't suppose you know anything personally about Donald Habeck."

"In fact, I do." Morton folded his arms across his chest and turned away from Fletch. "My sister's son, years ago, was accused of stealing a car and then running over someone in it. Intoxication, grand theft, vehicular homicide, at the age of eighteen."

"I'm sorry to hear that."

"It was awful. The boy was your average frustrated, sullen teenager who just went wild one night." With his back still toward Fletch, Morton said, "We hired Donald Habeck. I mean, he's the sort you hire when things look really awful."

"At any price."

"Yes. At any price."

"What happened to the kid?"

"Intoxication charge was dismissed. Habeck proved the police had used the blood-alcohol testing equipment incorrectly.

The charge of car theft was reduced to using a car without permission of owner. I suspect Habeck bribed the owner to say he knew the boy and there had been a misunderstanding regarding use of the car. And the vehicular homicide was found to be the fault of the car manufacturer. Apparently that model car had been proven to have something amiss with its steering mechanism." Morton sighed. "My nephew was sentenced to three months probation, no time in prison."

"Wonder they didn't give him the keys to the city."

Morton turned slowly on his heel. "We're still ashamed of the whole thing. My sister and I, well, we ended up feeling like criminals, like we committed a crime."

"In hiring Habeck."

"I think, in miscarrying justice." Morton shrugged. "My nephew, with just enough of a misdemeanor on his record to make him an understanding person, is now a teacher in a San Diego high school, married, three kids of his own. But, you know, I can't think of him without feeling guilty."

"Did Habeck leave your sister with any worldly wealth?"

"Not much. She had to sell their new house, their second car, cash in their savings, and accept a little help from me."

"What did you think this morning when you heard Habeck had been killed?"

"I've been thinking about it all day. When you live by the sword . . ." Behind his thick glasses, Morton's eyes were focused as if reading from a page close to his face. "Ironic, somehow. I see his ghost hurrying up from his corpse to defend the person who murdered him . . . for good long-range results, or bad. . . ."

"But always for money."

"Yes. He used his brilliance to twist the legal system for money. Scoff at him. Hate him for it. But, when it came right down to it, we paid that money, gladly, to save Billy from an utterly ruined life, to give him a second chance, which he, at least, took. I'm not sure how many of Habeck's clients take that second chance, how many of them are just free to maim, kill, destroy again.''

"Thanks for the book.''

"If you do meet Tom Farliegh, tell me if you think he's worth a feature story.''

"What time are you going to be done?''

"Never.'' Fletch was sitting at another borrowed desk in the city room. Having gone through his notes, he had just picked out items from the voluminous Habeck file he wanted copied.

"What's it today?'' Barbara asked over the telephone. "Wedding announcements? Deaths? Or writing headlines for other people's stories?''

"Hey, I'm working hard for you, kid. I'm trying to plant an item in Amelia Shurcliffe's column about jodhpurs. And the place to buy them is Cecilia's Boutique.''

"Anything would help. I'm so sick of wearing them.''

"You have to wear them in the store?''

"Yeah. A plum pair, would you believe it? Customers are supposed to come in, see me in my jodhpurs, say, 'Oh, darling, they're divine,' and buy themselves, or their daughters, a pair.''

"But do they?''

"No. They look me up and down obviously wondering if I'm sufficiently trendy even to wait on them. I'll meet you at the beach house, right?''

"It's an awfully long drive.''

"I only have the house another few days. Until the wedding.''

"When you gave up your place, why didn't you move into my apartment? It would have been much simpler.''

"What's wrong with having a beach house for the week before we get married?''

"Why don't you spend tonight at my apartment? That way I won't have to drive all the way out and back.''

"Hey. I'm getting paid for house-sitting. I know it's not much, but we need the money, right?"

"Right. It's just that I'd sort of like to stay in town and keep checking on a few things."

"I hear someone got bumped off in your parking lot this morning."

"True."

"A lawyer of some kind."

"Some kind."

"One of the ones you see in the newspaper all the time. A Perry Mason type. Murder trials, and big drug deals."

"Habeck. Donald Edwin Habeck."

"That's right. Interesting story. I mean, it should be interesting. I look forward to reading Biff Wilson about it."

Fletch said nothing.

"Fletch, you're not doing anything on that Habeck story, are you?"

"Well, there was a coincidence. I was just about to meet him when—"

"You'll get fired."

"Some confidence you've got."

"You haven't written enough wedding announcements yet, to take on a big story like that."

"I haven't taken it on. I just intend to sit and watch it."

"You've never *just sat* in your life."

"Well, maybe not *just sit*."

"Does anyone know you're sticking your nose into this story?"

"Barbara—"

"We're getting married Saturday, Fletch. First, you don't have time for any such story. Second, it really would be nice, when we come back from our skiing honeymoon, if you had a job. I'm pretty sure Cecilia won't have offloaded all her jodhpurs by then."

"Relax. If I turn up something interesting, something

useful, you think the newspaper would turn the information down?"

"Fletch, have nothing more to do with this story. Get away from it. Jealousies on a newspaper can't be any different from anywhere else."

"Anyway, I've been assigned to a different story altogether."

"What is it?"

"I'd rather not tell you, just now."

"Why not?"

"Well, it's not too far removed from wedding announcements, births, deaths. A travel story. You might say it's a travel story. It might even turn into a medical story."

"You're not making much sense."

"That's because I haven't really got ahold of the story yet. I'm writing it for the society pages."

"Fletch, I don't think there have been any society pages in this country for half a century."

"You know what I mean: the life pages, living, style. You know, the anxiety pages."

"You should be all right doing a piece for the anxiety pages."

"Sure. Anxieties, we all have 'em. You see, I was using my new influence to feed Cecilia's jodhpurs into Amelia Shurcliffe's column."

"Nice of you. When will you get to the beach house?"

"Soon as I can."

"What does that mean?"

"It means I have to run off some copies from a file. And then make one phone call."

"Only one?"

"Only one."

"And it has nothing to do with Habeck?"

"No, no," said Fletch. "Nothing to do with Habeck. Has to do with this other story. The one for the anxiety pages."

*   *   *

Fletch hesitated, just slightly, before pushing the button which would make selected copies from Habeck's file.

Sitting at his borrowed desk, he hesitated again, just slightly, before picking up the phone and dialing an in-house number.

"Carradine," the voice answered.

"Jack? This is Fletch."

"Who?"

"Fletcher. I work for the *News-Tribune*."

"Are you sure?" The financial writer's tone was mildly curious. "Oh, yeah. You're the guy who committed that headline a couple of months ago, what was it? Oh, yeah: WESTERN CAN CO. SITS ON ITS ASSETS."

"Yeah, I'm the one."

"That one, eh? Guess we're all young, once."

"Don't know why everybody objected to that."

"Because we'd all heard it before. Did you call for forgiveness, Fletcher, or do you have a hot tip for me on the international debt?"

"You know that guy who was murdered this morning?"

"Habeck? No. I didn't know him. Saw him once at a lunch for the Lakers."

"A couple of guys here are saying he was very rich."

"How rich is very rich?"

"That he was about to give away five million bucks."

"I doubt it. He was a worker. A high-priced worker, but a worker. I doubt he had more than he'd earned. What were his assets? A partnership in an admittedly prosperous law firm. What's that worth, year by year? Also, whatever he had been able to accumulate over a lifetime of work. Maybe he invested in something and struck it rich, but, if he had, I expect I would have heard of it. He was too much of a street person ever to have inherited anything much. And, again, if he had married great wealth, we would have known about it."

"What about the mob?"

"You think he was associated with the mob?"

"A criminal lawyer—"

"Sure, he probably had mob clients. But the mob doesn't make anybody rich but the mob. Despite what you read, the mob's biggest problem is financial constipation. The riskiest thing they do, at least regarding their own safety, is dispersing money. In fact, it's such a problem for them I don't know why they bother making so much."

"What's your guess as to how much money Habeck had when he died this morning?"

"Just a guess?"

"Take your time."

"Working hard all his life, paying his taxes reasonably well, giving little away, not making any big, stupid investments, not running through too many wives, which are a lot of big *if*s, I'd say he'd be pretty lucky to have five million dollars of his own."

"So," Fletch said. "Sam wins the office pool."

"Who's Sam?"

"Oh," Fletch said. "He drives one of the *News-Tribune* delivery trucks. The downtown run."

Fletch gathered the selected copies from the Habeck file. On top of the stack he put the volume Morton Rickmers had loaned him, *The Knife, The Blood*.

Then he hesitated a long moment before picking up the phone and dialing the number he had once thought belonged to a pizza-delivery establishment.

The voice that answered was young, female, strong, clear, healthy, and friendly. "Ben Franklyn Friend Service. You want a friend?"

Putting thoughts of anchovies and pepperoni out of mind, Fletch said, "I just might."

"Well, we're an escort service. Available twenty-four hours

a day. Your place or ours. But first, will you tell me who recommended you to Ben Franklyn?''

Fletch swallowed. ''My father.''

The girl hesitated. ''You have any problems, son?''

''Not that I know of.''

''Nice guy, your dad.''

''Yeah, he's a good old guy.''

''Doesn't want you to be alone in the big city, huh?''

''He doesn't—uh—want me making friends—uh—I can't get rid of. Uh.''

Suddenly, he had become very warm in the city room.

''I see. What's your dad's name?''

''Oh, I doubt he ever used your services himself. I mean, personally.''

''You'd be surprised. What's his name, anyway?''

''Uh. Jaffe. Archibald Jaffe. Never mind about him. My name is Fletcher Jaffe. I'm the one who's coming. I hope.''

''Okay, Fletcher. Why don't you come to the service? We'll check out your health.''

''I'm fine, thank you.''

''Oh, we're sure you are. By health, we mean just everything. We're friends like you never had before. We take care of all of you. You do exercise, don't you?''

''Oh, yes.''

''Well, we want to check out your skin tone, your muscle tone, your diet. Exercise you through to sexual fulfillment. You've never had friends like us before.''

''I'm sure.''

''We take you all the way, my man, from simple stretches, through deep breathing, to ecstasy.''

''Ecstasy! Wow!''

''You don't believe?''

''I've just never heard *ecstasy* used in a sentence before. I don't think. I mean, not conversationally.''

''You've never called Ben Franklyn Friend Service before.''

"Not for anything without cheese."

"What?"

"Never mind."

"You going to come right over?"

"Not right now. Someone's waiting for me. How about tomorrow?"

"Sure. I guess we can fit you in."

"Ha ha."

"What time?"

"Eleven o'clock."

"In the morning?"

"Right. I want to have my skin toned up."

"Fletcher Jaffe. Eleven o'clock tomorrow morning. We'll see you then. All of you. And you'll see all of us."

The phone clicked.

Fletch hung up.

And then did some deep breathing exercises.

13

"Wow!"

"These bugs are gettin' to me."

"Heck with the bugs. Listen to this."

Sitting on the beach in her swimsuit, Barbara Ralton was scratching her elbow with one hand and her back with the other. "Fletch, the bugs really take over the beach when the sun gets this low."

"Appropriate for what you're about to hear. Listen." His back propped against her beach bag, Fletch read:

> *Young flesh,*
> *taut skin,*
> *tight over muscle,*
> *smooth over joints,*
>   *Revealed*
>   *Realized*
>   *Explored*
>   *Exploited*

Felt
Most perfectly
    Reviled
    Revolted
    Explained
    Exploded
Sharp
Hard
Shining
Steel
    in a blade
draws across the flesh.
Blood bubbles, then
mimics the slit,
becomes a line
    of blood;
finding its own way, it
pours down the skin,
thick, red fluid
flowing over the soft
rose pink of skin.

Touch your tongue to the blood.
Bathe your lips in it.
Suck it through your teeth.
Let your eyes see above the slash
the skin draining, turning white,
whiter next the blood, and
watch the palpitations as
skin
reverberates with the ever-quickening
heart rhythm urging
out the blood to air, to
redness, to
flow.

What penetrates more
perfectly the warmth of flesh
than the coolness of steel?
    in truth,
were they not just
made for each other?

Barbara, bugs on her, was no longer scratching. She said, "That's sick."

"Pretty sharp," Fletch said.

In the red of the setting sun, she shuddered. "Punk."

Fletch ran his fingernail along her calf. "But do you get the point?"

"A little lacking in metaphor," she said.

"But consider the irony."

"Weird!" She moved the book in Fletch's hand to see the cover. "What's that supposed to be?"

"It's a poem by Tom Farliegh called *The Knife, The Blood*."

"That's poetry? Not exactly 'How do I love thee? Let me count the ways...'"

"I guess it's called the Poetry of Violence. Tom Farliegh is its inventor, or chief current practitioner, or something."

"Where did you get it, a motorcyclists' convention?"

"Tom Farliegh may or may not be Donald Habeck's son-in-law."

"For a son-in-law I'd rather Attila the Hun."

Fletch rolled onto his stomach. "It is sentimental, of course."

"I prefer Browning."

"At least he gives flesh and a knife their values."

"Oh, yeah. He does that. And why, Irwin, are you carrying around a book of poetry by Habeck's son-in-law the night that Habeck is murdered?"

Even facing away from the sun, Fletch squinted. "Don't you find it interesting?"

"Fascinating!" she said falsely. "Is the whole book like that?"

"I'll read you another." He reached for it in the sand.

"Not before supper, thank you." She stood up. "Flies and satanic poems. Did you bring anything for supper?"

"Yeah," Fletch answered. "There are some pretzels in the car."

"Great. I could tell you stopped somewhere on your way home. You arrived in nothing but swimming trunks."

"I know how to prepare pretzels."

"Come on. I brought lamb chops. I'll show you how to prepare them."

"I'm going to jump in the ocean." Fletch began to get up slowly. "Wash the sand off."

"You can tell me all about your new assignment," Barbara said, beach bag under her arm like a football. "The one that has nothing to do with people getting bullets in the head."

"Yeah, I'll do that," Fletch said absently.

> *in truth,*
> *were they not just*
> *made for each other?*

14

"So what's your assignment?" At the stove, Barbara wore an apron over her swimsuit.

Fletch munched a pretzel. "Research on Ben Franklyn."

Dark outside, light inside the beach house, the huge plate-glass windows reflected them.

"Somehow Ben Franklin doesn't strike me as news."

Fletch found the brown paper bag in which Barbara had brought the chops, potatoes, peas, and milk. In it, he put Donald Habeck's suit, shirt, tie, drawers, socks, and shoes. "Got some string?"

"Look in that drawer." She pointed with the potato masher. "What's new about Ben Franklin?"

"Healthy sort of man. Very contemporary." Fletch tied the string around the package. "Inventive. Diplomatic. Always liked the ladies. A businessman, too. He was a good businessman, wasn't he?"

"How burned do you like your chops?"

"If you're asking, stop cooking." He tossed the package on the floor near the front door.

Sitting at the table, Barbara said, "I'm calling your mother."

"What did I do now?"

"You're getting married Saturday. Don't you think Jessica ought to hear from me, her daughter-in-law-to-be?"

"Oh, sure."

"Give her the opportunity to come to the wedding, you know? Make her feel really welcome."

"I wrote her. Don't know if she can afford to come. She's a poor writer, you know. I should say, she's a writer, and she's poor. And if we pay her way from Seattle, we won't be able to afford a honeymoon."

"Still, her son's getting married."

"Naked?" Fletch asked. "Do you still mean for us to get married naked?"

"No." Barbara scooped mashed potato into her mouth. "I haven't been able to get rid of that eight pounds."

"Ah," smiled Fletch. "So you do have something to hide."

"I'll ask you once more about your father."

"What about him?"

She asked, "What about him?"

"He died in childbirth." Fletch shrugged. "That's what mother always said."

"Modern American marriage." Barbara sighed and looked at their reflection in the window.

"Yeah," Fletch said, "what's it for?"

"What do you mean, 'What's it for?'?"

"Alston asked me at lunch if I was sure I want to get married. That was just after I asked him to be my best man."

"Alston works for Habeck's law firm, doesn't he?"

"Yeah."

"Is he happy there?"

"Not very."

"What did you answer?"

"I don't remember."

"Lawyers are always asking difficult questions. That's their job. Makes 'em feel superior, I think. Helps them create the illusion they're worth their fees."

"Frank Jaffe said something or other about the only point in getting married is if you intend to have children."

"He's right. Almost."

"Do we intend to have children?"

"Sure." Barbara's eyes glanced over the rough wooden floor of the beach house. "We have to have money, first. You're not earning much. In fact, you're not in a very high-paid profession. I'm not in a profession at all. Kids cost a lot."

"Someone mentioned that today, too."

"What did you do, go around today developing a brief against marriage?"

"I went around today announcing the joyful news you and I are getting married Saturday, and everybody asked, *Why?*" Barbara stared at Fletch. "In fact, I'd say for the most part, people's reaction was, *Bleh!*"

"That's not very nice of people."

"No. It isn't."

"Just because other people make bum marriages . . ."

"What criterion do we have, but other people's marriages?"

"I think our getting married makes sense."

"So do I."

"We can support each other."

"Right. Today I tried to help you get out of Cecilia's jodhpurs."

"Build toward a family, a way of life."

"As long as I keep accepting one miserable assignment at the newspaper after another."

"Companionship. Grow old together, seeing things from

somewhat the same perspective, having the same memories, protecting each other.''

"Correct," said Fletch. "You know anybody who's doing it?"

"Doesn't mean we can't."

"No. It doesn't."

"I definitely think we should get married," Barbara said.

"I do, too," Fletch agreed. "Definitely."

"Just think of marriage the way you think of everything else," Barbara said. "Playing through to truth. Only in marriage, you're playing through to a truth of you, and me, and us."

The telephone rang.

Startled, Barbara looked at it. "Who could that be?"

"I asked Alston to call. He may have some things to tell me about Donald Habeck."

"Habeck." Barbara carried her plate to the sink. "You're crazy."

"Yeah." Fletch stood up to answer the phone. "Factor that in, too."

15

"Hate to admit it, ol' buddy," Alston said. "But you just might be right."

"Of course I am." Fletch settled into a Morris chair by the phone. "About what?"

"As best I could, without my fingers getting caught in the files, I've been able to dig up a few things for you: Habeck's latest big case; his current big case; and—this is where you may be right—what old client of his just got out of the pen with, maybe, an irrepressible urge to send a bullet through Habeck's skull."

"There is one?"

"First, his last and current big cases. Doubtlessly you have comprehensive newspaper files on both."

"Yes. I got them this afternoon."

"So you know the current big case concerns the chairman of the State House Ways and Means Committee being charged with a kickback scheme. Bribery."

"Yeah."

"He's charged specifically with having accepted fifty-three thousand, five hundred dollars from an architectural firm contracted to design a new wing on the State Penitentiary at Wilton."

"Hope the state senator had them design a nice cell with a southern view for himself."

"Doubt he'll ever see it, if he did. The maneuvers here are too sophisticated for me to understand. I don't mean legal maneuvers, I mean political maneuvers. Habeck has filed all kinds of motions and petitions I don't understand. He's doing the most amazing fox-trot through the courts with this case. I don't understand why the courts put up with this kind of wriggling."

"Habeck was just trying to let the case get to be old news as far as the public is concerned, wasn't he? After a while the public, and the courts, too, I suppose, lose their anger over a case like this. We become tired of reading about it. Indifferent to what happens. Right?"

"Right. It would help if you journalistic types blew the whistle on this kind of maneuvering once in a while. Reported in depth the history of such a case. Demand that the courts make final disposition of it."

"Yes, sir."

"So you'd be interested in Habeck's personal notations on the records of this case?"

"You bet."

"The first notation says, *Get this before Judge Carroll Swank.*"

"Ah. The idea being that Judge Swank owes something from the deep, dark, shadowy past to Senator Schoenbaum."

"One assumes so. Some indebtedness safely hidden. You boys would never be able to find it."

"Or, Senator Schoenbaum holds something in the blackmail line over the aforesaid Judge Swank."

"Judges may deliberate like self-righteous prigs, but they must live as pragmatists."

"I'll write that down."

"A second note on the file in Habeck's own writing might also interest you. It reads, *Actual kickbacks Schoenbaum admits to over eight hundred thousand dollars. Tax-free, note. Plan fee in five-hundred-thousand-dollar range.* Both these notes are near the beginning of the file. The rest of the file is just a record of Habeck's jerking the courts around."

"Until he gets the case in front of Judge Swank."

"And that's when he really jerks the court around."

"Meanwhile, Senator Schoenbaum is vacationing in Hawaii."

"Yes. Poor jerk thinks he's going to come out of this a rich and free man."

"Well, he's half-right."

"I don't see Schoenbaum as anybody who wants to ventilate Habeck's head."

"No."

"The other cases Habeck is pleading, and there are more than twenty, are all being worked up by underlings, poor beavers like me. Several cases of embezzlement, two vehicular homicides, a half-dozen cases of insurance fraud, as many as ten cases of parental kidnappings—you know, when a member of a divorced couple loses the custody battle and arranges to have his own kid kidnapped?"

"That many?"

"It's a big business. If I ever decide to leave Habeck, Harrison and Haller, I might decide to go into it. I'd feel more useful."

"Gives one pause to think."

"Plus one rather funny case about a milkman."

"I met a witty milkman once."

"This one is real witty. Listen. First, he rented a sable coat for his wife, for a month, on credit."

"Loving husband."

"Then he walked his sable-adorned wife into a Rolls-Royce showroom, and leased a Rolls-Royce for a month, on credit."

"Liked good cars, too."

"With his wife in the sable coat, both of them in the Rolls-Royce, he was able to rent a small mansion in Palm Springs."

"Why shouldn't a milkman live well?"

"With the coat, the Rolls, and the house, he then went to a local bank, and wangled a five-hundred-thousand-dollar cash loan."

"Wow."

"And gave up his job as a milkman."

"Yeah. Why should he need to work with all he's got?"

"He returned the coat, the car, and canceled the lease on the house. And skipped to Nebraska."

"You can buy a lot of cows in Nebraska for five hundred thousand dollars."

"Even the bank didn't care, for three years, because the guy kept paying them interest out of the principal he had borrowed."

"Don't tell me. He was charged with Understanding America Too Well."

"Eventually, the well ran dry, of course, and the bank went after the retired milkman."

"Why would Habeck take on a case like that? I don't see how the milkman can pay him much."

"Okay. Habeck took on the milkman's case. As soon as the bank heard that, they began to shake in their collective boots. Habeck, Harrison and Haller bought a few shares in the bank, and then threatened the bank with full exposure. Charged loan-forcing, incompetent administration, and a loan policy so inept that clearly the bank's charter should be revoked. After all, Fletch, they made a half-a-million-dollar loan to a milkman!"

"Oh, boy. So the bank is going to swallow the five-hundred-thousand-dollar loss, or whatever part of it the milkman didn't pay back out of principal?"

"Not only that, two of the partners in the bank, who also happen to be bank officers, are buying back the few shares of stock Habeck, Harrison and Haller own at what you may describe as well above market value."

"Phew. What I'm learning about the law. Tell me, Alston, is that called 'settling out of court'?"

"I think it's called having a bank by the short hairs, and tugging."

"I think it's called blackmail. Of course, I never went to law school."

"At law school, it's called blackmail."

"So far today, I've learned Habeck, Harrison and Haller, as a law firm, is actively in the burglary business, the blackmail business, judge fixing . . . what else do you guys do for a living?"

"Don't ask."

"You sure all law firms aren't this way?"

"Absolutely not."

"What happened to the milkman?"

"He moved to New York State, where he's employed as—"

"A milkman!"

"No. As some kind of a psychotherapist. During his three years in Nebraska, he qualified for some kind of a degree, got a professional certification which permits him to earn a living being understanding."

"I'll bet he's good at it."

"I'll bet he is."

"Upward mobility, Alston."

"The American dream."

"Through judicious use of credit."

"The name of the game."

"The creation of another debt-free professional."

"Warms my heart."

"The legal system works, Alston."

"Don't you ever forget it."

"And a bank had to sharpen its loan policy, from which we all benefit."

"Habeck's last case that reached the newspapers was about a year ago."

"The case of the Fallen Doctor."

"Yeah, the doctor who organized a certain number of his patients into drug pushers. The doctor was a wreck himself."

"And Habeck got him off by charging the Narcotics Bureau with entrapment."

"Ultimately, yes. First he went through a lot of dazzling footwork regarding the sanctity of the patient-slash-doctor relationship. To wit, doctors are not to be entrapped by the confidences of patients who turn out to be narcs."

"And, tell me, Alston, how did Habeck, Harrison and Haller get paid for that job?"

"There was a million dollars of cocaine never found by the authorities."

"Good God. Burglary, blackmail, drug pushing . . . why doesn't someone bring charges against Habeck, Harrison and Haller?"

"Who'd dare? In fact, talking to you right now, I feel my pants slipping down around my ankles."

"I appreciate that, Alston."

"Where you may be right is that a Habeck client got out of jail last Tuesday. And he's not a very nice person. He served eleven years the hard way. And I don't understand why Habeck took on the case in the first place."

"No personal notes?"

"All the files, except for a microfilm record of the case, are in the warehouse in Nevada and I can't get to them."

"He must have had a reason."

"A child molester. A real sweetheart. He had two trained German shepherds. Apparently he'd enter a housing project, first attract little kids with his dogs. Then the trained dogs would herd and hold the little kids in a corner of the building, or the play yard, and this son of a bitch would then make free with them."

"Jesus."

"Say one for me. Takes all types, uh?"

"Jesus!"

"Lots of little kids gave evidence. There were lots of witnesses to the event with which he was finally charged. I guess he had been getting away with it for a long time. He counted on the dogs to help him make his escape. What he didn't count on were a couple of black brothers who weren't intimidated by German shepherds and kicked their heads in."

"And he got only eleven years?"

"Habeck must have done something for him."

"Eleven years!"

"I'm sure they were eleven hard years, Fletch. Child molesters are not popular in prison. They get very few invitations to the cellblock cocktail parties."

"What's his name?"

"Felix Gabais. Employed at various jobs, bus driver, school-bus driver, taxi driver. Lived with a crippled sister in the Saint Ignatius area. Would be about forty-one, forty-two years old now."

"If Habeck got him out of prison in eleven years on that kind of charge, I can't see why he'd go gunning for Habeck."

"He's crazy, Fletch. I mean, a guy who works all that out with trained dogs has to be crazy. Talk about premeditation."

"I guess so."

"In this case, he's had eleven years to premeditate."

"Alston, I have another thought. Supposing someone killed or maimed one of your loved ones. And Habeck got him off scot-free, or something meaningless, a suspended sentence, or something. Wouldn't that incline you to go after Habeck?''

"Come again?''

"I heard of a case today in which Habeck was involved. Drunken teenager stole a car and killed someone with it. Habeck got him off with just a sentence of probation. What about the victim's family? Wouldn't they have reason to be pretty mad at Habeck?''

"I can see them wanting to harm the drunken kid.''

"But not Habeck?''

"That would take too much thinking. First, in anger, I think people want to see people get the punishment they deserve. When the courts don't give perpetrators the punishment they clearly deserve, yeah, I think even the most decent people feel the temptation to go out and beat the perpetrator over the head themselves.''

"But, if they think twice...''

"If they think twice, they're angry at something vague, you know, like *the legal system,* or *justice,* or *the courts.*''

"You don't think anyone ever focuses on the defense attorney who twists the legal system to get genuine bad guys off free?''

"It's possible. Someone bright, maybe.''

"Someone bright who sees a pattern in what Habeck is doing.''

"And, maybe, has a personal grudge.''

"And knows there is no way of ever bringing Habeck to justice.''

"Yeah. Such a person might be able to justify shooting Habeck in the head. But, Fletch, think of the numbers. Over Habeck's thirty-five-year career, the numbers of victims' loved ones and families who have watched Habeck send the perpetrator to the beach instead of to jail must number in the hundreds, the thousands.''

"I suppose so.'' Fletch took *The Knife, The Blood* from the table beside the telephone. "Anyway, I already know who killed Habeck."

"Bright boy." Alston sighed. "Why didn't you tell me that in the first place? Instead of spending all this long time talking to you, I could have gone jogging."

"You can still go jogging," Fletch said, turning the pages.

"I don't want to get mugged by a milkman."

"Listen to this." Fletch read:

> *Slim, belted hips*
> *Sprayed across by automatic fire,*
> *each bullet*
> *ripping through,*
> *lifting,*
> *throwing back,*
> *kicking*
> *the body at its*
> *center.*
> *Thus*
> *The Warrior In Perfection*
> *bows to his death,*
> *twists,*
> *pivots and falls.*
> *Waisted, he is wasted*
> *but not wasted.*
> *This death is his life*
> *And he is perfect*
> *In it.*

"Jeez!" Alston breathed. "What's that?"

"A poem called *The Warrior in Perfection.*"

"You and I know a little better than that, don't we, buddy."

"Do we?"

"That dancing beauty just isn't there."

"It isn't."

"That's the sickest thing I've ever heard. It makes me angry."

"If I'm right, and I'm not sure that I am, it was written by Donald Edwin Habeck's son-in-law."

"Oh. Anybody who'd write that would do anything for kicks."

"I read one to Barbara called *Knife, Blood* and suddenly she decided she had to come off the beach to get dinner."

"I think you're right. You needn't look any further for the murderer of Habeck than the snake who wrote that poem."

"I think he's worth talking to."

"So, the newspaper wants you on this story?"

"No, Alston, they don't."

"Trying to prove yourself, boy?"

"If I come up with something good, do you think the newspaper will turn it down?"

"I have no idea."

"I'm getting married. I've got to get going in life. So far, I'm playing dumb jokes on the newspaper. And the newspaper is playing dumb jokes on me."

"You're taking a risk."

"What risk? If I don't come up with anything, no one will ever know it."

16

Barbara stood wrapped in a towel over Fletch in the Morris chair.

"You want to know why we're getting married?"

"The world keeps asking," Fletch answered.

She dropped the towel on the floor.

She stood before him in the dimly lit beach house like a sculpture just finished.

"This body and your body moving in concert through life, in copulation and out of copulation, coupled, always relating to each other, each movement to each, however near or separated we may be, will measure our minuet in this existence, tonight, tomorrow, and all tomorrows,"

Fletch cleared his throat. "I've heard worse poetry. Recently."

"Are you coming to bed?"

"I guess I'd better." Fletch stood up, thinking of the immediate tomorrow. "It's now, or maybe never again."

17

Barbara entered the bedroom, head down, reading the front page of the newspaper.

"Dammit," Fletch said from the bed. "Next time you house-sit, please check to make sure there are curtains on the bedroom windows first, will you?"

"Biff Wilson made the front page."

"Of course."

"Or Habeck did."

"The sun isn't even up yet."

"You want to hear this?" Folding one leg under her, Barbara sat on the bed.

"Yeah."

" 'Nationally famous criminal attorney, partner in the law firm of Habeck, Harrison and Haller, Donald Edwin Habeck, sixty-one, was found shot to death in his late-model blue Cadillac Seville this morning in the parking lot of the *News-Tribune*.' "

"This bedroom faces west, but still this room is as full of light before dawn as a church at high noon Sundays."

" 'Police describe the murder as, quote, in the style of a gangland slaying, unquote.' "

" 'Gangland'!"

"That's what it says. 'Mr. Habeck's law partners, Charles Harrison and Claude Haller, issued a joint statement before noon this morning.' "

"I'll bet they did. Dropped all other work and put themselves right down to it."

" " "The legal profession has lost one of its most brilliant minds and deft practitioners with the passing of Donald Habeck. His incisive understanding and innovative use of the law as a defense attorney, especially in criminal cases, made Donald Habeck an example to attorneys nationally, and somewhat of a popular hero. We mourn the passing of our partner and dearest friend, especially under such despicable and inexplicable circumstances. Our heartfelt sympathy goes out to Donald's widow, Jasmine, his son Robert, daughter Nancy in parenthesis Farliegh, and his grandchildren." ' "

" 'Innovative,' " Fletch said. "First time I've heard that word to mean crooked."

"Was he crooked?" Barbara asked.

"There was a moment yesterday when I referred to Habeck as a *criminal lawyer* I was afraid someone would think I was making a joke."

"Some wordsmiths, these guys. 'Despicable and inexplicable circumstances.' "

"Lawyers are the only people in the world who get to say, 'Words don't mean what they mean. They mean what we say they mean.' A deft practitioner of the law. Ha! A perverter of the legal system."

"You seem to have formed a personal opinion, Fletch."

"I hear what I hear."

"Don't let personal opinion get in your way. There are other perfectly good ways you can destroy us over this story."

"You're right."

" 'Habeck's wife, Jasmine, was placed in seclusion by her doctors and therefore was not available for comment.' "

"There must have been a first Mrs. Habeck. Any reference to her?"

"Not that I see. 'Neither Harrison nor Haller would comment on the nature of Habeck's death pending police investigation.' "

"It was no gangland slaying."

" 'According to John Winters, publisher of the *News-Tribune*, Donald Habeck had requested a meeting with Mr. Winters for ten o'clock this morning to seek advice regarding the announcement of a charitable contribution Mr. Habeck intended to make in the city. "I did not personally know Donald Habeck," John Winters said. "Naturally, all of us here in the *News-Tribune* family express our regrets in his family and friends." ' "

"Wise old John Winters. Hold the sleazy lawyer at arm's length even in his death. Amelia Shurcliffe said no one would dare declare Donald Habeck either a friend or an enemy. I guess she was right."

" 'Mr. Habeck's body was discovered by *News-Tribune* employee Pilar O'Brien while she was reporting to work. Police Lieutenant Francisco Gomez stated Mr. Habeck had been shot once in the head at apparently close range by a handgun of as yet undetermined caliber. The gun was not discovered at the scene of the crime.' "

"It was not a gangland slaying."

" 'A graduate of the state system of education, and for years a visiting lecturer at the law school, Habeck . . . ' Blah, blah, blah. The report goes on to recount his most famous cases." Barbara turned to an inside page. "At great length. Want me to read all that?"

"I went through all that yesterday. Even I know how to write obituaries."

"I think son-in-law Tom Farliegh should be arrested, charged, convicted, and imprisoned immediately." Barbara refolded the newspaper.

"You think Tom Farliegh murdered Habeck?"

"Tom Farliegh wrote that poem you read me last night. Isn't that enough reason to imprison him? A man who writes a so-called poem like that shouldn't be left loose to walk around in the streets."

"It was not a gangland slaying."

"Am I'm supposed to ask you why you keep saying that?"

"Are you asking?"

"I suppose so."

"In order to drive into the parking lot of the *News-Tribune* you have to stop and identify yourself and state your purpose to the guard at the gate. But anyone can walk in and out. Habeck's car was parked more toward the back of the lot than the front. I just can't see professional gangsters stopping and saying anything to the guard at the gate, driving in, doing their dirty deed, then driving out again. I also can't see a professional gangster parking his car outside the gate, walking in, popping Habeck in the head, and then walking out. Can you? A professional gangster would have hit Habeck somewhere else."

"Strange no one heard the shot."

"A small-caliber handgun makes a pop so slight, especially in a big, open-air parking lot, you could mistake the sound for a belch after eating Greek salad."

Barbara stretched out beside him on the bed.

"Guess I should start the long drive back to the city," Fletch said.

"You don't have to go yet."

"How do you know? There are many, many things I want to do today. And some I don't."

"Don't forget you're having dinner with Mother and me tonight. To discuss the wedding."

Fletch glanced at his watch. "We really did wake up awfully early. I guess we have time."

"I know." Barbara cupped her hands behind his neck. "That's because I took down all the window curtains in here last night, before you arrived."

18

"Good morning," Fletch said cheerily to the middle-aged woman in an apron who opened the door to him at 12339 Palmiera Drive, The Heights. Her eyes narrowed as she recognized him as the man who had run through her kitchen the day before wearing nothing but a denim shirt hanging from his waist. He gave her a big smile. "I'm really not all the trouble I'm worth."

"Yes?" she asked.

"I just want to deliver this package." He handed the grocery bag filled with Donald Habeck's clothes through the doorway to her. "I'd also like to see Mrs. Habeck, if possible."

The woman kept the door braced with her feet when she took the package with both hands. The string had loosened. "In seclusion," she said. "Under sedation."

One of Donald Habeck's black shoes dropped out of the bag.

"Oh, my," Fletch said. He picked up the shoe and put it on top of the bundle in her arms.

The woman drew her head back from the shoe.

"One other question," Fletch went on. "There was an older woman here yesterday, sitting by the pool. Bluish hair, red purse, green sneakers. Do you know who she was?"

The woman looked at Fletch through narrow slits over Donald Habeck's shoe.

"She said she was Mrs. Habeck. She acted strangely."

"I do not speak English," the woman said. "Not a single goddamned word."

"I see."

She closed the door.

"I'll be back to see Mrs. Habeck when she's feeling better!" Fletch shouted through the door.

Getting into his car in the driveway, Fletch looked up at the house.

A window curtain in the second story fell back into place.

19

"Thank you for seeing me," Fletch said slowly, "so promptly."

He was surprised the curator of contemporary art at the museum was seeing him at all, let alone at nine-thirty in the morning without an appointment. He expected museum curators to keep relaxed hours. He also expected any museum curator to be standoffish with someone presenting himself in blue jeans and T-shirt, however fresh and clean, sneakers however new and glistening white, who said he was from a newspaper.

He also did not expect any museum curator, however contemporary, to be sitting behind a desk in a Detroit Tigers baseball cap. On the desk, beside one huge book with MARGILETH written in script on the glossy cover and a few folders, was an outfielder's mitt and a baseball.

"You're from the *News-Tribune*," curator William Kennedy confirmed.

"Yes. I was assigned to report on the five-million-dollar

gift to the museum that was to be announced by Donald and Jasmine Habeck." Fletch smiled slightly at his accurate use of the past tense. "A lady in your Trustees' Office said she thought the gift was to be made to this department."

"I'm glad to talk to someone, anyone, about it," Kennedy said.

Fletch asked, "Are you from Detroit?"

"No." Kennedy took off his baseball cap and looked at its logo. "I just admire excellence, in any form."

"I see."

"I also collect video-cassettes of Nureyev, Muhammad Ali, and Michael Jackson. Recordings of Caruso, McCormack, Erroll Garner, and Eric Clapton. Do you think I'm odd?"

"Eclectic."

"I'm a perfectly happy man." Kennedy reached for his baseball mitt. "I don't know why everyone isn't like me."

"Neither do I," Fletch said.

"Do you collect things?"

"Yes," Fletch said. "People."

"What an interesting thought."

"I don't use people, just collect them. It gives me some interesting memories on the long drive."

"Is that why you're a journalist?"

"I suppose so. That, and a few other reasons."

"You have less of a storage problem than I have."

"First, I need to confirm with you that Mr. and Mrs. Donald Habeck were giving this department of the museum five million dollars."

"I'm not sure." Kennedy tossed the ball up into the air and caught it in his mitt. "And if they were going to actually make such an offer, in writing, I'm not sure we would accept it."

Fletch raised his eyebrows. "Wouldn't a museum accept money from any source?"

"The source doesn't bother us. In my fifteen-year museum

reer to date, I've never seen money turned down because of
source, even if it were tainted money. Remember that old
heeze about Mark Twain? A minister came to him saying
at a gangster had offered him money to fix the church's
of. Twain asked, 'Why are you hesitating?' The minister
id, 'Because it's tainted money.' 'That's right,' Twain said.
'ain't yours, and t'ain't mine.' ''

"You collect good stories, too?"

"As they come along."

"I think I'm hearing you saying that you considered
abeck's money tainted."

Kennedy shrugged. "We know he was a tricky lawyer."

"By 'tricky' do you mean crooked? I think I'm collecting
olite ways of saying crooked."

"How often do you hear of lawyers going to jail?"

"Not often."

"Doctors get sick, but lawyers seldom go to jail."

"Why would a museum turn down money?"

"Because of the stipulations that come with the money. Let
e explain." Kennedy put his mitted hand on top of the
aseball cap on his head. His other hand spun the baseball on
e desk. "Late last week, Donald Habeck made an appoint-
ent to see me. I was dismayed when my secretary told me
ne had made the appointment. We had never pursued Donald
labeck. I have never heard that he cared anything about art,
r the museum. Therefore, I suspected he wanted to talk me
ato being an expert witness for a case of his—something of
at sort."

"And you wouldn't have agreed?"

"I don't think so. I have been an expert witness in court,
f course. But only when I have felt I was on solid ground,
ould trust whichever side of a case requested me. I don't
ake a career of it. Only when I feel need for me is
astified."

"And you didn't feel you could trust Donald Habeck?"

"I didn't know anything about him, other than an impre sion of him that has come through the newspapers a television press. Vaguely, my impression was that, through lot of tricks, he kept people who ought to be in jail out of it. had never met the man."

Fletch noted how quick people were to say they had nev met, or had scarcely met, Donald Habeck.

"So Habeck was given an appointment, but not invited lunch," Kennedy continued. "He came in last Wednesda afternoon, sat in the chair you're sitting in, and surprised th hell out of me by saying he was thinking of giving th museum five million dollars."

"What was your first question?"

Kennedy thought a moment. "My first question was, 'C your own money?' Immediately, I was suspicious, of I don know what."

"And he confirmed it was his own money he wanted t give away?"

"Yes. I then said, as politely as I could, that I had neve heard he was interested either in art or the museum. H answered that he was very interested in art and, furthermore that he had identified what he referred to as 'a vast hole' i our present contemporary collection."

"That got your attention."

"It certainly did. I could hardly wait to hear what 'hole' h felt was in our collection. Ours is not the strongest collectio of contemporary art in the whole world, but it is very stron and really quite well balanced, thanks to my predecessor an myself." Kennedy was again playing catch with himself "He said he wanted the five million dollars spent exclusivel on acquiring contemporary religious art."

After a moment, Fletch said, "That's a puzzle."

"Isn't it?" Looking at Fletch apologetically, Kenned said, "As you know, or don't know, there is almost n contemporary religious art. I mean, all art is religious, isn'

In its own way, even the profane. Art depicts man in his
relation to nature, himself, his fellow persons, and his deity.
Not all of it may be worshipful, but each piece of true art, to
me, is a powerful acknowledgment of the nature of our
existence.''

"How did you answer him?"

"Politely, I asked him whom he thought we should be
collecting. In true legalistic fashion, he answered that we are
supposed to be the experts in that, and that if we felt we
couldn't find viable contemporary religious art to acquire,
I'd take his money elsewhere.''

"A tough guy even in his giving.''

"Wait. You haven't heard everything. Gently, I tried to
explain to Mr. Habeck that if there were much viable contemporary religious art, I'd be the first to seek it out and acquire
Of course, prayer-card art, like the poor, is ever with us.
Some churches have developed very contemporary-looking
designs for their crosses, and stations thereof. But unless you
consider a Jesus with female breasts on the cross a viable
statement, there isn't much new in the field. As critics and
curators, we find ourselves nowadays, perhaps mistakenly,
considering the various religious genres, from Creation to
man-at-the-stake, closed history.'' Kennedy tossed the ball
high and caught it. "Then I realized I was lecturing the poor
man, and that was not why he came here. I could see he was
getting angry. I was on the wrong track altogether. So, more
personally, I asked him why he wanted to contribute so much
money.''

"A question we all have.''

"I expect the answer will astound you. After a few
moments of writhing in that chair, I'm sure looking as
uncomfortable as any witness under his own cross-examination,
Habeck blurted out that his life was over, that he was packing
in; no one cared a tin whistle for him; he was dispossessing
himself of all of his property, and''—Kennedy threw the ball

high in the air; he had to lean forward to catch it—''I
intended to spend the rest of his life in a Roman Cathol
monastery.''

After a moment of silence, Kennedy threw the ball acro
the desk at Fletch.

Catching the ball, Fletch said, ''Glunk.''

''Thought that would surprise you,'' Kennedy said. ''Yo
see why I'm happy to talk to you this morning. A ve
strange circumstance indeed.''

''My, my. Who'd have thought it?''

''Aren't people amazing? Well worth your collecting.''

''He wanted to become a monk?''

''Yes. So he said. A Roman Catholic monk. Spend the re
of his life reading Thomas Merton, or something. Matins an
evensong. The whole bit.''

''He always wore black shoes.''

''What?''

''Never mind.''

''Needless to say, we've had some staff meetings aroun
here to discuss this whole Habeck business. No one ha
known what to think. Then, yesterday, when I was driving o
to lunch, I heard on the car radio Habeck had been murdere
When he said last Wednesday that his life was over, he wa
more right than he knew.''

''If he wanted to give away five million dollars and go int
the monastery, why didn't he give the money to the monas
tery, or to the Church?''

''I asked him that. He said he was too old ever to fulfill
ministry. Furthermore, that he would have too much to learn
And, he wanted the peace an quiet of a monastery. He said h
was tired of talking and arguing and pleading. Would yo
believe that?''

''So establishing a collection of religious art at the museu
would do his public pleading for him?''

''I guess. He hoped such a collection would inspire reli

ious feelings among contemporary people more than any
ermons he could ever give, or ever want to give. If I
nderstood him correctly.''

Fletch tossed the ball back to Kennedy in a high arc. ''I
on't get it.''

''He said he'd have something more than a million dollars
eft over, and that money he would give to the monastery.''

''What about his wife? His kids? His grandchildren?''

''He didn't mention them. Except to say no one cared a tin
histle for him. His words exactly.''

Kennedy tossed the baseball back to Fletch.

''The museum as church, uh?''

''A museum is partly a church. Maybe entirely a church.''

''So how did you leave it with him?''

''I was so startled, I suggested he think it over. I think I
ven dared suggest he talk it over with his wife, his children,
is law partners.''

Fletch tossed the ball back in as high an arc as the room
ould take. ''Curator as minister, eh?''

''Or shrink.'' And I told him we'd talk it over here. I
ndicated very strongly to him that I didn't feel we could take
is five million dollars with the restriction that it be spent
olely on acquiring contemporary religious art. It wouldn't be
air to him to accept money on conditions we couldn't
bserve.'' He tossed the ball back to Fletch. ''If he could find
ome wording which would make the money available to us
o use, with the understanding that we would acquire valid
ontemporary religious art when and if it became available,
hen maybe we could accept his money.''

Fletch arced the ball back at the curator. ''And he, being a
awyer, was perfectly sure that he could develop such wording.''

''Probably. The story of his murder I read on the front page
f your newspaper this morning said he intended to see your
ublisher regarding the announcement that he was giving five
nillion dollars to something in the city.''

"The museum was what was mentioned to me."

"Did you write that piece in this morning's paper?"

"No. Biff Wilson."

Kennedy tossed the ball into his glove. "It was a goo
piece."

"It was okay," Fletch said. "For an obituary."

20

In the very small reception room of the Ben Franklyn Friend Service, the young-middle-aged, distinguished-looking woman gave Fletch the once-over from behind her small wooden desk.

"If you take your left here at the corner," she said, pointing a manicured hand, "and left again in the middle of the block, you'll find yourself in the alley."

"Ecstatic!"

"Our delivery door is about halfway down, on the left." Over her pink sweatsuit she wore a long rope of pearls. "The door is clearly marked."

"Pure ecstasy!"

The woman frowned. "You are making a delivery, aren't you?" She looked more the type to be sitting at a checkout desk in a public library.

"What am I delivering?" Fletch asked.

"Linens. Towels."

"Me."

"You?"

"Me. In all my parts. Head, shoulders, hips, and knee joints, right down to the ankles. And everything in between." Fletch swallowed hard.

"Do you have an appointment?" She opened a desk calendar. "You're just not the sort . . ."

"Sort of what?"

Her eyes confirmed that he was wearing a T-shirt, faded jeans, and very white, new sneakers. ". . . the sort we usually see."

"I was welcomed by the museum dressed this way."

"Your name?"

"Jaffe."

"Ah, yes: Fletcher Jaffe." She made a pencil check in the IN box beside his name.

"You've heard the name before?"

"We don't pay that much attention to names."

"Jaffe is a name to which you should pay attention."

"That will be one hundred and fifty dollars."

"Good! I'll pay it!" He dropped seven twenties and a ten on the desk. "Make sure I get a receipt."

She looked quizzically at him. "Our clients don't usually ask for receipts."

"I do."

"I'll make out a receipt for you before you leave."

"Why not now?"

"Well, you might want to add on some extras."

"Extra whats?"

The woman seemed embarrassed. "Tips. Whatever. "

"I see."

"You're not married, are you?"

Fletch shook his head. "No, ma'am. No one goes through my pockets."

"Diseases?" Her eyes enlarged as she looked at him. "Are you willing to swear you have no diseases?"

"This place is harder to get into than a New England prep school."

"I asked you about diseases."

"Chicken pox."

"Chicken pox!"

"When I was nine." Fletch pointed out a pockmark on his left elbow. "I'm better now, thank you."

The woman sighed. She pressed a button on the desk intercom. "Cindy? Someone's here to see you."

"Ah, Cindy!" exclaimed Fletch. "I was hoping for a Cindy. Nobody wants a Zza-zza, Queenie, or Bobo this hour of the day."

"I've seen you somewhere before," the woman said, almost to herself. "Recently."

"I'm around town," Fletch said breezily. "A bit of a *boulevardier.*"

"Oh, Cindy," said the woman. "This is Fletcher Jaffe."

In the door stood a woman in her early twenties. She was dressed only in well-cut nylon gym shorts, sneakers, and footies. Her shoulders were lightly muscled. Her perk breasts were tanned in the round identically with the rest of her body. Muscles were visible in her stomach. Her black hair and wide-set eyes matched perfectly and had the same sparkle.

Looking at Fletch, she wrinkled her nose.

"Good morning, Cindy." Fletch again swallowed hard. "Glad you came to work early today."

Through the street door came another young woman. She was wearing white jeans and a loose red shirt. She had fly-away blond hair.

Approaching the desk, she openly studied the scene: Fletch standing in the middle of the small reception room; Cindy presenting herself in the doorway.

"Marta!" she whimpered to the woman at the desk.

"I can't help it, Carla," Marta answered.

"You told me I should sleep in, this morning!"

"I also told you," Marta said forcefully, "never to wear that color red. It doesn't go with your hair coloring."

"I know." Carla giggled. "It makes men in the street look away."

In the interior doorway, Cindy tossed her head. Fletch followed her.

He followed her down a paneled, carpeted corridor.

"You a cop?" she asked.

"No."

"I hope you are," Cindy muttered. "Time this place got busted." She slowed her walk. "Do me a favor, though, will you?"

"Anything."

"Bust this place if you want. See where it will get you. But don't bust me personally, okay?"

"What makes you think I'm a cop?"

"I'm splitting the end of this week. I swear to you. I don't want the hassle."

"If I'm a cop, you're ugly."

Even in the dark corridor, her skin had a lovely sheen.

She smiled at the compliment.

She opened a heavy drawer built into the wall, and pulled out another pair of well-cut nylon shorts. "These about right? Waist thirty?"

She tossed them to him.

"Sure."

She led him into a brightly lit room to the left off the corridor.

In the room was a single-frame exercise rig.

The walls were covered with mirrors. Mirrors hung from the ceiling. At one place there was even a mirror on the floor, inset into the carpet.

Fletch stood on the floor mirror and looked up and around. Through the angled ceiling mirrors he saw himself from directions he had never seen himself before. In the mirrors on the four walls he saw his body replicated to infinity.

Cindy closed the door to the corridor. "Where did you get your tan?"

"On my face."

"Anywhere else?" She crossed the room, went through a door to a bathroom, came back immediately, and tossed him a towel.

Standing on the mirror, looking around at himself everywhere, Fletch said, "Me, me, me."

"You got it, honey."

He held the towel and the shorts in his hand.

"Take a shower," she said. "Use the soap. Change into just the shorts, and come back."

Fletch held the shorts up. "These shorts ain't got nothin' in them."

"They will have," she said. "I expect."

The shower soap stung.

When he reentered the room, Cindy was at a small, recessed bar mixing a drink.

She glanced at him. "I thought so."

"You thought what?"

She was bringing him the drink. "What vitamins do you take?"

"P."

"Never heard of it."

"All the best beers have it."

She handed him the drink. Her other hand dropped five stuffed olives into his hand.

He sniffed the drink "What's in it?"

"Orange juice."

"Okay." He munched the olives.

"Some protein powder."

"That sounds healthy."

"A little yeast."

"Sounds explosive."

"And some ground elk's horn."

"I was hoping you'd say that."

"An aphrodisiac, you know?"

"Anything else?"

"No."

"Specialty of the house?"

"Drink it, honey. Perfectly safe."

He sipped it. "Yummy."

"Chug-a-lug," she said.

"Really," he said, choking a little. "You thought of marketing this stuff?" Even while drinking it, his throat felt dusty. "Elixir of Ben Franklyn."

"Come on." She took the empty glass from him and put it on the recessed bar.

Then she took his hand and led him to the exercise machine.

"You know how to use these things? Of course you do. Lie down on your back. You're going to do bench presses. I have it set for one hundred and twenty pounds. That about right?"

"We'll see."

He lay down on his back on the bench. His knees were bent, his feet on the floor.

Looking up, he saw himself and the top of Cindy's head, and her shoulders, in the mirror.

"Lift," she said.

He lifted.

"That's about right," she said. "Feel good?"

"Like ice cream on a hot summer's day."

"Do eight in a row, slowly."

She sat on him, straddling his thighs. She spread her hands on his lower stomach, thumbs touching.

As he lifted, she pressed her hands into his stomach muscles.

He felt a sensation such as he had never felt before.

He groaned.

"Don't drop it," she said. "Makes a loud noise."

He let the weights down quietly and looked into her eyes.

"Come on," she said. "You're going to do eight of them in a row. I'm giving you every motive. Breathe."

He breathed and lifted.

On the third lift, he found his legs straightening, his heels sliding along the rug.

She did not fall off his thighs. Through the mirror he saw that she had hooked the calves of her legs around the legs of the bench. At each lift she pressed the palms of her hands into his stomach muscles.

"Breathe," she said.

"That, too?"

After he did eight lifts, she flicked the front of his shorts with her fingernails. "You're healthy enough. I thought so."

He raised his knees.

"I'll take your sweat," she said.

She leaned forward and put her breasts, her stomach on his. She raised her legs and put her thighs on his. She rolled on him, just a little.

As soon as he gave in to irresistible impulse and put his arms around her back, she was up and away.

She stood under the chin-up grips. "Come on."

"Who said exercise has to be boring?"

As they moved in the brightly lit room, their infinite reflections in mirrors on all sides made it seem as if each were a legion moving with martial precision.

"Put your hands on the back of the grips."

Standing on his toes, he stretched totally and put his hands around the grips.

"No," she said. "Put your hands further back on the grips." He did so. "Now do a chin-up." He did so while she watched. "Again," she said.

While he was lifting himself a second time Cindy jumped

up and grabbed the grips just in front of his hands. Her body knocked against his.

She lifted herself with him, their bodies just brushing. She stared into his eyes as they lifted themselves slowly, together, lowered themselves to full stretch, up again.

"Now, stay up," Cindy said.

"As if I had a choice."

She wrapped her legs around his hips.

Slowly she relaxed her hands on the grips.

His body took her weight.

She wrapped her arms around his neck.

"Now let us down slowly."

She opened her mouth and put her teeth hard against his taut neck muscles.

As he lowered them, every muscle, ligament, tissue, and piece of skin in his body above his waist was stretched to its maximum.

There was a delirious crackling up his spine, a small explosion in the back of his head.

As his feet settled on the floor, his knees buckled.

Tangled, they both fell on the mat.

Cindy laughed. "Not everybody can do that."

Their legs were tangled. He put his arms around her. His shoulder muscles felt inflamed, inflated.

She kissed his neck, where she had bitten him.

"I'm lapping up blood," she giggled.

"Gym class was never like this."

"You went to the wrong school."

"I always suspected that."

"We've got lots to do yet," she said.

"Will I be up for it?"

"I'll see to that."

Cindy had not yet untangled herself from him when the door to the corridor opened.

She jumped. She looked up at the doorway in genuine surprise.

21

"What's your game?" Marta asked Fletch from across her desk in the executive office of the Ben Franklyn Friend Service.

"Game?" Sitting in a small wooden captain's chair in front of the desk, Fletch looked down. He was still breathing somewhat heavily, still sweating, and the front of his flimsy yellow shorts indicated to any observer that his attention was still elsewhere. "Warden, I'm suffering."

Marta picked up the phone on her desk and pushed three buttons. Into the phone, she said, "Cindy? Get dressed. Then come in here."

"Take pity on me!" Fletch said.

Reluctantly, he had followed Marta down the dark, carpeted corridor to the office behind the reception room. Walking, Marta had more of an atheletic spring in her step than sexy wriggle in her hips.

"You'll calm down in a minute, boy."

"I don't think so. You may have created a permanent condition here."

"Don't you wish."

The ferns in this office were alive. *Venus de Milo* stood on a pedestal in one corner. On a wall was *September Morn*. Another wall had a large panel of color photographs of women weightlifters, flexed.

On Marta's desk was a stack of bills which looked suspiciously like seven twenties and a ten.

"Am I being expelled from the Ben Franklyn Friend Service?" Fletch asked. "Won't you be my friend?"

"I asked you what you're playing at."

"I'm just a red-blooded boy out for a morning of sport."

"Like hell you are." Marta fingered the pearls draping her stomach. "I remembered where I saw you before."

"I know!" Fletch said. "I just remembered, too. Sunday, at the Newcomers' Coffee, at St. Anselm's Church."

"You're right about Sunday," Marta said. "You want something. And I think I know what."

"You'd be right." Leaning forward, elbows on knees, Fletch put his face in his hands. "Nothing so wicked has happened to me since Sue Ann Murchison's parents came home early from the first *Star Trek* movie and caught us on the couch."

"I saw you on Sunday. You ran in the Sardinal Race."

"I didn't get any understanding then, either. They threw me out. It was a real cold night. There's a danger in brittleness, you know. If I hadn't kept my hips absolutely straight as I went down their front walk . . ."

"You hound-dogged the girls all through the race."

". . . why, I wouldn't be here today."

"Why?"

"If you excuse me, I think I'll go for a run now."

"Sit down."

"I've got to do something!"

"You've got to answer me, is what you've got to do. I asked you: Why did you follow us all through the Sardinal Race Sunday?"

Fletch sat back down in his hard chair. "Because I'm a dirty old man."

"I asked you: Why?"

"Because I used to be a dirty young man."

"You are a young man," Marta insisted. "A transparently healthy young man."

"Bursting."

"You are good-looking. In fact, I expect some women would consider you exciting to look at."

"Some women consider cabbage exciting to look at."

"A hundred and fifty dollars." Marta riffled the stack of bills on her desk with her fingers. "You can get anything you want, probably more than you want, without walking a full city block."

"Mind if I go try it right now?"

"Sit down, please. I was suspicious the minute I saw you. A hundred and fifty dollars is a lot of money. And that's just for starters."

"You know how to cool the client, huh?"

"The minute you walked in here, I knew no one like you was laying down two hundred dollars or more just to get a sexual thrill."

"I was enjoying it. I was headin' for ecstasy, when you opened that door."

"Then I remembered where I saw you before. I'll ask you one more time: Why did you stay right behind us through the entire Sardinal Race Sunday?"

"All right," Fletch said. "I confess. I'm a student of advertising. Publicity, actually. I was studying your technique." He held his hands out to indicate wriggling hips. "Your technique really worked. I mean, you really got mileage out of your publicity."

Marta's smile was droll. "Really . . ."

"Didn't I see a big spread on the Ben Franklyn Friend Service on the sports pages of the newspapers, yesterday? Two pictures, at least. Was it the *Chronicle-Gazette?*"

The woman's smile became genuine. "The *News-Tribune.*"

"Yeah. That's right. All for the price of a dozen T-shirts. That's real mileage."

Marta said, "You're a spy."

Fletch widened his eyes at her. "I'm a spy?" He dropped his voice to a near whisper. "You mean, from Red China?"

"You're studying us all right." Marta nodded. "Is that it? That's why you followed us Sunday. That's why you came here this morning. You're studying our operation."

"Oh, you mean an industrial spy," Fletch said more loudly. "From Japan."

"After you learn what we do here, you intend to open one of your own exercise-to-sexual-ecstasy pavilions."

"You phrase things so well," Fletch said. "Truly, you have a natural talent for advertising and publicity."

"Isn't that true?"

"*Moi?*" Fletch asked. "Look at me. At my age, where could I get the money to open one of these gymnasiums-of-delight?"

"I don't know, but you're here."

"I don't even know how much one of these exercise machines costs, but, I'm sure, plenty. All these mirrors. Lights. Bathrooms. Ground elk's horn."

"Someone could be backing you."

"Heck, lady, at my age I couldn't get financial backing from a milkman."

Marta shuddered. "Don't call me 'lady.' "

"Right. Sorry."

"So, then: Why are you here, Fletcher Jaffe?"

Fletch looked at his toes. "I thought by now you would

have figured that out,'' he said, not knowing what his next line of defense was, but hoping for one.

"You want a job." Marta looked pleased with herself.

"You got it," Fletch said quickly.

"I had to be circumspect." Marta straightened her back.

"I understand."

"In this business," Marta said, "one has to be careful."

"Of course." Fletch gulped. "Naturally. Me, too."

"Talking around, testing each other out, before we lay our cards on the table."

"You're good at it," Fletch said.

"That's why you've been making this strange approach to us. *Solicitation* is such a dirty word. You wanted to see if we'd make the offer to you."

"Right," Fletch said through his Adam's apple.

"You thoroughly expected your one hundred and fifty dollars back this morning." She picked it off the desk and handed it to him. "Here it is."

He took it.

She sat back in her swivel chair, and turned sideways to the desk. "At the moment we only have two suites operating for women, three days a week, Tuesday, Wednesday, and Thursday, when our male traffic is apt to be down. Don't worry. You'll make more money those three days than you could at any other profession, except of course, maybe neurosurgery. The women have a separate entrance, of course, but we're talking the same thing. The principle here is that sex is far more ecstatic after hard exercise. You know, exercise as foreplay." Listening to her, trying to swallow his Adam's apple, staring at her, Fletch thought Marta remarkably like Frank Jaffe sitting in his swivel chair behind his desk, trying to get across a few principles of journalism. "When it comes right down to it, of course you know, we don't expect you to use your own personal, shall I say, intimate equipment." She chuckled. "Except your fingers, of course. Unlike women,

men can't bear that much traffic. Men can't phony it. Our clients understand that. We have machines, vibrators, mechanical dildos which I find quite satisfactory. We even have a vibrating dildo machine on a wide, leather belt you can strap on yourself, if you're not absolutely repulsed by the woman. Of course, we expect you to solicit an extra charge, for that service.'' There was a rap on the door. Marta called, ''Come in, darling!''

Cindy opened the door and stood just inside it. She was dressed in loafers, white knee socks, a short kilt, and a light blue, buttoned down, preppy dress shirt with the sleeves rolled up. Without expression, she watched Marta's face.

''Say hello, again, to your new colleague, darling.'' Marta stood up. ''Fletcher Jaffe will be joining the staff of the Ben Franklyn Friend Service. I want you to take him to lunch, Cindy, and give him the benefits of your wisdom and experience.''

Now Cindy was watching Fletch without expression.

Fletch's throat was dry.

''He made a real smart approach to us,'' Marta said. ''He knew he couldn't come here and just ask for a job, without making himself awfully vulnerable. He gave me a hard time,'' she chuckled. ''Is he a cop? I asked myself. A spy? The cops wouldn't send anyone that young. And no one his age could run a place like this. Sexual dysfunction? Not from what I saw watching you two through the mirror.''

''You're some detective,'' Fletch croaked.

He stood on wobbling knees.

Marta came around the desk and put her hand on the back of his neck. ''He's exactly what we need, to build up the female side of this business. Isn't he, Cindy?''

''Sure.'' Cindy was still watching him. ''I guess.''

''He's just perfect. I've been looking for you, boy.'' She squeezed the back of his neck. ''Exactly what we need. Welcome aboard. You can start work anytime.''

"Thanks."

"Tell him everything, Cindy. Show him the ropes."

Fletch said to Cindy, "Mind if I take a shower before I get dressed?"

"*I'd* appreciate it."

"Have a nice lunch, kids. Today you're lunching on the Ben Franklyn Friend Service. But, remember, high protein, both of you, and watch the starch and fats." Back behind her desk, Marta beamed at Fletch. "And remember, Fletch. My door is always open."

22

"That never happened before," Cindy said. "Marta just opening the door and bursting in that way. I couldn't imagine what was happening." They were walking from her car to Manolo's sidewalk café. "Of course, I knew there was something weird about you. Something different. Remember my asking you if you were a cop?"

"You asked me to bust the Friend Service, but not you personally."

"Just in case you were a cop. You need the sense of privacy that that closed door gives you, you know? Set the right mood, control the client."

"Satisfy him, too."

Fletch carried his jeans and his T-shirt rolled up in his hand.

When he was about to get dressed, Cindy had walked into the bathroom and tossed him a T-shirt and a pair of light shorts. "Marta said you were to wear these. She said you understand about public relations." Across the front of the

T-shirt and across the front waist of the shorts was written, in small letters, YOU WANT A FRIEND? and across the back of the T-shirt and the back of the shorts, BEN FRANKLYN.

Cindy had suggested lunching at Manolo's Café. Fletch suggested someplace else, but Cindy said Manolo's was the in place at the moment.

So they went along the sidewalk, Fletch a walking billboard, hoping no one knew precisely what the commercial message he was flashing meant.

Marta had been pleased to see him wearing the shorts and shirt. His job was secure.

"Of course, Marta can watch us through the mirrors anytime she wants."

"The mirrors are windows from their reverse side?"

"Not all of them. Just some."

"What does that do to your sense of privacy?"

"It's good. Makes you feel safe, you know, in case something goes wrong. In case you get some kook in there, who turns violent or something."

"You get kooks often?"

"No. But when you sense something might be wrong, there's a little button you can push in the bar that signals someone to come watch through the mirror."

"I see."

"And, of course, Marta sells the seats, and there are the cameras."

"What?"

"Behind the big wall mirrors, there are seats, in one or two of the gyms, you know, for voyeurs. Old, fat, repulsive, I don't know what they are. People who would rather watch it than do it."

"Men and women?"

"Sure. Marta nicks them one hundred bucks a seat."

"You perform for them?"

"We like to. I mean, supposing we get a reasonable

young, healthy guy in there. Like yourself. Marta would have invited you back for a freebie, say, Friday night. You would have come back, and I would have put you through the routine, the only difference being that people would have been watching.''

"And I wouldn't have known it."

"All you would have known was that you were getting the routine free."

"And what would it have meant to you?"

"More money. Also, having people watching somehow enhances the experience, you know? Especially when you're doing it all the time."

"Beats the sense of privacy?"

"Sure it does. Haven't you ever done it in public?'

"Not intentionally."

"Sometimes Marta rents us out for parties. We do it on the floor, after dinner. A guy and a gal, two gals, two guys. Really turns the old dears on. It's fun. You'll see. And the tips are marvelous."

"You said something about cameras."

"Yeah, that's necessary. To avoid difficulties. They're behind one of the smaller mirrors, in every gym. A videotape camera and a still camera. We get shots of every client."

"Why?"

"Well, sometimes they're drunk, or angry, or get frustrated. You know, clients are the same in any business, I suppose. They complain, threaten. If they seem truly dangerous to us, Marta shows them the pictures. That quiets them, you bet. It's not just that they're doing this, you know, it's that the pictures make them look so ugly and clumsy, big, gray guts hanging out, hairy asses sticking up being beaten by the exercise machines."

"And the pictures are used for blackmail sometimes, right?"

"Sure. Especially if the client stops being a client, and we know who he really is. Once you walk in the door of the Ben Franklyn Friend Service, a piece of you stays there forever.''

"You've made a friend for life.''

"It's a good business.''

"Yeah,'' said Fletch. "It's up there with a solid law practice.''

"Oh, look. There's a free table.

"So,'' said Fletch, stretching his legs under the shade of the café table. "Are you the prostitute with the heart of gold?''

With his arms folded across his chest, all his commercial messages were out of view.

"I don't think a heart of gold would pump very well,'' Cindy answered. "I have a better place to put my gold.''

"Have you made much gold at Ben Franklyn?''

"Enough to leave the stupid place. Marta doesn't know yet. Please don't tell her. We want it to be a surprise, end of the week. Friday's my last workday. Got something else to do Saturday. Sunday, we're off to Colorado. For good.''

"You're escaping.''

"You bet.''

"But, if you're making so much gold . . .''

"It's not very nice of me to say this. I mean, you're just joining the service, and I'm leaving. I should say only good things, I guess. You may not believe this, but, frankly, Fletch, the Ben Franklyn Friend Service is sort of a sleazy place.''

Fletch tried to look surprised.

"I'm just fed up with it,'' Cindy said. "You remember when you were in the reception area that frowsy blond who came in and started kicking up a fuss?''

"Yeah.''

"That was Carla. She was jealous because I got you as a client. She wasn't even expected in this morning, for cryin' out loud.''

"She gets first pick of the clients?"

"She gets the first pick of everything. Hours, clients, gyms."

"Seniority has its benefits, in any business."

"Seniority! She's been there three months, I've been there two and a half years, since it opened, for cryin' out loud!"

"There's jealousy in every business, I guess. What's she got you haven't got?'"

"Didn't you hear Marta say something about her wanting Carla to sleep late this morning? Guess who crept out of a double bed, and tiptoed out of a bedroom this morning, so Carla could sleep late?"

"I see."

"Marta."

The waiter Fletch had had the day before recognized Fletch. He looked around hopelessly, probably for another waiter. Reluctantly he approached.

Cindy leaned forward and said to Fletch with great vehemence: "I don't care what business you're in. No one should get special perks or advancement because of sex!"

Fletch cleared his throat. He looked up at the waiter.

The waiter said, "So interested to see you're alive and well today."

"Thank you, I think."

"And what will your 'usual' be today? I can't wait to hear. In fact, I'm sure our chef, who didn't sleep a wink last night, reliving your order of yesterday, cringes in his kitchen this noon upon the possibility of your return."

"You ate here yesterday?" Cindy asked.

"A memorable experience, Ms.," said the waiter. "In fact, we've asked the dining-out critic of the *News-Tribune* to pass us by until this particular customer either moves out of state or passes on to his eternal damnation of hiccups."

Fletch said to Cindy, "I just ordered a—"

The waiter held up his hand. "Please, sir. It does not bear

repeating. Having heard your order yesterday, I barely got through the rest of the day and the night myself. If we can't believe each day can be better than the last where would we be?''

Fletch said to Cindy. "Do you think he's insulting me?''

"Oh, no," said Cindy. "I think he's trying to instruct you in the finer points of fast food.''

"Fast food takes refinement?''

"You bet." She said to the waiter, "Anyway, I'm ordering for him today.''

"Oh, thank God! Sir, someone has finally taken you in hand!''

"He'll have five scrambled eggs.''

The waiter looked at her, astounded. "That's it.''

"And a chocolate egg-cream," Fletch muttered.

"Yes," Cindy said. "You see, from now on, a certain kind of demand is going to be made upon his body, in his new job.''

"He doesn't want to hear," Fletch muttered.

"And you, Ms.?''

"I'll have a banana split, three kinds of ice cream, fudge sauce, marshmallow, and chopped nuts.''

"What will that do for you?'' Fletch asked.

"Make my tummy happy.''

Fletch said to the waiter, "I'll have you know this young woman this morning has already fed me a dose of ground elk's horn.''

The waiter said, "I could have guessed that.''

"It was not," Cindy said. "That's a fake. I think it's really pulverized cow's horn.''

"Oh, sigh," said the waiter. "What happened to those nice people who used to say, 'Just a Coke and a hamburger rare'?''

"Young people can't get any respect from waiters," Fletch

muttered, "no matter what they do for a living. No matter what they talk about."

"What's my job description?" Fletch asked between sucks of his chocolate egg-cream through a straw. "Call boy?"

"You're a whore, sir, like the rest of us, and don't you forget it." Cindy picked up her spoon. "If you think anything else, you lose control, of yourself, of your client. It's a profession, you know. You must not lose control. Losing control can be dangerous."

The waiter had brought their lunches announcing, "Five aborted chickens and a bowl of frozen udder drippings."

Fletch asked of Cindy, "How did we end up here?"

"We were brought up the same, I expect. All Americans are, to some extent." With her spoon she was spreading the whipped cream and the marshmallow evenly over her ice cream. "We were brought up primarily as sexual objects, weren't we? I mean, what were all the vitamins, pediatrics, orthodontistry really for? Why did parents and schools make us play sports? To learn a philosophy, to learn how to win, how to lose? Nonsense. Parents and coaches protested, complained, argued with referees and each other more than we did. For health reasons? Nonsense. How many of your friends survived school sports without permanent knee, back, or neck injuries?" Cindy put a heaping spoonful of ice cream, fudge sauce, marshmallow, and whipped cream in her mouth. "Must be outdoors, doing things, but not without sun block-age, to preserve the skin. Lotions morning and night. The sole purpose was to create beautifully shaped legs, arms, shoulders, flat tummies, in gleaming, fresh skin."

"I'm a sex object?" Fletch asked.

"That's all you are, brother. Growing up, what was the intellectual discipline you were given? The theology? philosophy? culture? Me, a thirteen-year-old girl, comes running home from school, bursting into the house, and says, 'Mama,

Mama, I got an A in mathematics!' And Mama says, 'Yes, dear, but I've been noticing your hair is losing its sheen. Which shampoo are you using?' "

Quietly, Fletch was eating his plate of eggs.

"Who were held up to us as heros?" Cindy asked. "Teachers? Mathematicians? Poets? No. Only those with beautiful bodies, athletes and film stars. They are the ones interviewed on television continuously. And are they ever allowed to talk about how they really become as fast on their feet, or how they get themselves into the character of a role they're playing? No. All they're ever asked about is their sex lives, how many times they've been married, and to whom, and what each affair was like. Prestige, Fletch, is in how many people you can attract to your bed."

"Therefore, you became a whore."

"Isn't that what it's all about?"

"Very clear-sighted of you."

"I think so."

"You enjoying your banana split?" It was half gone.

"Very much."

"I can see that."

"Very much."

"But, Cindy, I, uh, have some qualms, about, uh, actually doing it, uh, you know, for money."

"I hardly ever *actually do it*. At the spa, the machines beat the clients. They get all stressed and strained, and I see that they get excited, and I jerk 'em off before they know what happened. Then they get apologetic that they couldn't contain themselves and I 'missed a really good time,' in quotes. When I'm out at night as an escort, mostly I sit in the restaurants and the clubs watching some old boy drink himself blue in the face. I just listen to him, sort of. Usually, that's all he really wants. It's very boring. When he's totally drunk, I hustle him back to his hotel room, strip him, and put him in his bed. Next morning, he thinks he's had a wonderful time, done wonderful things with a wonderful girl. He hasn't. You'll learn. I've probably made love to fewer men, or, fewer times with a man, than that secretary over there.''

She nodded to a young woman at a nearby table with an older man. On their table, besides their lunches, were notepads, pens, a folder of paper, and a calculator.

Cindy said in her throat, '' 'Cept I get paid more.''

Fletch said, ''Maybe I mean emotionally. How am I supposed to handle, you know, being paid for being intimate emotionally? I worry a little about that.''

''That's so much bullshit handed out by the psychiatrists. And let me ask you: Who's more intimate with a client, a whore or a psychiatrist?''

''Uh . . .''

''I know their text by heart. The guilt trip. Whores have an enormous need for love, but we don't know what love is. Our only way of valuing ourselves is by setting a price on our affections, our attentions. Isn't that true of psychiatrists, too? Man, they're just projecting. I don't care. They have to make a living, too. I just wish they wouldn't lay their own sickness off on us.''

''But you, Cindy, after two and a half years of this, how can you ever really, truly relate to a man again, have a genuine experience?''

''I don't want to. I never did before. I never will.'' She was scraping her ice-cream bowl clean with her spoon. ''See, that's where everybody's wrong, at least about me. About many of us. I mentioned a friend to you, a real friend. She works at Ben Franklyn, too. We've made our money. Next week, we're splitting. We're going to Colorado, going to buy a dog-breeding ranch, and live happily ever after.''

''You're lovers?''

''You bet. See, making love to a man means nothing to me. Emotionally. Morally. Whatever those words mean. I don't care about men. Going to bed with a man doesn't

other me any more than it would bother you to go to bed
with a boy, or a dog."

Fletch said, "What kind of a dog?"

Cindy sat back from her empty bowl. "The way I was
brought up, eating that ice cream was more of a sin for me
than going to bed with a man. Or men. Or a whole track
team." She looked at her empty bowl. "I enjoyed it."

"Things are different, for me," Fletch said.

"I suppose so. That's your problem."

At the corner of the block, walking toward them, was a
yellow skirt familiar to Fletch. So was the dark blue, short-
sleeved blouse above the skirt.

"Oh, my God."

Cindy stretched her arms a little. "But, for you and me
basically it's the same thing, I expect. I was developed into a
supposedly brainless, cultureless beautiful body, a sexual
object, and told men are materialistic oppressors and making
babies is a no-no. I'm not really an athelete. I'm not an
actor."

Fletch had sat up straight. Under the table he had moved
his feet into a sprint position. His eye measured the distance
between his table and the door of Manolo's. "Oh, wow."

"It comes time to make a living," Cindy continued. "What
am I supposed to do? Pretend I'm a big intellect? Or, worse,
pretend I'm a worker-ant?"

The woman approaching them spotted Fletch.

Then she spotted Cindy.

Fletch said, "Oh, no."

With certainty, Cindy said, "I am doing exactly what I am
supposed to be doing. I am exactly who I am supposed to
be."

"Fletch!" the woman said.

"Uh . . ."

Cindy turned around. Delight came on her face.

"Barbara!" she squealed.

Cindy jumped up and hugged Barbara around the neck.

Barbara hugged Cindy.

Fletch stood up. "Ah, Barbara..."

When the hugging and squealing abated, Barbara looked a Fletch. She was still holding Cindy's hand.

Barbara said, "I didn't know you two know each other!"

23

"You have a hickey on your neck," Barbara said to Fletch.

The waiter had brought a third chair to the table, heard with relief they wanted nothing more than the bill, and gone away.

"A passion mark," Barbara added, looking closely at him from under the shade of the umbrella. "It wasn't there when you left me this morning."

Fletch fingered the mark on his neck. "I, uh . . ."

Cindy's eyebrows wrinkled in confusion.

"And that's not the way you were dressed when you left this morning." Barbara put her hand on his rolled T-shirt and jeans on the table. "How come you're in shorts?"

Fletch folded his arms across his chest.

"What does your T-shirt say?" Barbara leaned forward and moved his arms. " 'You want a friend?' What does that mean?" She reached into his lap. "Your shorts say the same thing."

"They do," Fletch admitted with dignity.

"Did you get a bargain?" Barbara asked.

Fletch croaked, "How do you two know each other?"

"We're old friends from school," Barbara said easily.

"You are? Old friends?"

"Yeah."

"Good friends?"

"I've mentioned Cindy to you. She's been advising me the wedding."

Fletch said: "Ah!"

"Fletch!" Cindy yelled. She hit her forehead with the he of her hand. "You're that Fletch!"

Accusingly, Fletch asked Barbara, "And why aren't y wearing jodhpurs?"

"Ho, ho, ho," Cindy laughed.

"I change for lunch," Barbara answered. "I hate t beastly things."

"This is the Fletch you're marrying on Saturday?"

"In the flesh." Barbara put her hand on his thigh. "Fletc you're awfully hot. You're sweating. Your face is red. You a right?"

"Ho, ho, ho," said Cindy.

"Oh, my God," said Fletch.

"But how do you two know each other?" Barbara aske

"Ho, ho, ho," said Cindy.

"I, uh, we..." said Fletch.

"Is there something funny?" Barbara asked.

"Not really," said Fletch

"Ho, ho, ho," said Cindy.

"After we're married," Barbara said, "I have the sma hope Fletch comes home at night dressed something like t way he goes out in the morning."

"Ho, ho, ho." Cindy was choking with laughter.

"Barbara," Fletch said slowly and seriously, "Cindy and met in the course of business."

"Ho, ho, ho!" laughed Cindy.

The secretary and the older man at the nearby table wer frowning at this disturbance.

"The course of business?" Barbara asked.

"The course of business!" Cindy laughed.

"In the course of business," Fletch affirmed. "Now, Barbara darling, if you'd just—"

"Barbara darling!" yelled Cindy.

Not understanding Cindy's raucous good humor, Barbara said to Fletch, "Oh, by the way. I just heard on the car radio that someone has confessed to murdering Donald Habeck."

Fletch snapped forward in his chair. "What?"

"A man named Childers, I think. Went to the police this morning and confessed to killing Donald Habeck. A client of Habeck's—"

"I remember," said Fletch. "The trial ended two or three months ago. He was accused of murdering his brother."

"Well, this morning he admitted murdering Habeck."

"But he was acquitted. I mean, of murdering his brother."

"So you needn't trouble your little head about the murder of Donald Habeck anymore. You can go back to doing the job you're assigned to do."

"Yeah," Fletch said grimly. "Thanks."

"We can get married Saturday, we can have a honeymoon, and maybe you'll even have a job when we get back."

"That's right." Cindy had stopped laughing. She was looking at Fletch with new eyes. "You're a reporter!"

Fletch sighed. "Right."

"For the *Chronicle-Gazette*," said Cindy.

"For the *News-Tribune*." Fletch looked a dagger at Barbara.

"What's going on?" Barbara asked.

"Cool," said Cindy. "That explains everything!"

Fletch said, "I'm afraid it does."

"Have you written anything for the newspaper I might have read?" Cindy asked.

"Sunday," Fletch said. "Did you read 'Sports Freaks at End of Line'?"

"Yeah," Cindy said. "Sure I did. The lead piece

in the sports section. Real good. Did you write that?''

Fletch said, ''Just the headline.''

''Oh.''

''What were you doing?'' Barbara grinned gamely, as asking to be let in on a joke she might have already ruine ''Being undercover?''

''Thanks for asking,'' Fletch said.

Cindy began laughing again. She clapped her hands. ''Super!

'' 'Super,' '' Fletch quoted grimly.

The waiter gave the bill to Fletch. ''Serving you, sir,'' said th waiter, ''is an affliction I'd hate to have become an addiction.

Fletch stared at him.

Cindy took the bill. ''No. This is on the company, remember? She laughed out loud again. ''You might say, it's on the house!

''Anyway, Cindy,'' Barbara said. ''We're going to be ma ried on a bluff, overlooking the ocean. Did I tell you tha The weather's supposed to be nice Saturday.''

Cindy was paying the bill in cash.

''Remember, we're having dinner with my mother tonight, Barbara said uncertainly to Fletch.

''Tonight for dinner,'' Fletch said somberly, ''I'm havin my head on a plate.''

''Cindy,'' Barbara said. ''Around the corner there's a sports sho There's this great-looking skiing suit in the window. You know, for o honeymoon. Want to walk over with me and see how I look in it?'

''Sure,'' Cindy said. She left the waiter a generous tip.

The two women stood up from the table.

Fletch remained, elbow on the table, chin on his hand.

''See you, Fletch,'' Barbara said.

Fletch didn't answer.

Cindy said happily, ''See you, Fletch! At the wedding Saturday!''

After Cindy had gone a few paces, she turned around again doubled over in laughter. ''Fletch!'' she called. ''You'r being married on a bluff!''

24

"Hello? Hello?" Fletch knocked loudly on the frame of the screen door. Inside the bungalow a television was playing loudly but nevertheless was drowned out by a child crying, other children yelling, and the noise of some mechanical toy. "Hello!" he shouted.

The front porch was a junkyard of broken toys, a scooter with its neck twisted, a crunched tricycle, a flattened plastic doll, a play stove that looked like it had been assaulted with an ax.

On the television, a woman's voice said, "If you tell Ed what you know about me, Mary, I'll see you rot in hell."

Inside the house, a woman's voice shouted, "Keep up that bawlin', Ronnie, and I'll slay you silly!"

A man's voice said, "Now, now. Let's get this eating process completed. The kiddies must eat, Nancy. Keep up their strength!"

Associate Professor Thomas Farliegh's bungalow was eight blocks from the edge of the university campus. Other humble houses surrounding it had vestiges of paint on them and at least undisturbed stands of weeds in their front gardens. Farliegh's house was yellow and gray with rot, a front window was smashed in its center, and the front yard was packed dirt, holding, among other things, a wheelless, collapsed, rusted yellow Volkswagen.

Driving to Farliegh's house, Fletch had heard a repeat of the radio news report Barbara had mentioned. Stuart Childers had confessed to murdering Donald Habeck. He had confessed— and been released.

Fletch stood as close to the screen door as he could and shouted as loud as he could, "Hey! Hello!"

Noise within the house dimmed fractionally.

A shadow the other side of the screen door grew into a woman who said, "Who are you?"

"Fletcher."

"Who? I don't know you. Better come in."

Inside it was discovered it was not the screen door which had made him less audible.

"Are you a student?" the woman asked.

"I'm from the *News-Tribune!* The paper!"

"Tom's back here," she said. "I don't know if he's corrected your paper yet." She led him into the kitchen at the back of the house. "You said your name is Terhune?"

The house smelled of diapers, burned food, spilled milk, and ordinary household dirt.

"I'm from the newspaper," Fletch said.

In the kitchen, beside the blaring television set, a battery-operated toy tank treading noisily along the floor, up and down piles of laundry, garbage, and books, were five children, all of whom seemed to be under the age of seven. Two were in diapers, three in underpants. Each seemed to have been freshly bathed that morning in used dishwater.

A short, bald, chubby man was at the chipped kitchen table spooning mushed prunes into an infant in a high chair.

The man's eyes, visible as he glanced up at Fletch for a brief instant, were a startlingly pale blue. Four of the children also had blue eyes, but none as light as his.

The woman said nothing.

"What?" Fletch asked.

The television said, ". . . transporting a cargo of dum-dum bullets . . ."

The woman turned it down, which left just the noises of the tank overcoming all obstacles on the floor, two children shouting and kicking each other, and one small child sitting on a torn cushion against the wall bawling lustily.

"Ronnie," the woman said to the bawling child, "stop crying, or I'll kick you in the mouth." Her threat went unheeded. Her feet were bare.

"Do you have a car?" the woman asked Fletch.

"Yes. Are you Nancy Farliegh?"

"He wants to see you," the man at the table said.

"I'm sure he wants to see you, Tom. Something about a paper."

"I want to see you, Nancy. I'm from a newspaper."

"Oh," she said. "About my father's death." She was wearing a loose, bleach-stained skirt and a green, food-stained blouse. Her arms and legs were thin and white, her stomach distended. Her hair hung in greasy strands. "I don't care to say anything about that, but I do need a ride."

"I'll give you a ride."

"Our car is broken," the man at the table said. "Smashed. *Kaput*. Ruined."

"I should have gone yesterday," Nancy said.

"Yes, yes," the man said. "Bobby likum prunes."

"Sit down." Nancy picked up a pile of newspapers and a telephone book from another chair at the table, and dropped them on the floor. "I'll just change." She looked down at her clothes. "Tom, should I change?"

The child on the cushion stopped bawling. Determination entered his face.

"Never change, darlin'."

The determined-looking child got up from his cushion. He crossed the floor. He caught the tank and picked it up. He hurled it through the window.

Now three children were in the middle of the floor shouting and flailing each other. Hair-pulling seemed their best strategic device. It caused the best shrieks.

"I'll just change," Nancy said.

Fletch looked through the kitchen window. In the yard, the toy tank was assaulting a collapsed baby carriage.

He sat down.

"Choo, choo, choo, choo!" said Tom Farliegh. "Now the choo-choo comes to the open tunnel. Open the tunnel!" The baby opened her mouth. Tom stuck the mushed prunes into it. "Now," he said, scraping the bottle of the jar clean, "chew, chew, chew, chew."

"Social Security," Fletch quoted. *"The sidewalks of the city/Offer up without pity/Little old ladies to be mugged."*

"Ah!" Tom wiped the baby's mouth gently with a crusted rag. "You're familiar with my work."

"Do you call it the Poetry of Violence?"

"That's what it's called." Tom lifted the baby from the high chair and placed her carefully on the floor.

He crossed the kitchen to where an even smaller baby was lying in a plastic basket-chair on the edge of the stove, looking like something to be roasted. The man was shaped like a rutabaga. He brought the baby in the basket-chair to the kitchen table.

"Your poetry is different," Fletch said.

"Different, yes." Tom was trying to unscrew the cap off a bottle of baby formula. "Why don't you call it beautiful?"

He handed the bottle to Fletch, who unscrewed the cap and handed it back.

"Would *beautiful* be the right word?" Fletch asked.

"Why not?" Tom screwed a nipple onto the bottle. "Choo,

choo, choo.'' The baby opened his mouth. Tom inserted the bottle. ''There must be a beauty in violence. People are so attracted to it.''

Holding the bottle tipped to the infant's mouth, he looked down at where four children now fought and cried on the floor. One was bleeding from a scratch on an arm. Another had a new welt over an eye.

''That's why I have so many children,'' Tom Farliegh said. ''Look at their fury. Isn't it wonderful? Unbridled violence. I can hardly wait until this crop get to be teenagers.

''May your dreams come true,'' Fletch prayed. ''How many do you think will make it?''

''You are attracted to violence,'' Tom said.

''Not really.''

''Do you watch football?''

''Yes.''

''They aren't violent?'' Tom's hands were the softest, pudgiest Fletch had ever seen on a man. ''The vast preponderance of human entertainment is violent.'' He nodded at the television. ''That instrument of popular human communication dispenses more violence in a day than most humans, without television, normally would see in a lifetime. What attracts us to such violence?''

''Fascination,'' said Fletch. ''It is the second greatest puzzle, in life, that people are willing to do unto others violence which, apparently, they want done unto themselves.''

''Beauty,'' Tom said. ''The fascinating beauty of violence. The ultimate irony. Why has there never been a poet before to admit it?''

''*Slim, belted hips/ Sprayed across by automatic fire/ each bullet/ ripping through,/ lifting,/ throwing back,/ kicking/ the body at its/ center.// Thus/ The Warrior In Perfection/ bows to his death,/ twists,/ pivots and falls,*'' quoted Fletch.

''Beautiful,'' said Tom.

''I have seen such things,'' said Fletch.

"And it is beautiful. Admit it." Tom Farliegh tipped the baby bottle higher. *"Waisted, he is wasted/ but not wasted.// This death is his life/ And he is perfect/ In it."*

"What courses do you teach at the university?"

"The works of Geoffrey Chaucer. Another course comparing the works of John Dryden and Edmond Spenser. Also, my share of freshman English courses."

"You teach *The Faerie Queene?*"

"Oh, yes." Tom took the bottle out of the baby's mouth. There was a small quantity of formula left in it. He put it to his own mouth, and drank it.

The baby cried.

Tom took the bottle to the sink and rinsed it.

Fletch asked, "Did you do violence to your father-in-law?"

"Yes," Tom said. "I married his daughter. He never forgave either of us."

"He never came to see his grandchildren?"

"No. I doubt he knew how many he had, or their names. Too bad. He would have appreciated them."

Fletch watched one Farliegh child throw a carrot at the head of another. "I think so."

"There was no honesty in Donald Habeck."

"You're living in squalor here," said Fletch. "Your father-in-law was a multimillionaire."

"Did I murder my father-in-law?" The short, pudgy man turned around from the kitchen sink and dried his hands on a piece of newspaper. "There would have been no irony in it."

"No?"

"No. It's the innocence of victims which makes a poetry of what happens to them. And I'm a poet."

"Did you know he intended to give almost his entire fortune to a museum?"

"No."

"If he had died without a will, as I understand lawyers are apt to do, your wife might have inherited enough for you to take up poetry full-time. That is, if his fortune were still intact. Are you saying poets aren't practical people?''

"Some are.'' Tom Farliegh smiled. "Those who get published in *The Atlantic* and win the Pulitzer Prize. They might be practical enough to do murder. But, surely, you're not accusing the most unpopular published poet in the country, of practicality?''

Nancy Farliegh reentered the room. She was wearing ballet slippers, a hotter-looking full skirt, and a once-white blouse gray from repeated washing. An effort had been made to brush her hair.

"Are we ready to go?'' she asked.

Not knowing where he was going, Fletch stood up.

"Morton Rickmers, the book editor of the *News-Tribune*, might like to do an interview with you, Mr. Farliegh. Would you be available to him?''

"See?'' Tom Farliegh grinned at his wife. "I'm reaping the benefits of my father-in-law's sensational murder already.'' To Fletch, he said: "Sure, I'm available to him. I do anything to deepen my unpopularity.''

25

"Is it all right to leave him with the children?" Fletch buckled himself into the driver's seat.

"Why do you ask?" Nancy Farliegh found her seat belt.

"Your husband sees beauty in violence. Those kids are beatin' up on each other in front of him."

"He's better with the kids than I am. He has much more patience."

"Much more tolerance." He turned the ignition key. "Where are we going?"

"The Monastery of St. Thomas, in Tomasito."

"Tomasito!" Fletch looked at her. "That's a hundred kilometers from here!"

"Yes," she said. "It is."

"I thought I was just dropping you off downtown."

"My brother is in the monastery." Nancy stared at the unmoving landscape through the windshield. "It is a cloistered monastery. I don't think he yet knows Father is dead. I feel I must go talk to him. I have no other way to get there."

156

"Your brother is a monk?"

"A monk, a monk," she said. "I suppose Tom could make a vicious nursery rhyme from that: *A monk, a monk/ hiding in a trunk/ to have nothing to do/ with his father, the punk.* Not very good."

"Not very."

"Guess I'll leave poetry to my husband. I'll just keep birthing his little monsters."

Fletch put the car in gear. "Sorry," he said. "There's a hole in the muffler."

"I don't hear it."

"Are you a Christian?"

"Me? God, no. Bob's going into the monastery was his own thing. It had nothing to do with the family, I mean, our upbringing, at all. I suspect he's trying to atone for the sins of his father. Aren't they supposed to be visited on the son? He's got his job cut out for him."

Across from the university, Fletch drove up the ramp to the freeway and accelerated.

He said, "Someone who talked with your father just last week told me your father said he intended to enter a monastery."

Nancy gasped. "My father?" She laughed. "I knew newspapers print nothing but fiction."

"It's true," Fletch said. "At least it's true that somebody said it."

"Maybe my father would enter a monastery if he heard the Judgment Day Horn. It would be just like him. A clever legal defense."

"He was getting older."

"Not that old. About sixty."

"Perhaps he wasn't well?"

"Hope so. If anyone deserved leprosy of the gizzard, he did."

"Were you never close?"

"Emotionally? I don't know. I never saw him that much,

growing up. Black suit and black shoes coming and going in the driveway. Intellectually? After I grew up, I realized how he'd been screwing the system all his life. A real destroyer of values. For profit. He never believed in good, or evil, or justice; any of the things we have to believe in, to center our lives, to focus. He believed in having his own way, despite the social consequences; in lining his own pockets. He was the most completely asocial and amoral man I ever knew. If he weren't educated as a lawyer, he probably would have been a psychopathic killer himself." After a moment, she laughed wryly. "My father, a monk!"

"Your husband," Fletch said, "extolls violence."

"You don't see a difference?" Nancy asked. "My husband is a teacher. A poet. At sacrifice to himself, he's pointing out the beauty in violence. We are attracted to it. He's making us confront the violence in ourselves. He's teaching us about ourselves. His poetry wouldn't be so damned effective, if it weren't true."

"What sacrifice to himself?"

"Come on. People cross the street when they see him coming. They won't even talk to me. We haven't been invited to a faculty cocktail party in three years. Most of the faculty want to get rid of him. He could never get another job teaching. We're going to end up in Starvation Lane. Just so Tom can make this statement, not about the nature of violence, but about the nature of you and me. Don't you understand?"

"Anyway." Fletch stretched in his car seat. "This man, who should know, told me your father intended to give five million dollars to the museum. The money was to be spent on contemporary religious art. He was going to give the rest of his worldly goods to a monastery, which he was going to enter."

Nancy shrugged. "He had an angle somewhere. I'd guess someone had the goods on him. The Justice Department. The

Internal Revenue Service. The American Bar Association. I expect that after the dust settled, you would have found my father living luxuriously somewhere with his sexy, pea-brained young wife behind the facade, the protection of some religious or cultural foundation, all brilliantly, legally established, and funded, by himself.''

"Maybe. But did you know your father had stated the intention of disposing of his worldly goods?''

"I read something of the sort in the newspaper. This morning's newspaper. After he was murdered.''

"No one had told you before?''

"No.''

Fletch said, "It's always hard to prove that you don't know something.''

They rode without speaking for a while. They listened to The Grateful Dead on the radio.

Finally, Fletch said, "At your father's house yesterday, I met a woman who was about sixty years old, white-haired, or blue-haired, whatever you want to call it, wearing a colorful dress and green sneakers. I asked her if she was Mrs. Habeck, and she said she was. All she'd say about your father was that he wore black shoes and wandered away. She referred to Habeck, Harrison and Haller as *Hay, Ha, Haw*.''

"Ummm,'' Nancy said.

"That your mother?''

"Um.'' Nancy shifted in her seat. "What it says on your shorts is correct. You can be a friend, I guess.''

"That's not quite what the legend means.'' Fletch had changed T-shirts. He had hoped his own, pure T-shirt, left outside his shorts, had covered the advertisements.

"You put your finger on it,'' Nancy said. "Growing up, my father and I ignored each other. He wasn't interesting. When I got older, I learned contempt for him. 'Brilliant legal practitioner.' Bullshit. He was a crook. When he put Mother away, had her legally committed to a home for the mentally unwell, I absolutely despised him. I never spoke to him again, or voluntarily saw him again. Sorry. I didn't tell the exact truth, before. I hate the son of a bitch.''

"Oh.''

"Mother didn't need to be thrown out of her home. Confined to an institution, however swank and gentle. She's just pixilated.''

Fletch remembered Mrs. Habeck looking down at her green sneakers and saying, *I don't have any privacy.*

"Pixilated," Nancy repeated. "Year after year, Dad left her alone in that house. No one wanted to know her. At first, she tried to get out, go do things, you know, join the Flower Club. The other ladies didn't want her. Some sensational case of my father's would be in the newspaper, a small editorial outcry about Donald Habeck getting a not-guilty verdict for some rapist. And Mother's flower arrangements wouldn't get into the show. Her phone wouldn't ring. Once, when I was a teenager and getting independent, Mother marched downtown and got herself a job behind the counter in a florist's shop. My father put a stop to that, quick enough. Poor, damned soul. She moldered alone in that house. Talked to herself. She began setting the dining-room table for luncheon and dinner parties, for six people, eight people, a dozen. There were no people.'' Tears streamed down Nancy's face. Her voice sounded dry. "What could I do? I went home as much as possible. She used to go to six different hairdressers in one day, just to have people to talk to. Her hair was getting burned out. Then she took to spending all day in the shopping malls, buying everything in the world, lawn mowers, washing machines, towels. There were about twenty washing machines delivered to the house one week. When she was being packed up to go to the Agnes Whitaker Home, it was discovered she had over two thousand pairs of shoes! She liked to talk to the salespeople, you see.''

Fletch took the turning for Tomasito. "Does she escape from the home often?"

"Almost every day. At first the institution staff would be alarmed and call me, I suppose call my father. Scold her when she came back. But she's harmless. She has no money, no credit cards. I have no idea how she gets around. Have never been able to figure that out. On nice days, I guess she goes and sits in the park, walks around the stores pretending she's buying things, goes back to her old home and sits by the pool."

"Yeah. That's where she was yesterday."

"She must appear to Jasmine as sort of the Ghost of the First Wife." Nancy laughed. "So what. She turns up at my house two or three times a week. Sits and watches the television. Sits and watches the children. Tells them absolutely crazy things, like about the time she made friends with a great black bear in the woods, and the bear taught her how to fish. The children adore her."

"And she loves the children?"

"How do I know? She keeps showing up."

"And you don't think this woman should have been confined?"

Nancy's jaw tightened. "I don't think she should have been left in isolation for years. I don't think she should have been socially ostracized. No. I don't think she should have been thrown out of her home. When strange symptoms began appearing, I don't think my father needed to continue what he was doing. They could have retired, started another life somewhere. Or, if it was too late, some sort of a paid housekeeper-nurse could have been hired to stay with her, give her some company." Nancy was silent for a long moment, the muscles in her jaw working. Then she said, "My father got rid of her through some legal trickery, divorce and confinement, because he wanted to marry pea-brained Jasmine."

"You don't like Jasmine, of course."

"Like her?" Nancy looked across the car at Fletch. "I feel sorry for her. The same thing is happening to her as happened to my mother."

They went down a ramp from the freeway onto a two-lane road through fairly decent farmland.

Nancy said, "I heard on the television this morning that someone confessed to my father's murder."

"Yes," Fletch said. "Stuart Childers. A client of your father's. Accused of murdering his brother. Acquitted two or three months ago."

"So?" Nancy said.

"He was released by the police immediately. I don't know why."

Nancy said, "What are you getting at, friend?"

"I don't think it was a gangland slaying," Fletch said, "despite the suggestion in this morning's *News-Tribune*."

"You think I did it?"

"Someone in the family heard your father intended, or said he intended, to dispose of all his worldly goods, for reasons sacred or profane. Incidentally, my source reported that your father said, last week, that no one gave 'a tin whistle' for him. His words."

Nancy snorted. "I suppose that's true."

"Someone decided to do him in before he decided to do the family out. You, your husband. Your mother, for your sake or the sake of your kids. Your father's second wife."

"You don't understand Tom."

"He may be the important poet, the intellectual you say he is. But where was he Monday morning?"

"At the university."

"What time is his first class on Mondays?"

Nancy hesitated. "Two in the afternoon."

"Okay."

"Poverty is important to Tom. The fact that he, his work is

being scorned. It makes the sacrifice more real, the poetry,'' she stuttered, ''most significant, monumental.''

''You weren't brought up in squalor,'' Fletch said. ''Your daddy may not have bounced you on his knee, but you had a stocked refrigerator in a clean home, with a swimming pool in the garden. Plus a lot of washing machines.''

''Frankly, friend, I don't want a penny from my father. People are still getting mugged, raped, and murdered because my father took their money.''

''Ah, the beauty of violence!'' Fletch said. ''You've got five kids crawling around the floor. You said you are headed for Starvation Lane. Not many mothers let their kids starve, if there's an alternative.''

After a moment, Nancy said, ''Monday morning I was home alone with the kids.''

''Great witnesses. Got any other?''

''No.''

Fletch slowed as they passed a sign saying THE MONASTERY OF ST. THOMAS. He turned right through the gates.

''There's a guard at the gates to the *News-Tribune* parking lot,'' he said. ''Checking cars. I see someone, knowing your father was going to the newspaper that morning to arrange for the announcement of his giving away his fortune, walking into the parking lot, shooting him as he was getting out of his car at the back of the lot, and walking out again, unquestioned.''

The car was rising on the road through a well-kept forest.

''Who, Mother?''

''She does have her own way of coming and going,'' Fletch said. ''And her own point of view. And what does she have to lose? She's already been committed as insane.''

''You haven't mentioned Jasmine.''

''I haven't met Jasmine. By the way, your father has a cook now.''

''Good. Jasmine has someone to talk to. I doubt she can fry eggs.''

"A young wife, possibly about to be left high and dry through her husband's spiritual conversion or his legal trickery..."

Atop a gardened knoll ahead of them was a large, stuccoed, Spanish-style building.

"Tom's self-image would be destroyed by our having money," Nancy said. "My mother couldn't focus on anything long enough to do murder. I don't care enough about my father or his money to have murdered him."

"And then there's Robert." Fletch put the car in the gravel car park and turned off the engine.

"Now you're really crazy."

"I'll wait here for you."

Her hand on the car door handle, Nancy didn't move. Again she stared through the windshield at unmoving scenery.

"I'm sorry for you," Fletch said. "This will be tough on both of you. I'll be here."

"No," Nancy said. "Come with me, will you, friend? This place gives me the creeps."

26

"Have you been in a monastery before?" Robert Habeck took Fletch by the elbow and steered him toward a backless bench across the small courtyard.

"No," Fletch answered. "The silence is ear-splitting."

"I heard the noise of your car." Robert smiled. It seemed an admonition.

Fletch and Nancy Habeck Farliegh had been shown silently into a small, cool waiting room immediately inside the main door. They sat on a carved wooden bench.

In a few minutes, the abbot entered. He did not greet them, or sit down. Nancy explained she had come to the monastery to tell her brother their father was dead. The abbot nodded and left without uttering a single word.

Waiting, Nancy explained to Fletch that this room and the small, adjacent, high-walled courtyard were the only places females were allowed in the monastery. She had last visited Robert after her first baby was born, almost seven years ago.

Since then she had written him once a year, at Christmas. She had never had an answer from him.

They waited a little more than forty-five minutes.

When Robert entered the room, he smiled and held out his hands to his sister. He did not embrace her or kiss her. He did not say anything.

Nancy introduced Fletch as "a friend."

Looking down at Fletch's shorts, Robert asked, "Are you a Quaker?"

"What? No."

Robert's ankle-length white robe was belted by a length of black rope. He wore sandals. He was scrawny and balding. His beard looked like it had been struck by a plague of locusts.

His eyes went from the dull, inward-directed to a more lively substitute for verbal communication.

Following them across the courtyard, Nancy said, "I have five children now, Robert. Tom still teaches at the university, but he's becoming quite well known as a poet. Mother is still at the Agnes Whitaker Home. Physically, she's quite well. We see her often."

Robert sat on the bench, and looked up at them with happy eyes.

Nancy sat beside him.

Fletch sat cross-legged on the ground-stone path in front of them.

"Robert, I have something difficult to tell you." Contrary to everything she had said, Nancy then began to weep. "Father is dead." She sobbed. "He was murdered, shot to death, yesterday, in a parking lot."

Robert said nothing. His eyes became inward-directed. He did not look at, reach out a hand to, touch his sister in any way. He offered her neither sympathy nor empathy.

Desperate to collect herself, Nancy wiped her eyes with the hem of her heavy skirt.

Finally Robert sighed. "So."

"I don't know what's happening about the funeral," Nancy said. "Jasmine . . . the partners . . . Robert, will you come to the funeral?"

"No." He put his hand on the bench and looked around the small courtyard as if he wanted to get up and go away. "Here we are used to death . . . the flowers . . . the farm animals. . . . It comes to us here. We need not go out to it."

Fletch asked, "Do you ever get to leave here?"

"Who would want to?"

"Do you ever leave here?"

"Sometimes I go in the truck, to the markets. In the station wagon, to the dentist."

"Do you ever go alone?"

"I am never alone. I carry the Savior with me in my heart."

Nancy put her hand on Robert's hand. "No matter what we thought of him, Robert, it's a shock, it's hard to take, that he was murdered. That someone actually took a gun, and ended his life with it. Stood before him. Shot him."

"Ah, The Great Presumption," Robert said, clearly speaking in capitals. "Why do people keep making The Great Presumption, that we each have the right, moral and legal, to die a natural death? When so many, many of us die by accident, violence, wars, pestilence, famine. . . ."

Nancy glanced at Robert, then looked at Fletch. She moved her hand.

"Well . . ." Fletch said, "your father died of violence."

"Murder makes it seem that someone has corrected God." Robert smiled. "We must believe someone has. But, no. One cannot really correct that which is perfect."

Nancy straightened the hem of her skirt over her knees with shaking hands.

"Robert," Fletch said, "the story is that yesterday morning, your father went to the *News-Tribune* to consult with the publisher, John Winters, about the announcement of your father's intention to donate five million dollars to the art museum. He had had a meeting at the art museum, to discuss this gift. The museum was not sure that it wanted such a gift, as long as your father stipulated that the money be spent exclusively on contemporary religious art.''

Robert looked interested.

''Furthermore,'' Fletch continued, ''your father told the curator at the museum that he intended to give the rest of his wealth to a monastery, which he intended to enter, to join.''

At first, Robert raised his eyebrows and stared at Fletch.

Then his jaws tightened. He squeezed his eyes shut. Elbows on his knees, hands clutching each other, Robert lowered his head.

Nancy and Fletch glanced at each other.

Finally, Fletch asked, ''Are you angry?''

''That man,'' Robert said through clenched teeth.

Fletch asked, ''Was he possibly trying to come to you? His son?''

Looking at Fletch, Nancy's eyes popped.

Robert said, ''That man.''

Fletch asked, ''Do you believe any of what I've just told you?''

For a long moment, Robert sat on the bench silently, apparently holding himself together with effort. He breathed deeply through his nose. ''Impossible,'' he said. His breathing became easier. ''Nancy wrote me that my father, after disposing of my mother, institutionalizing her, took a second wife. . . .''

''Jasmine,'' Nancy said.

Robert's eyes opened. Much of the strain left his face. ''I don't suppose she's dead?''

''No,'' Nancy answered.

''One may not divorce a wife,'' Robert said, as if elucidating a fine point of law, ''for the sake of entering a monastery.''

Fletch said, "Oh."

"So all this is not true," Robert said. "Like the rest of my father's life. It is some complicated lie. Even if he were free, months, if not years, of prayerful instruction and reflection would be required."

Fletch looked down at the ground stone between his folded legs. "He had perhaps more than another million dollars to donate to a monastery."

Looking at Fletch, Robert said nothing.

Fletch turned the question. "Robert, you must believe in redemption. Is it totally inconceivable to you that your father could make such a change in his life at the age of sixty, sixty-one?"

"My father," Robert said with difficulty. "My father spent his life shortcutting the law. In fact, short-circuiting it. There is no shortcut to eternal paradise. One cannot short-circuit the laws of God."

Nancy uttered a short laugh. "Robert. You sound so unforgiving."

Finally, Robert turned to his sister. "And are you forgiving?"

"No," she said. "Not of what he did to Mother."

"One never knows," Robert said. "Perhaps the man died within the grace of God. I sincerely doubt it."

Fletch had the impression Robert did not want his father's company either in the monastery, or in paradise.

"What he did to Mother," Robert said. "What he did to all of us."

"What did he do to you?" Fletch asked.

Robert's eyes became as inflamed as the subject's of an El Greco portrait. "He taught us the one thing that must not be taught children, that must not be taught society: that one can commit evil with impunity, if one lies about it successfully." Robert's voice rose. "And do you expect that a person with such a philosophy, such a practice, can ever come to God?" His voice lowered, but his hands, even his shoulders shook.

"I am spending all my adult life trying to separate mysel
from such a wicked belief. It is the one belief which car
destroy society. It is the one belief which can corrupt irretrievably
a person's soul." Trying to smile at Fletch, Robert asked
"And do you believe a person with such a mind-set could
confess, with honesty, and come to God?"

Fletch felt he ought not answer.

Robert modulated his voice. "What he did to us that is
unforgivable is that he corrupted us beyond belief."

Fletch stood up from the ground-stone path.

Robert spoke, looking at his callused fingers. "It doesn'
matter who killed him. We are all murdered by life, by our
own way of life, by how we live. Of course he died a violen
death. His life condoned, encouraged violence. We are all
victims of ourselves." Nancy was standing up, too. "All that
matters is that he died in God's grace. Although I can'
believe he did, and is condemned to suffer in hell through all
eternity, we will not know. Such was his life; such was his
death: all between his Divine Creator and himself."

"Despite the circumstances," Nancy said, straightening
her skirt, "it's good seeing you, Robert."

Robert did not rise from the bench. Robert did not answer.

"Right," Fletch said. "Try to get some peace."

Between the waiting room and the monastery's main door,
Fletch said to Nancy, "Wait one moment for me, will you?"

He crossed the foyer and entered a small outer office lined
with filing cabinets.

He then went through an open door into larger, well-
furnished office, where the abbot sat behind a large, wooden
desk. The abbot looked up from some eye-saving pale green
papers on his desk.

"Pardon the intrusion," Fletch said.

The abbot didn't say he did, or didn't, pardon the intrusion.

"Robert's father, Donald Habeck, not only died yesterday,

he was murdered." There was no response apparent from the abbot. "It is important for us to know if Donald Habeck came and talked with you, recently."

The abbot pondered as if this might be a trick question from the body of scholastic philosophy.

"Yes," the abbot finally said slowly. "Donald Habeck came to see me recently. Yes, we talked."

"More than once?"

The abbot looked at the open door behind Fletch.

"When he came to see you," Fletch asked, "did he also see Robert?"

"To my best knowledge, Robert did not know he was here," the abbot answered.

"Was Robert here yesterday morning?"

"Monday morning? I expect so."

"May I ask the nature of your conversation with Donald Habeck?"

"No."

"You can be subpoenaed," Fletch said.

"You have my address," the abbot answered. "I am always here."

Nancy awaited Fletch in the car.

Before Fletch had the key in the ignition, she said, "I need a beer break. The odor of sanctity makes me want to puke."

27

"Cecilia's Boutique. Cecilia speaking. Have you consid
ered jodhpurs?''

"Good afternoon,'' Fletch said. "I ordered a pair o:
jodhpurs for my wife, this morning. A color you don't have
in stock?''

"There's a color we don't have in stock?''

"Special order. Green, white, and black stripes, vertical a
the thighs and calves, horizontal at the knees.''

"We certainly don't have that in stock.''

"It's all right. I understand. You're a small shop. Can'
have all the jodhpurs in the world in stock.''

"I thought we did,'' Cecilia said beguilingly.

"I told the salesgirl, who said her name was Barbara, tha
I'd call her this afternoon with my wife's exact size.''

"That would be Barbara Ralton.''

"May I speak with her, please?''

"Of course.''

After a pause, Barbara said, "Hello?''

172

"Hiya, sweetie."

"Fletch? How did you get through to me?"

"I lied. But it's all right. I can forgive myself. When people are corrupt enough to oblige lies, I oblige them."

"Where are you?"

"In the only bar in Tomasito."

"Tomasito? What are you doing there?"

"Having a lukewarm beer."

"You went a long way for a beer."

"Listen, Barbara, I won't be able to have dinner with you and your mother tonight. There are things I still have to do."

"You promised."

"I promise for tomorrow night."

"That will leave only two days till the wedding."

"Absolute promise."

"Fletch, did you hear on the radio that the police released the man who confessed to Habeck's murder?"

"Yes."

"Oh, no. That's why you're in Tomasito! That's why you're going to be late tonight! The week we get married, you are determined to get yourself fired over that Habeck story!"

"Barbara? I had another assignment from the *News-Tribune*. But, you know, somehow or other the rug got pulled out from under my feet on it."

"The travel story. What has Cindy got to do with a travel story?"

"You can go a long way with Cindy. How did she like the ski outfit?"

"She liked it. I bought it. Cindy has excellent taste in sportswear."

"I'll say. Er, Barbara, do you have any idea what Cindy does for a living?"

"Yeah. She works for one of those diet-health spas. Which is why I was so surprised to see she had a banana split for lunch. I guess she can take such a thing, but she sets people like me a real bad example."

"She works it off, I guess. One way or another."

"I forget which spa she works for. One of the fancy ones, downtown, I think."

"Do you think she might be gay?"

"Cindy? Lesbian? No way. I've seen her out with lots of men."

"I'm sure you have."

"Cindy's real nice."

"Yes, she is. See you tonight."

"You are coming to the beach house?"

"Absolutely. I'll just be late. You might put some curtains up in the bedroom."

"Don't you like getting it up early?"

"Not that early."

28

"Hey! Damn it all! Open up!" Again Fletch pounded on the door. Again he looked to the street corner. Again he tried the doorknob. Again he read the sign: EMERGENCY EGRESS ONLY. MAIN ENTRANCE AROUND CORNER. AGNES WHITAKER HOME. He was about to sprint again. He banged the door one more time with his fist. "Hey!"

It opened.

Inside, on the cement floor, were green sneakers.

"I saw you through the window," Mrs. Habeck said. "You'd better come in."

Fletch entered quickly and closed the door behind him.

"Why was that policeman chasing you?" Mrs. Habeck asked.

"Damned if I know." Fletch breathed deeply. "Just after I parked, about five blocks from here, this cop jumped out of his car, yelled at me, and started chasing me. His partner got stuck in traffic. Thanks for letting me in."

"You certainly had a good lead on him," Mrs. Habeck

said admiringly. "Of course, you're dressed for running. If it's the police's job to catch people, why don't they wear shorts and sneakers too?"

In the utility hall where they stood, her flowered dress seemed particularly bright.

Fletch said, "I don't know your first name."

"Why should you?" Mrs. Habeck turned and led him through a door and along a corridor. "I've been awaiting you, you'll see. But now you're late. They'll be setting supper for us soon. A ridiculously early hour, I know, but, as you know, institutions set out their three meals within the same eight-hour workday. As a result, some institutionalized people are too fat; some are too thin: none can outrun a policeman, I'm sure."

They went into a large room at the front of the building.

A television at the back of the room played a quiz-game show for three depressed-looking people. A man in a full suit sat at a bridge table, mulling over a hand of cards. The three empty positions at the table had cards neatly stacked in front of them. At the side of the room, a young woman in jeans and a T-shirt that said PROPERTY I.C.U. ATHLETIC DEPT. worked a computer terminal.

Fletch and Mrs. Habeck sat in chairs in a front corner of the room. She had an excellent view of the street from her window.

"My name is Louise," she said.

"Is that what your friends call you?"

"Don't have any friends," Louise Habeck said. "Never have, since I was married. My husband's friends genuinely didn't like us, you see. None of our friends did. Your shorts ask if I want a friend. Well, I did want a friend, at one time. It's like wanting a cup of tea in a desert. I'm sure you know what that's like. After a while of not having a cup of tea, it becomes all right. You stop wanting it." She lifted a large, brown, paper shopping bag from the floor beside her chair and put it in Fletch's lap. "I've been nothing less nor more than Mrs. Habeck for a good long time now."

In the bag, neatly folded, were his jeans, T-shirt, undershorts, and socks. They smelled clean. At the bottom of the bag, he could feel his sneakers.

"You did wash my clothes for me!"

"I said I would."

"My favorite sneakers!"

"My, they made an amusing noise going 'round in the dryer. The noise a camel might make, after having been trained for an Olympic track event."

He changed from his new, white sneakers to his old, dirty, holey sneakers.

She watched him wriggle his toes in them.

"You might have been able to run away from the policeman even faster, if you'd been wearing those." Outside the window, the policeman stood, arms akimbo, on the curb. "My husband, of course, always wore black shoes. Somehow or other, he always managed to wander away in black shoes."

They watched the police car come down the street, make a U-turn, and pick up the policeman.

"I honestly don't know what the policeman's chasing me was all about," Fletch said. "Maybe I should have stopped and asked, but there's a lot I want to do yet today."

"I love the way you arrive places," she said. "Yesterday, reeking of bourbon. Today, chased by a cop. Reminds me of no one whatsoever."

"You depart places pretty well." He remembered her disappearing yesterday with his clothes.

"Oh, yes," she agreed. "Once you're put out of your own home because you're too much trouble, after that, you know, departing anywhere becomes easy. Like not wanting a cup of tea."

"Tea," he said. "Yes."

"Sorry I can't offer you any," she said. "All these people

around here dressed in white are not paid to fetch and carry.''
A large man dressed in white was now standing just inside the
recreation-room door. ''They make that quite clear when you
first arrive. They're paid to stand around like dolts and
grimace.'' She grimaced at the large dolt. He didn't see her.
His eyes were totally bloodshot. ''Scat!'' she said to him.
''Go set supper!''

The well-dressed bridge player put down his hand, took the
seat to his left, and picked up that hand.

''I'll be a cup of tea,'' Fletch said.

She smiled and nodded with understanding.

''Tell me,'' Fletch said gently. ''Do you know by now your
ex-husband is dead?''

She laughed. She slapped her knee. ''That would make
him ex enough! Ex-pired!''

Again, in her presence, Fletch did not know if he ought
laugh.

He cleared his throat. ''I've spent today visiting your
family.''

''You're trying to discover who done Donald in!'' she said
gleefully.

''Well, I'm trying to get the story. Trying to understand . . .''

''There's no understanding Donald. Never was. If he
himself told me he was dead, I'd wait for the obituary, before
believing it.''

''Obituaries,'' Fletch said solemnly, ''are not always to be
believed either.''

''I hope they had some source for the news of his death
other than himself. Or his office.''

''They did. He was shot to death. In the parking lot of one
of the newspapers.''

''He must have a jury deliberating somewhere.''

''What do you mean?''

''Donald always calls attention to himself when he knows a

jury is going to bring in a positive verdict. He says it's good for business.''

"He didn't shoot himself," Fletch said. "The gun wasn't found.''

"It wandered away," she said. "Wandered away on black shoes.''

"Yes. Okay. Tell me, do you often go back to your old house and sit in the garden? The gardener didn't know you.''

"Not often. Usually I don't sit there unless I know no one's there. I'm used to that house being empty, you know. Sometimes Jasmine surprises me. She comes out of the house and sits with me and we talk. She's discovered living with Donald is lonelier than living alone. He wanders away, you know.''

"On black shoes. What was special about yesterday?''

"Yesterday? Let me think. Oh, yes, Donald got shot.''

"I mean you stayed at the house even though the gardener was there.''

"Such a nice day.''

"When I met you yesterday, did you know Donald had been killed?''

"I knew it some time. I don't know whether I knew it before or after meeting you. Meeting you didn't seem that significant, originally. You weren't drunk, were you?''

"No.''

"You smelled it.''

"Did you know before I told you that Donald intended to announce he was giving five million dollars to the museum?''

"I washed your clothes for you. *Bumpity-bumpity-bump!* went the sneakers in the dryer. Exactly like a camel running the four-forty.''

The bridge player was now in the fourth position at the table.

"How do you get around, anyway?''

"Vaguely.''

"I mean, how do you get around the city? To your daughter's house, to—"

"I sit in an open, empty car. When the driver comes back, from shopping or whatever, I tell him or her where I want to go. They take me."

"Always?"

"Always. I'm a little, old, blue-haired lady in a bright dress and green sneakers. Why wouldn't they? Sometimes they have to go someplace else first. I go, too. The secret is that I'm never in a hurry. And," she noted, "sometimes I get to see places I wouldn't otherwise see."

Fletch frowned. "Your daughter did somewhat the same thing this afternoon."

"Did she? I never explained to her how to do it. She never asked. But, poor dear, she hasn't any money, either."

"I went with your daughter to the Monastery of St. Thomas this afternoon and spoke with Robert."

"That sinner!"

"Why do you say that?"

"Have you ever heard of the sin of omission?"

"No."

"Robert's omitting life in that monastery. I suspect he'd rather be in jail, but he knew his father would prevent his going to jail, no matter what he did. I think some people want to be in jail, don't you?"

"Shooting his father would accomplish two goals, wouldn't it?"

"Splendidly!"

"I think I heard your son, the monk, actually saying something like he doesn't much care if his father goes to hell."

"Oh, we all felt that way about Donald. Didn't you?"

"Didn't know him."

"Not a pity."

"When Nancy was telling Robert their father was dead, she wept."

"Nancy! I brought her up to be such a pretty girl and, for a while there, she was such a whore."

"Was she?"

"She married her college professor, you know. What's his name?"

"Tom Farliegh."

"Yesterday you didn't know his name. Today, you do. You see? You've learned something."

"Not much."

"I try to get his name around, in my own small way."

"Rather a strange man, don't you think?"

"Oh, he's a darling. Very good to me. He publishes my poetry."

"What?"

"Well, he gets it published. Under his own name, of course."

Fletch sat forward. "What?"

"Well, you just indicated you wanted to learn something."

"What are you saying?"

"That little book, *The Knife, The Blood*. Those are my poems."

Fletch stared at the blue-haired lady in the corner of the Agnes Whitaker Home's recreation room. "You do like playing with words."

"Very much," she said firmly. "Very much."

"Ex-pired husband. With sounds. *Hay Ha Haw*."

"They're good poems, aren't they?"

"I think I believe you. The Poetry of Violence written by . . ."

"The few critics who reviewed the poems referred to them as that. 'Poetry of Violence'? I suppose so. Poetry of Truth and Beauty. I don't like labels."

"Your writing those poems changes the meaning of them altogether."

"Does it? It shouldn't."

"It changes the perspective. *The sidewalks of the city/ Offer up without pity/ Old ladies to be mugged.* If you think a young man wrote that, it seems cruel. But if you know a sixty-year-old woman wrote it—"

"I don't know about criticism. I know Tom needed to publish something, to keep himself employed at that university. His own poems wander around on black shoes like Donald. Never can get ahold of them. So verbose they should be verboten. Well, they are forbidden, essentially. Couldn't get them published. So I gave him mine. He has my five grandchildren to support."

"My God. Life is crazy."

"Interesting thought."

"Tom talks as if he wrote those poems!"

"He's supposed to. It's a secret, you see. Even Nancy doesn't know. You mentioned perspective. Who'd publish the poems of a little old lady in a private mental home? Tom is a university professor. If he presents something to a publisher, at least it will be read. Right? I can't help it if the world's perspective is crazy."

"When people are corrupt enough to oblige lies, you oblige them."

"Tom's working on the second volume now. I'm helping him. It's very difficult for him, you see. When a person has to lecture almost every day in fifty-minute lumps, it must be nearly impossible for him to think in terms of a simple, concise line, each word pulling more than its own weight, a cadence that works in the briefest moment. Don't you think?"

"I have no idea."

"But you see, I, on the other hand, have lived more or less in silence. A silence so profound that when a sound, a word emerges into it, I realize it in the most complete sense, hear

it, feel it, touch it, taste it, turn it over and over, in its
isolation, in my isolation. Sound, to Tom, in his busy life,
with five children, must be resisted, somewhat. Sound to me
is cherished, and I coax it into fullness, into meaning.''

"Explored, exploited, explained, exploded," Fletch said.
"Expired."

"I do think I've identified for Tom a previously unadmitted,
shall we say? source of beauty. He's getting the hang of it.
Pretty soon some of these poems will be entirely his." Louise
Habeck looked around the recreation room. "And pretty soon
it will be time for supper."

"There's a story I've heard," Fletch said slowly, "that
Donald Habeck was taking a turn for the religious."

"Donald was always religious," Louise Habeck said.

"No one else seems to think so."

Louise Habeck shrugged.

"He was a liar," Fletch said. "A paid liar, a professional
liar. You yourself said you wouldn't believe him if he told
you he was dead."

"A liar has a regard for the truth such as the rest of us do
not have," Louise Habeck said. "A liar believes that truth is
somehow difficult, mysterious, mystical, mythical, unobtainable,
to be pursued. I'll bet you that while Demosthenes was
wandering the earth, searching for an honest man, he was
selling gold bricks on the side and cheating his landlords. To
the rest of us, truth is as obvious, as common, as plain, as a
simple poem."

"Would you believe Donald would retire into a monastery?"

"Oh, yes. It would be just like him. Just what he would
do. He was forever poring over religious tracts, books of
sermons, proofs of this and that."

"How could his children not know that?"

"They know nothing about him, other than what they read
in the newspapers. Nobody did. After you read about Donald
in the newspapers, you don't want to know him."

"Did he ever take instruction in any religious faith?"

"All of them. That's how he spent most of his evenings. That's why I never saw him. The children never saw him. Never knew him."

"Listen," Fletch said softly, "Donald Habeck had a mighty unusual lady we both know committed to a mental institution."

"Yes," Louise Habeck said. "Me. It was very kind of Donald, very correct. Living here is much nicer than living with him. I get to watch other people eat. All of the people here"—she waved her arm around the room—"are better company than Donald was. I come and go as I please. People give me rides. They talk to me, usually. I tell them stories about Peru. And Donald was right: I was buying rather too many washing machines and lawn mowers."

"Have you ever been to Peru?"

"No, but neither have they."

"Mrs. Habeck, your son is a monk who can't find peace. Your daughter and grandchildren live in squalor. Your son-in-law is a pudgy impostor."

"What does that have to do with Donald?"

"Donald could have helped them, gotten help for them, at least have been accessible to them, tried to know them, see them."

Louise Habeck stared at the floor between them for a long moment. "Donald wandered away," she said, "after God. I hated him for it." Somewhere in the building a soft gong sounded. Her eyes rose to meet his. "The poetic irony would be," she said, "if Donald were shot before he could escape his life of lies."

"Did you shoot him?"

She smiled. "At least now I know where he is."

People were hurrying out of the room.

"Come on," she said. "I'll show you out the side door. It's much simpler than going through all that rigamarole at the front door. Your not signing in would confuse your signing out.''

"Thanks for doing my laundry," he said, following her. "Although your delivery system leaves something to be desired."

Walking down the corridor ahead of him, she said, "Washing your clothes, I came to love you."

At the Emergency Egress Only, Fletch said, "Okay if I come by someday and take you for a cup of tea?"

Louise Habeck shook her head. "I doubt I'll be thirsty."

29

Fletch rang several times and waited several minutes but no one answered the door at 12339 Palmiera Drive. The sun was lowering. It was getting cooler. There were no cars in the driveway, no wreath on the front door. Louise Habeck was in a home for the mentally unwell. Robert Habeck was fretting in a monastery. Nancy Habeck was living in squalor with a husband who was a fraud. And Donald Habeck was dead, murdered.

And Jasmine?

Fletch backed up from the front door and looked up at the curtain that had moved as he was leaving that morning.

It moved again.

He smiled, waved at the curtain, turned, and walked to his car at the curb.

As he was getting into his car, the front door of 12339 Palmiera Drive opened. The silhouette in the door was as the gardener had drawn it in the dirt.

Fletch closed his car door and started back up the flagstone path.

She came down the steps to the walk. Behind her, the door closed.

"Oh, damn," she said. "I just locked myself out."

"Are you Jasmine?"

She nodded. She was older than she looked at a distance. Older, heavier, face more scarred by cosmetics, eyebrows more plucked, hair more dyed.

"My name is Fletcher. I work for the *News-Tribune*."

"How am I going to get back into the house?"

"Cook's not here?"

"I couldn't pay her. She went."

"Why did you come out?"

"I was curious." Jasmine was wearing an unmournful, low-cut, yellow sweater blouse, lime-green slacks, spike-heeled shoes. "That bundle of clothes you dropped off this morning. They were Donald's clothes."

"Sorry I couldn't have them cleaned before I dropped them off."

"Are they part of the investigation?"

"No."

"I mean, I know they weren't the clothes he was, uh, dead in."

"No. They were just his clothes. I was returning them."

"Oh." That seemed to satisfy her. She looked worriedly at the house.

"Jasmine, I'm puzzled."

"Aren't we all. I mean, really!"

"Did Donald discuss giving five million dollars to the museum with you?"

"No."

"Not at all? He never mentioned it to you?"

"Not a peep. To the museum? I read in the paper he was planning to give money away to somebody."

"Did he ever mention religious art to you? Show you any?"

"I don't even know what it is. Religious art? I thought only people could be religious."

"Did he ever talk about religion to you?"

"No. Lately he's been reading big books instead of sleeping. Big novels."

"Did he ever mention to you his visiting the monastery in Tomasito?"

"Where his son is? No. I've never been there."

"Did he ever suggest to you that he might like to enter a monastery?"

Her eyes widened. "No!"

Fletch too looked at the house. "So. We're all puzzled."

"He lived like a monk," she said. "Up all night, reading. *War and Peace. The Brothers Karaminski.*"

Fletch's eyes narrowed. "Harm no more?" he said. "Something like that. Go away and do no more harm?"

"Yeah," she said. "He said something like that. Two or three times." She shrugged. "I never knew what he was talking about. When he talked."

"He never mentioned going away with you?"

"No. Why should he?"

Fletch shook his head. "I get less puzzled for a second, and then more puzzled. You are Jasmine Habeck, aren't you?"

"No. The newspaper was wrong about that."

"Your name is Jasmine?"

"Only sort of. We never married. Donald never divorced his first wife. Louise. Have you met her?"

Fletch heard himself saying, "Yuss."

"Sort of weird lady. Sort of nice, really. She'd sit and say nothing for the longest while, and then she'd ask, 'Jasmine, what do you think of the word *blue?*' and I'd say, 'I don't think about the word *blue* all that much,' and then she'd say something really weird like, 'Blue Donald blew away in a blue suit.' Really! Very strange.''

"I'm becoming less puzzled."

"That's good."

"You were just living here as his friend?"

"Well, sort of I had to, you see." She shifted on her heels. "Maybe you can tell me what to do."

"Try me."

She took a step closer to him. "I'm in the Federal Witness Program, you see."

"Oh."

"I testified in a trial in Miami against some bad guys, for the government. They really weren't bad guys, I didn't think so, they had lots of money, and didn't care whether it was day or night. But they were in trouble, and the government said I should help them out, testify against them, or I could go to prison, too, and I hadn't done anything bad, taken a few jewels from Pete"—she pointed to a turquoise ring on her finger—"my favorite fur, so I said, 'Sure,' hung around a long, long time, went to court and answered all sorts of dumb questions about seeing the naked women working in the coke-cutting factory, things like that, you know? So I was to be protected by the federal government. You think I should call someone in Washington?"

"What did all that have to do with Donald Habeck?"

"Nothing. I was in this lawyer's office in Miami, and Donald came in to see a friend. At that time they were going to send me to St. Louis when I was done, and my girl friend, this Hispanic *chanteuse*, said that's where the Bibles are printed and it's awfully muggy there, and that didn't sound like me. Donald invited me for a drink. Two days later I came back here with him. We was never married." She concluded with, "My real name isn't Jasmine, of course."

"Of course."

"No one's is, I think."

"I suspect not."

"I mean, have you ever actually met anyone named Jasmine?"

"Never before. Not even now, I guess."

"That's why I chose it. If I had to go be anoniminous, at least I wanted an outstanding name. Wouldn't you?"

"I suppose so."

"So what should I do now Donald's dead? Call someone in Washington, or what?"

"What federal officer did you deal with in Miami?"

"That's the trouble. I can't think of his name. It was either John or Tom."

"What about Habeck's partners? Do they know you are in the Federal Witness Program?"

"I don't think so. I think they thought I was Mrs. Habeck Part Two. The few times we were together they never spoke to me. I mean, except for, 'Get me a drink, will you, Jasmine?' Pete and those guys were much nicer. At least they knew I was a woman, you know what I mean? They didn't treat me as no equal, for God's sake. I'm glad I came out here with Donald before I finished testifyin' against them."

"I see." Fletch looked at a few of his toes through the tops of his sneakers. "So you're sitting here without any money, any friends. . . ."

"Yeah. I want a friend."

"You're not Donald Habeck's widow, you're not even Jasmine. . . ."

"I'd be little Miss Nobody, 'cept I was married twice once."

"Do you have any idea of Donald's plans for you, if he went away, if he went into a monastery?"

"I had no idea he was going into a monastery. It must have come over him sudden like. I had a girl friend like that. Suddenly it overcame her to be a WAC."

"I guess we'd better get you in touch with some federal officer here in town."

"I thought of talking to the mailman about it. Well, I mean . . . really."

"Someone will call you."

"Plus, I'm locked out of the house." She turned around and looked at the quiet brick house floating on rhododendrons. "My fur is in there."

He started toward the house with her. "Is there a burglar alarm? I didn't notice."

"No. Isn't that stupid? Think of a big criminal lawyer like that, and his house don't even have a burglar alarm. He should have known some of the guys I knew!"

"I think he did, Jasmine. I think he knew all of them."

30

"I see someone's arse sticking up from the bushes!" Definitely, that was Frank Jaffe's voice. No other voice was that gravelly. "And on that arse is written 'Ben Franklyn Friend Service'!"

In the dark, in the bushes in front of the *News-Tribune*, momentarily Fletch wondered if he went all the way in his imitation of an ostrich and stuck his head into the ground he would disappear entirely from view.

Instead, he stood up and turned around. He had not realized he had moved so far into the building's security lights.

"'Evening, Frank. Time you'd gone home."

"Oh, it's you!" Frank Jaffe exclaimed in mock surprise. "Don't you think we've given that particular institution of physical excess enough free advertising this week?"

"Yes. I do."

"Then why are you in front of the *News-Tribune* building waving a flag at passing traffic advertising their services?"

The manila envelope and the pencil Fletch had taken from his car were on the ground behind the bushes.

"That's not really what I'm doing, Frank."

"What else are you doing?"

"I'm looking for a gun, Frank."

"You're looking for your gum?"

"Okay."

"How could you drop your gum way over there in the bushes?"

Fletch held up his index finger. "Don't you feel that wind?"

"You were trying to throw up in the bushes," Frank accused.

"No, I wasn't."

"You were trying to catch a buggerer?"

"Frank . . ."

"Besides advertising their services across your arse, have you penetrated any deeper into the whorehouse story?"

"I wanted to talk to you about that, Frank."

"Clearly you've exposed yourself. Are we going to expose them?"

"Frank, I think the story is going to take a little longer than we originally thought."

"Ah," said Frank. "Really getting involved, are you, boy?"

"Something unpredictable has happened . . . a setback . . ."

"Discovered you really dig this assignment, that it? Getting your bones ground at office expense, who wouldn't? Ah, Fletch, I wish all the employees at the *News-Tribune* threw themselves into their work as enthusiastically as you do! I knew you'd like this assignment, once you got into it!"

"I threw myself into it, all right, Frank—"

"That's my boy!"

"Trouble is, you see, this girl, Cindy—"

"Now, I'll bet, even *you're* asking yourself why you're getting married Saturday!"

"Well, you see, Barbara—"

"Carry on, Fletcher, whatever you're doing. But, please The publisher and I would both appreciate it if, in keeping your chin up, you keep your arse down!"

"All right, Frank."

"Good night, Fletch."

"Good night, Frank."

31

"Is Lieutenant Gomez in?"

The counter in the lobby of the police station was so high it made even a helpful citizen feel like a humble miscreant.

"Why do you want to know?" the desk sergeant asked.

"I want to talk to him," Fletch said. "I want to give him something."

"Leave it with me. I'll see that he gets it."

The sign on the desk said SERGEANT WILHELM ROHM.

"I'd like to talk to him. Is he in?"

"What's in the big envelope?" Sergeant Rohm read the advertisement on Fletch's clothes.

"What I want to give him."

"Delivery service from a whorehouse; that's pretty good. What's in the envelope, handsome? A case of clap for the lieutenant? It won't be his first."

"A gun."

"Used?"

"I think so."

"I'll give it to him."

"He's not in?" The sergeant took the envelope and felt the contents. "Don't mess up the prints," Fletch said.

"Ah, a junior G-man," the sergeant said. "I can see you're used to working under covers."

"At least let me write the lieutenant a note."

"Sure." The sergeant slid a turned-over booking sheet and a ballpoint pen across the desk. "Write anything you want stud. We just love full confessions. Sometimes even the lawyers find them an obstacle to getting their clients acquitted."

"Why was Stuart Childers released?"

"What's that got to do with you?"

"Curious."

"Stuart Childers is always released. He comes in here once a day. Sometimes twice. He confesses to any murder he hears about on the radio. Also robbery, arson, and aggravated littering. He must have really gotten a kick out of his day in court. Wants to play defendant again."

Fletch wrote:

Lieutenant Gomez:

Your search for the Habeck murder weapon couldn't have been extensive. Guard checking cars at News-Tribune *parking lot gate indicates murderer walked into and out of parking lot. I followed logical walking path from back of parking lot, where Habeck was murdered, to street, and found this gun in the bushes in front of* News-Tribune *building tonight. I lifted it with pencil through trigger ring, so prints should be complete. Also look forward to ballistics report. Tell your pal, Biff Wilson, I'm always glad to be of assistance. Clearly he needs help writing obituaries.*

I. M. Fletcher

"You writing your life's story?" The desk sergeant was trying to ignore a weeping black lady at the other end of the counter. "I'd love to know what it is you male whores do that's worth paying for. Nobody's ever offered to pay me."

Fletch handed him the folded note. "Put this in the envelope with the gun, will you?"

"Sure, stud. I'll take care of it." He put the note on top of the envelope.

"Please," Fletch said. "It's important."

"Sure, stud, sure. Now why don't you get out of here before I throw you in a cell where you'll get to do whatever you do for free?"

32

"What are you two doing, playing *Uncle Wiggly in Connecticut*?"

"Yeah." Cindy quoted: " 'I was a nice girl, wasn't I?' "

Barbara and Cindy were in lounge chairs on the deck of the beach house. The small, round table between them held their glasses, a half-empty bottle of Scotch, and an ice bucket.

"A banana split for lunch and Scotch at night," Fletch said. "Better be careful you don't go to hell, Cindy."

She stretched her arms. "That's okay. I'm retiring real soon."

"Yeah," Fletch said. "You're going to the dogs."

There was a quarter moon over the ocean. Far out to sea a good-sized freighter was moving south.

"Have a drink," Barbara said. "Join us."

"Yeah," Cindy said, "you've had a long day, I think, getting a job this morning, when you already had one, then a business lunch . . ."

"You don't know the half of it."

"A discouraging day, too, I think," Barbara said.

"Yeah, yeah," Cindy said. "Discouraging, presenting yourself so well at the job interview, then being discovered a liar, an impostor, so quickly at lunch."

The women laughed.

In the kitchen Fletch half-filled a glass with tap water.

"Poor Fletch," Barbara said. On the deck he added Scotch and ice to the water in his glass. "He was so discouraged he drove himself all the way to Tomasito, just for a drink."

"A warm beer," he muttered. "What's to eat?"

"Nothing," Barbara said. "Remember, you canceled dinner with my mother."

"We haven't eaten," said Cindy.

"It's ten o'clock," Fletch said.

"We've been talking," said Cindy. "Story of my life."

"Maybe you'll go for pizza," said Barbara.

Fletch sat in the chair near the railing. "So Cindy . . . Did you ruin my prospects for employment? Did you tell Marta I'm an impostor? That I'm not really a male whore but rather an honest journalist out to screw the Ben Franklyn Friend Service?"

"I thought about it," Cindy said. "I thought a lot about what to do. This afternoon my clients didn't get my undivided attention. Seeing I wasn't controlling the situation as well as I should have been, one guy came on real strong. I had to make an accident to cool him off. One of the lift bars swung against his nose accidentally-on-purpose." She was dressed as she had been at lunch, in a short kilt and loafers. "It's okay. No blood got on the rug."

"You were ready with a towel," Fletch guessed.

"I'm always ready with a towel. Men are always spilling one fluid or another."

Barbara took a gulp of her drink.

"Did you tell Marta, or not?" Fletch asked.

"I decided either I had to tell Marta who you are and screw

you,'' Cindy said, ''or tell Barbara who I am, and screw
Marta.''

''A tough decision.'' Fletch watched Barbara. ''So you've
told Barbara, your old friend, who you are, what you do for a
living . . . et cetera?''

''Yeah.''

Fletch asked Barbara, ''How do you feel about that?''

Barbara didn't answer immediately. ''I guess I understand.
I'm more surprised at myself, than anything.''

''What do you mean?''

''That I could have a friend and really know so little about
her. It makes me doubt myself, my own sensitivity, my own
perceptions.'' For a moment Barbara looked into the glass she
held in her lap. ''This is difficult to explain. I mean, now I'm
wondering who the hell you are, Fletch, the guy I'm going to
marry in three days. What don't I know about you? How
good are my perceptions?''

''Jitters,'' Cindy said.

''Today,'' Fletch said, ''I discovered things about a few
people I would never have guessed. I added some real
interesting people to my collection.''

''I mean, here we go along in life assuming everybody is
more or less as he or she appears to be, as he or she say they
are. Forgive my bad grammar. Enough of that he-or-she shit.
And, wham-o, in one minute over a drink or something you
discover they've been living this whole life, having thoughts,
doing things, being someone you never knew about, never
even dreamed possible.''

Cindy said, ''I think with orthodontics and psychiatry,
health care, clothing fashions, too, with the great American
idealization of normalcy, which doesn't exist, people think
they want to love people similar to themselves.''

''All that's the mother of prejudice,'' said Barbara. ''Eco-
nomics is the father.''

"It's the differences between people that we ought to love," said Cindy.

"If we were just exactly what people think we are," Fletch said, "we wouldn't have much of ourselves to ourselves, would we?"

"Yeah," Cindy giggled. "Hypocrisy is our last bastion of privacy."

"My." Barbara waved her glass in front of her mouth. "Pour a little booze into this trio and we pick up a philosophical text fast enough, don't we?"

"It wasn't much of a decision," Cindy said. "I'm leaving Ben Franklyn Friday. I don't mind letting the Ben Franklyn Friend Service know I have a sting in my tail."

Fletch said, "And there's Marta's fondness for Carla. . . ."

Cindy smiled at him. There was light coming through the window from the living room. "The human element is in everything we do. Isn't that what we're talking about?" She plopped two ice cubes into her glass. "Anyway, that's no way to run a business. People should not be allowed to win career advancement in bed."

Barbara giggled into her glass. "You're talking about a whorehouse here, Cindy! I'm sorry, old pal, but that's funny."

"My business has less to do with sex than you think," Cindy said.

"I'm sure."

"So what have you really decided?" Fletch asked.

"I've decided to help you get your story," Cindy said. "Let's expose Ben Franklyn."

"Great!"

"It will be my wedding present to you and Barbara. I was going to give you a collie when you came back from your honeymoon. . . ."

"A collie!" Barbara exclaimed. "If Fletch doesn't keep his job, we won't be able to feed ourselves!"

"Tell me what you need," Cindy said to Fletch.

"I need to know who owns the Ben Franklyn Friend Service."

"Something called Wood Nymph, Incorporated."

"That's beautiful."

"Nymphs would," Barbara giggled.

"Who owns Wood Nymphs?" Fletch asked.

"I have no idea."

"Nymphomaniacs always would," Barbara said. "Isn't that the point?"

"I need to know that. I need to know specifically and graphically what services you provide, and the specific fees for those services."

"I can tell you that right now."

"Please don't," Barbara said. "Not while I'm drinking."

"I'll need some sort of a deposition from you regarding the performances you put on for voyeurs. And that the man frequently doesn't know he's being watched, that his ass is being sold."

"Oh, charming!" said Barbara.

"Also, a description of the whole escort service, that you're really operating as call girls, call people. The parties at which you have performed, how that works, how much it costs. The whole blackmail thing, the cameras—"

"Cameras!" clucked Barbara. "Hypocrisy is the last bastion of privacy."

"Listen," Fletch said to Barbara, "a week ago you suggested you and I get married naked in front of everybody."

"I was kidding."

"Were you?"

"I thought I could lose eight pounds."

"Can you get all that by tomorrow?" Fletch asked Cindy.

"I'll try."

"Pizza," Barbara said. "I am feeling a distinct need for pizza."

Cindy looked fully at Fletch and asked, "What about a list

of our clients?'' She watched him closely as she waited for his answer.

"Sure," he said evenly. "Prostitution can't exist without the johns.''

"Will you publish their names?'' Cindy asked.

"I don't know," Fletch said. "I honestly don't know. I will present their names for publication.''

"Uh!'' Cindy said. "It's still a man's world, Master!''

"Will you please go get some pizza, Fletch?'' Barbara asked. "Better make mine pepperoni. Right now I don't think I could look an anchovy in the eye.''

33

"We called ahead," Fletch said to the counterman. "Three pizzas in the name of Ralton."

The sweating counterman did not smile at him. "It will be a few minutes."

The counterman then picked up a phone between two ovens. He dialed a number, and turned his back.

There were six other people waiting for pizzas. Four men, two in shorts, one in work clothes, one in a business suit. A teenaged boy in a tuxedo. A young teenaged girl in shorts, a halter, and purple high-heeled shoes. She also wore lipstick and eye shadow.

"Aren't you afraid of spilling pizza on your dinner jacket?" the man in running shorts asked the teenaged boy.

The boy answered him, apparently courteously, in rapid French.

"Oh," the man said.

Fletch opened the door to the vertical refrigerator and took out a six-pack of 7-Up. He put it on the counter.

"Schwartz?" the counterman called.

The boy in the tuxedo paid for his pizza and left.

The man in working clothes got his pizza next. Then one of the men in shorts. A woman in tennis whites entered and gave the name Ramirez. The young girl clicked out of the store on her high heels carrying her pizza like a tray of hors d'oeuvres.

"We must have called a half-hour ago," Fletch said to the counterman. "Name of Ralton?"

Again the counterman did not smile at him. "It will be a few minutes."

The man in the business suit picked up his pizza.

Two policemen strolled in. Their car was parked just outside the front door. They didn't give a name.

They looked at the counterman.

The counterman nodded at Fletch.

The cops jumped at Fletch, spun him around, pushed him.

Fletch found himself leaning against the counter, his hands spread, his feet spread. One cop had his hand on the back of Fletch's neck, forcing his head down. The other's fingers felt through Fletch's T-shirt, his shorts, checked the tops of his athletic socks.

"What did he do?" the man in running shorts asked.

The eyes of the woman in tennis whites widened. She stepped back.

"He was robbing the store," a cop answered.

"He was not!" the man said. "He's been standing here fifteen minutes!"

"He was about to rob the store."

"He gave a name! He was waiting for pizza!"

They pulled Fletch's arms behind his back.

He felt the cool metal of the handcuffs around his wrists, heard the click as they locked.

"He's robbed lots of stores," the cop said. "Liquor stores,

convenience stores. Once he got his pizza, he'd rob this store.''

"Oh," the man said.

The other cop said, "Even a robber's got to eat, you know."

"He doesn't look like a bad guy," the man in running shorts said. "Fast. You'd never catch him, once he started runnin'."

"Well," a cop said. "We caught him."

The man said to Fletch, "Your name Ralton?"

"No."

"That does it for me," the man said. "He gave the name Ralton. Phony name."

"His name's Liddicoat," said a cop. "Alexander Liddicoat."

"That's probably phony, too," said the man.

"Ramirez?" the counterman called.

The woman in tennis whites paid for her pizza.

"Let's go," the cop said.

Both hanging on to Fletch, they waited for the woman to go through the door with her pizza.

"Can we take my pizza with me?" Fletch asked. "I'll let you have some."

"Thanks anyway," a cop answered. "We just had Chinese take-out."

Outside they put him in the back of the police car carefully and slammed the door.

As they settled in the front seat, the cop in the passenger seat looked at his watch. "Eleven-forty. We take him all the way downtown, we'll never get back in time to go off duty at twelve."

"What's so special about him?"

"Dispatch said take him straight downtown to headquarters."

"Yeah." The driver started the car. "We run a taxi service."

"I could save you the trip," Fletch said. He was trying to fit his handcuffed hands into the small of his back against the car seat. "My name's not Liddi-whatever. I've got identification in my wallet."

"Sure. I bet you have. Might as well get goin', Alf."

"You've got the wrong guy," Fletch said.

The cop in the passenger seat said, "Twelve years on the force and I've never yet arrested the right guy."

The car started forward. "We didn't read him his rights."

The other cop looked through the grille at Fletch.

"You know your rights?"

"Sure."

"That's good. He knows his rights, Alf."

"Cruel and unusual punishment already," Fletch said. "Lettin' a guy smell pizza for fifteen minutes, then not lettin' him have any."

"Tell your lawyer."

The police car bumped over the curb from the pizza store's parking lot onto the road.

Fletch said, "Next stop, the guillotine."

34

"Fletcher?"

On the cell bunk that reeked of disinfectant, Fletch sighed with relief. The guard opening the cell door had called him Fletcher. Confusion regarding who he was was now over. Now he could go to his apartment and get some sleep.

He stood up. He figured it must be about four in the morning.

For about three hours he had lain on his bunk listening to two men, not synchronized, vomiting, one old man whimpering, another singing, for more than an hour, over and over again, the refrain *I'll be blowed, Lucy, if you will....* In the cell next to him, two male streetwalkers argued endlessly and passionately about barbers. One had asked Fletch how to get a job with the Ben Franklyn Friend Service. Fletch answered he didn't know, he was just a bouncer there. Fletch's cellmate was a portly, middle-aged man in white trousers and sandals who said he was a schoolteacher. The afternoon before, he said, he had stabbed one of his students.

There was blood on his trousers. After telling Fletch this, he curled on his bunk and fell asleep.

"Come on," the guard said. "Move it."

"Am I free to go?"

He followed the guard between the cells to the steel door.

While he was being booked as Alexander Liddicoat, for more than twenty incidents of armed robbery, Fletch's wallet and watch had been taken from him. Photographs of Alexander Liddicoat were with the warrants. Looking at them upside down, Fletch saw a remote resemblance. While handing it over, Fletch showed the booking officer identification in his wallet, his driver's license and press card, proving who he was. Without really looking at the identification photographs, the booking officer charged him with stealing the wallet of Irwin Maurice Fletcher, as well.

The other side of the steel door, Fletch turned right, toward the stairs to the booking desk and the lobby.

The guard grabbed him by the elbow. "This way, please."

They went to the left, past offices. Most of the doors were open. Lights were on, people working in the offices.

At the end of the corridor, they came to a closed door. The guard opened it with a key. He snapped on the inside light.

Six chairs were around a long conference table. Nothing else was in the room. High up on the far wall was a barred window.

"Wait here," the guard said.

"Why are you holding me?"

The guard closed the door behind him.

Fletch snapped off the light, crawled onto the table in the dark, and fell asleep.

The light snapped on. The door was open.

Lieutenant Gomez was standing over Fletch.

"You make yourself at home wherever you are, don't you?"

Fletch sat up. "What time is it?"

He was cold.

"Five-thirty A.M. The jailhouse swimming pool doesn't open for another half-hour. The mayor and his top aides are down there cleaning it for you now. They know you like to go skinny-dipping every morning."

"Glad to see you." Fletch remained sitting on the table. "You get to work early."

"Working on an important case," Gomez said. "The murder of Donald Edwin Habeck. You know anything about it?"

"Yeah. Read something about it in the newspapers." Fletch yawned and rubbed his eyes. "Did you get the gun?"

"What gun?"

"The gun I left for you last night. I left it upstairs at the desk for you, with a note."

Gomez repeated: "What gun?"

"I think it's the gun used to kill Habeck. I found—"

Gomez looked at the door.

Biff Wilson stood in the door, shaved and suited as well as ever, wrinkled and rumpled.

"Oh, hi, Biff," Fletch said. "Did you bring the coffee?"

Biff snorted. "I guess I was a wise guy once. Was I ever this much of a wise guy, Gomez?"

"You were never a wise guy," Gomez said. "Always the altar boy."

"I thought so." Biff closed the door. "I'm not even sure I remember precisely what it is one does to a wise guy."

"On the police, we break his balls," Gomez offered. "Do all the guys in journalism have balls?"

Biff stood closer to Fletch. "Hi, kid. I heard you were incarcerated."

"Case of mistaken identity," Fletch said. "Robber named Liddicoat. Apparently his picture had been circulated to all the liquor stores, pizza parlors—"

Biff said to Gomez, "Can we make the charge stick awhile?"

"Awhile," said Gomez.

"You can't," Fletch said. "Booking desk has already checked the identity in my wallet. That's how you know I'm here, right?"

"Wallet?" Biff asked Gomez.

"He didn't have a wallet," Gomez said. "Just a stolen wristwatch."

Biff nodded at Fletch.

"We were talking about a gun," Fletch said.

Biff looked at Gomez. "What gun?"

"A gun I found," Fletch said. "Outside the *News-Tribune.* I turned it in to Sergeant Wilhelm Rohm last night, with instructions to give it to Gomez."

"I don't know about a gun," Gomez said.

"You're a good boy." Biff stroked Fletch's leg with the palm of his hand. "A real good boy."

Fletch moved his leg.

"Muscle." Biff dug his fingers into Fletch's thigh. "Look at that muscle, Gomez."

Fletch got off the table and moved away.

"And what do those shorts say?" Biff squinted. "I can't quite read it, can you, Gomez? Some high-school track team?"

"Ben Franklyn Friend Service," said Gomez.

"Football," said Biff. "I think that means a football team."

"That's another story," Fletch said.

"I sure would like to know what you've found out," Biff said.

"Lots," Fletch said. "You write lousy obituaries, Biff."

"Why do you say that, Liddicoat?"

"For one thing, Jasmine and Donald Habeck never married. He never divorced Louise."

"Yeah? What else?"

Fletch looked from Gomez to Wilson and shook his head.

"What else?" Biff asked.

"Have you talked with Gabais yet?"

"Who?"

"Felix Gabais. Child molester. An ex-client of Habeck. Served eleven hard years. Released from prison last week."

"Have you talked with him yet?"

"Not yet."

"You've been bird-doggin' me all week, kid. Talked with everybody in the Habeck family, as far as I know, even the brother in the monastery. You're stealin' our thunder. What for, Liddicoat?"

Again, Fletch shook his head. "This was no gangland slaying, Biff. You're on the wrong track."

"You know better than we do, uh? The newspaper assign you to this story?"

"The museum angle."

"Oh. The museum angle. That make sense to you, Gomez?"

"No sense whatever, Biff."

"I think this kid ought to get lost."

Gomez said, "We can lose him."

"Some sort of bureaucratic tangle," Biff said. "You know, kid, once you get entangled with the cops, any damned fool thing's liable to happen."

"Sure," said Gomez. "We'll put him in the van for the funny farm this morning. It will be a good ten days before anyone straightens out that bureaucratic tangle."

"What will that get you?" Fletch asked. "A few days. You think I'd shut up about it?"

"Can't blame us for a bureaucratic tangle," Biff said. "I'm not even in this building this morning. You're not here either, are you, Gomez?"

"Naw. I'm never in this early."

"This is a real wise guy. Our offer of a few days' vacation

at the funny farm doesn't frighten him. We should stick a real charge on him, Gomez. Get him off my back forever. Is that what you do with wise guys? I forget.''

"Generally, Biff, if you're going to hit somebody, you should hit him so hard he can't get up swinging.''

"Yeah.'' Although speaking softly, the veins in Biff's neck and temples were pulsing visibly. His eyes glinted like black pebbles at the bottom of a sunlit stream. "I've heard that somewhere before. Let's hit him with a real charge, so he can't get up again swinging. Let's see. He was picked up as Alexander Liddicoat. While he was being booked, it was discovered he had a seller's quantity of angel dust in his pocket. You got any spare PCP, Gomez?''

"Sure,'' said Gomez. "For just such an occasion.''

Fletch was hot. "All because I'm bird-dogging your story, Biff?''

"Because you're a wise guy,'' Biff said. "There's no room for wise guys in journalism. Is there, Gomez?''

"You were always an altar boy,'' Gomez said to Biff.

"We play by the rules, kid. You get convicted for possession of a seller's quantity of PCP, Fletcher, and somehow I doubt John Winters and Frank Jaffe are going to want to see you around the *News-Tribune* emptying wastebaskets anymore. Or any other newspaper.''

"What am I supposed to say?'' Fletch asked. "That I'll back off and be a good boy?''

"Too late for that,'' Biff said. "I've decided you're a real wise guy. We want you gone.''

"I'm supposed to say I'll go away?''

"You'll go away,'' Gomez said. "At taxpayers' expense. We'll see to it.''

Fletch laughed. "Don't you think I'll ever come back, Biff?''

Biff glanced at Gomez. "Maybe. Maybe not. Who cares?''

"You'll care.''

"I doubt it. You spend a few years inside now, and, what with one thing and another, you won't even be able to walk straight when you get out. Not much of a threat." Biff said to Gomez: "Find out about this gun he's talking about. Where's the PCP?"

"Got some in the locker."

"Get it. We'll go to your office and rewrite this kid's booking sheet."

"Got some real coffee in the office. We'll have some real coffee."

"I could use some."

Fletch said, "Jesus, Biff! You're serious!"

"Have I ever made a joke?"

"Ann McGarrahan said you're a shit."

"She should know. Biggest mistake of her life was marryin' me. Everybody says so."

Gomez laughed. "You the reason she never had any kids, Biff?"

"Had something to do with it. The lady didn't like to be screwed by anybody with whiskey on his breath."

Fletch said, "Jesus!"

"Guess I won't be seeing you around anymore, kid," Biff said. "Can't say I'll miss ya."

"Biff—"

"Someone will come get you in a while," Gomez said. "Enjoy waiting. It will be a lot of years before you ever get to spend any time alone again."

"We're going to go cook your papers, kid." Biff held the door open for Gomez. "And, believe me, Gomez and I are the greatest chefs in the world."

Fletch stood alone in the fluorescent-lit room. The door had thwunked closed. Wilson's and Gomez's footsteps faded down the corridor. Muffled shouts came from the cellblock.

Louise Habeck crossed his mind.

Fletch looked up at the dirty, barred window. Even with the bars on the outside, an electric wire ran from the closed window into the wall.

There was no air-conditioning/heat vent.

The walls were painted cement.

Green sneakers, blued hair, and a flowered dress . . .

It was crazy. Fletch went to the door and turned the knob. He pushed.

The door opened.

He looked out. The corridor was empty.

His heart going faster than his feet, he ambled along the corridor and up the stairs.

There was no one at the counter of the booking office.

In the lobby the same black woman who had been weeping there the night before was now sitting quietly on a bench. The sergeant at the reception desk was reading the sports pages of the *News-Tribune*.

It took Fletch a moment to get the sergeant's attention. Finally, he looked up.

"Lieutenant Gomez and Biff Wilson are having coffee in the lieutenant's office," Fletch said. "They'd like you to send out for some doughnuts. Jelly doughnuts."

"Okay." The sergeant picked up the phone and dialed three numbers. "The lieutenant wants some doughnuts," he said into the phone. "No. He has his coffee. You know Gomez. If it ain't mud, it ain't coffee."

"Jelly doughnuts," Fletch said.

The sergeant said, "Jelly doughnuts."

35

"*News-Tribune* resource desk. Code and name, please."

"Hiya, Pilar. How're you doin'?"

"Good morning. This is Mary."

"Oh. Good morning, Mary."

"Code and name, please."

Still ravenously hungry, Fletch was glad at least to be back in his own car, headed for his own apartment. "Seventeen ninety dash nine. Fletcher."

Jogging to the bus stop, his eyes scanning the storefronts for a place open for breakfast, Fletch then realized he had no money. The police had stolen his wallet and keys. The thought amused him that if he robbed a convenience store, Alexander Liddicoat would be blamed.

His car was in the parking lot of a pizza store way out at the beach. He hitchhiked. The first driver who picked him up was a middle-aged man who sold musical instruments. He tried to interest Fletch in the roxophone. He was then picked up by a van filled with kids headed for the beach. At that hour of the morning they were passing around a joint of marijuana and already had finished one quart of white wine. A group of youngsters headed for the beach on a fine morning, each was near tears. It was past nine o'clock by the time Fletch arrived at his car, removed the parking-violation notice from it, hot-wired it, and started the drive back to his apartment. ,

"Messages for you," said the resource desk's Mary over the car phone. "Someone named Barbara called. Sounds like a personal message."

"Yes?"

"We're not supposed to take too many personal messages, you know."

"Ah, come on, Mary. Be a sport." Fletch's hunger, the morning's heat, the bright sunlight, made his eyes and head ache.

"Message is, 'Did you eat all the pizza yourself? All is forgiven. Please phone.' "

The reference to pizza made his tum-tum beat a tom-tom.

"Well?" Mary asked.

"Well what?"

"Did you eat all the pizza yourself?"

"Mary, that's a personal question. No personal questions, please."

"You did. I think you ate the pizza yourself. There's nothing worse than expecting someone to bring you a pizza and that someone eats it all himself."

"Mary, have you had breakfast this morning?"

"Yes."

"I haven't."

"You don't need breakfast, with all the pizza you ate."

"Is there another message?"

"I wouldn't forgive you. Yes. Ann McGarrahan wants to hear from you. Message is, 'Fletch, know you have your hands full with present assignment but please phone in. Beware B.W. and other social diseases."

"Okay."

"What's B.W.?"

"Mary, that's another personal question."

"I never heard of B.W."

"You're lucky."

"I thought I knew all the social diseases. I mean, I thought I knew of them."

"Fine. Now I need the address of Felix Gabais." He spelled the name for her. "In the St. Ignatius district."

"Aren't you going to warn me about B.W.?"

"Mary? Stay away from B.W."

"I mean, how do you catch it?"

"Sticking your nose in places it doesn't belong."

"Oh, we never do things like that. There's only one Gabais in the St. Ignatius district. First name, Therese."

"That's it. He lives with his sister."

"That's 45447 Twig Street. Mapping shows the address to be a half-block west of a car dealership on the corner."

"Thank you. One more: I need the address of Stuart Childers." Again he spelled the name.

"That's disgusting," she said. "Anyone who does that deserves B.W."

"Mary . . ."

"That's 120 Keating Road. Mapping shows that to be Harndon Apartments. Swank."

"Okay. Thanks."

"I shouldn't tell you this, I suppose, but Mr. Wilson called in a while ago. He wanted that address, too."

"Which address?"

"The one in St. Ignatius. Therese Gabais."

"Mary, you've already got B.W."

"Oh, don't say that."

"Be careful, Mary. B.W. can lay you up a long time."

*   *   *

"This is an answering machine," Fletch said into his apartment phone on the third ring. "I am not able to come to the phone just now—"

"Fletch!" Barbara shouted through the phone. "You don't have an answering machine!"

"Oh," Fletch said. "I forgot."

Fletch didn't have much. Across from the rickety, second-hand couch where he sat, posters were on the wall of the harbor of Cagna, on the Italian Riviera, of Cozumel, in eastern Mexico, of Belize, of Nairobi, Kenya, of Copacabana, in Rio de Janiero, Brazil. He hoped someday to have some really decent photographs on his wall, a proper collection. Someday, maybe, he'd have walls big enough to hold some decent copies of the paintings of Edgar Arthur Tharpe, Jr., the western artist.

"Are you all right?"

"Of course." On the chipped plate on the chipped coffee table in front of him there was very little left of his breakfast of scrambled eggs, waffles, and bacon. "Why do you ask?"

"You went out for pizza last night at eleven o'clock! And you never came back!"

"Oh, God! I didn't! Are you sure?"

"You never even phoned!"

"I did not eat all the pizza myself. I didn't get any of it."

"Were you in an accident, or something?"

"Or something. How come you're free to phone me? Cecilia finally get a customer for her jodhpurs?"

"I'm doing an errand for her, at the drugstore. We damned near starved to death."

"Did you lose those eight pounds you don't like?"

"I think I did."

"What did you and Cindy do?"

"Went to bed, finally. What else could we do? We waited for you until past one o'clock."

"Did Cindy stay the night?"

"Of course. What else? We'd had drinks, remember? She knew she shouldn't drive."

"Yeah."

"Damned inconsiderate of you. You could have at least phoned."

"I could've?"

Hung from the ceiling across the room was his surfboard, a thing of beauty, a joy forever.

"We were worried. I phoned the pizza store. The man said no one named Fletcher had been there."

"You ordered in the name of Ralton."

"Oh, yeah. I forgot. Where did you spend the night?"

"Long story. Mind if I tell you later?"

"Does it have to do with Habeck?"

"I guess so." Fletch looked at his plate. His headache was gone.

"Did you read Biff Wilson's piece this morning?"

"Yeah." The *News-Tribune* was on the couch beside Fletch. It was not reported that a gun, the possible murder weapon, had been turned in to police the night before.

"His piece strongly indicates, Fletch, that Habeck was bumped off by the mob because he knew too much."

Fletch sighed. "Maybe he's right."

"I mean, really, Fletch, how long has he been covering crime for the *News-Tribune?*"

"A long time."

"He must have contacts everywhere."

"He must have."

"I mean, sure, people must talk to him: the police, mobsters, informants. He probably has it all figured out."

"Probably."

"There's little point in your being up all night, losing sleep over it. There's no point at all in your losing your job over it."

"Listen, Barbara, I've got to shave and shower and get to work."

"Ate all the pizza, and slept late. And I'm marrying you?"

With a flick of his fingers, Fletch knocked the *News-Tribune* onto the floor.

"I'd have second thoughts, if I were you," Fletch said.

"Too late. I'm on my umpteenth thought. Remember you're having dinner with my mother tonight."

"Absolutely."

"Six o'clock at the beach house. If you disappoint her again, all her doubts about you will turn into certainties, for sure."

"For sure."

"You'll be there?"

"Absolutely."

"Okay. By the way, Cindy said to call her at twelve-thirty sharp at 555-2900. She'll answer the phone herself."

"Say again? That's not the number of Ben Franklyn."

"No. She said she'll just be there at that time, waiting for you to call. That's 555-2900. She'll have things to tell you then."

"Okay."

"Fletch, this is Wednesday."

"Already?"

"We're getting married Saturday. You absolutely must be at dinner tonight."

"Okay."

"There are things to discuss."

"Okay, okay."

"I've got to get back to work," Barbara said.

Fletch said, "Yeah. Me, too."

36

"I'm from the *News-Tribune*," Fletch said. The woman who opened the door of the ground-floor apartment at 45447 Twig Street was in a wheelchair. "Are you Therese Gabais?"

Her eyes were black, her face gray, her hair unwashed, uncombed. "We can't afford a daily newspaper. I don't like them, anyway."

"Has anyone else from the *News-Tribune* been here?"

She shook her head no.

The car dealership at the corner of Twig Street seemed to be offering special sale prices on rusty, six-passenger sedans. Fletch had parked near the dealership and walked the half-block, scuffing through the wastepaper and empty tins on the sidewalk. He almost stumbled over the legs of a woman asleep in a doorway.

He was watching for a police car, or Biff's car. While he breakfasted, talked with Barbara, shaved and showered, his doorbell had not rung. If it had rung, he planned to go through a back window and down the fire escape. Being falsely arrested as Alexander Liddicoat for more than twenty robberies was slightly amusing. Having Wilson and Gomez contrive real charges against I.M. Fletcher for drug dealing was totally alarming. The police had not appeared at Fletch's apartment. They were not now visible in the street.

But Wilson and Gomez had every reason to believe Fletch would show up at the Gabais apartment.

"Has anyone been here?" Fletch asked. "The police?"

Again the woman shook her head no. Her eyes were dull.

She wheeled her chair aside. Perhaps she next would close the door in his face.

Holding the door open, Fletch stepped into the foul odor of the apartment. "I'm looking for Felix Gabais."

Expression briefly came into her eyes as she looked up at him. She was surprised he was still there. "He doesn't want a newspaper, either."

Fletch pushed the door closed. "Need to talk to him."

There was a bed, a mattress and some blankets on a box, in the room.

Moving no further, the woman's attention went to a television turned to a quiz-prize show on a dark, heavy bureau.

Fletch stepped through the only door into another room, a kitchen, of sorts. There was a small refrigerator, a stove top, a sink. Everything was filthy. Empty food cans overflowed the sink. The smell of garbage and excrement was stinging. Against the wall on the floor was a double-sized mattress without pillows or blankets.

There was a massive, brown upholstered chair between the mattress and the refrigerator.

And in the massive chair was a massive man. His gaze remained on the corner of the walls behind the stove top. A half-finished quart bottle of beer was in one hand on the chair arm. Slobbered food and drink were on his shirt and prison-issue black suit.

Fletch sat on the edge of the mattress. "What have you done since you've been out of prison?"

"Bought this chair." Felix Gabais's free hand raised and lowered on the chair arm. "Bought that mattress." Felix looked at the mattress. "Bought beer." The counter in the corner beyond the refrigerator had more than twenty empty quart beer bottles. "Beer's the only thing that fills me up now." The fat creases on Felix's neck rearranged themselves as Felix turned his head and looked down at Fletch. "I'm doin' okay, first week out."

"Looks like you got enough to eat in prison anyway."

"Yeah. But she suffered." Felix tipped the bottle toward the other room. "No one took care of my sister in eleven, twelve years. Scrounging food stamps. Sends kids out for cat food. Eating cat food off scrounged food stamps, you got it?" Fletch nodded. "Look at this place. Landlord took the living room and the other bedroom away from her. Only 'cause he couldn't throw her out. See that wall he put up?" From the layers of filth on it, Fletch supposed the wall had been there for most of the eleven years. "You call that legal?" Fletch didn't opine. "What are you going to do about it? She didn't do anything wrong. Why should she suffer?"

"Did you do something wrong?"

Instantly, there were tears in Felix's eyes. "I shouldn't have been put in prison. I was sick. What would you call someone who bothers small children?"

"Sick."

"Sure. They had to put me away. Couldn't let me be loose. Had to keep me in prison until I was no good anymore. Had to wreck me. I don't know about prison, though. That's an awful insult to a sick person."

"At your trial, you didn't plead insanity."

"At my trial, I didn't say nothin'!" Felix made no effort to control his tears. "You know what a defendant feels like at a trial?" Fletch shook his head. "He's in a daze. He's shocked this could be happenin' to him. He's shocked by what he's hearin' about himself, about the things he did. All these people are talkin', talkin', talkin' about you and about the things you did. What they're sayin' has nothin' to do with what you've always thought about yourself. All the time they're talkin', you're sick. You're struck dumb, you know what I mean?''

"Your lawyer was Donald Habeck, right?''

"Mr. Habeck. Yeah. I could have said a lot, if he didn't talk so much. See, I had my reasons. I had my own idea of things. I could've explained.''

"You could explain molesting children?''

"I had things to say. I was just tryin' to make it up to them.''

"How did you pay Habeck? How could you afford him?''

"I never paid Mr. Habeck. Not a dime.''

"I don't get it. Why did he take your case?''

"I don't know. One day he walks into the jail and says, 'I'm your lawyer.' He never asked me nothin'. He never let me explain. I could have explained, from my perspective, why I was such a bad guy. He never let the judge ask me nothin'. Day after day after day I sat there in the courtroom while all these people came out, one after another, and said they saw me do this, they saw me do that, the two dogs, this, that, this, that.'' Felix put the bottle of beer to his mouth, but didn't swallow much. "Every day the television and newspapers made a big thing of it. They hounded my sister. They hounded my sister crazy. Showed where we lived. Drew maps. Showed the playgrounds, the schoolyards where I used to walk the dogs and meet the children.'' Felix was crying copiously. "The newspapers were lousy! Drove her stupid!''

"I'm beginning to understand.''

"You ever hear of trial by newspaper?''

"You were the case Habeck lost. Lost big. Why not? A child molester . . .''

"Why did he do it? Why did he let it drag on so long? Why did he tell 'em everything? Why didn't he let me tell 'em anything?"

"He used you for publicity. Through you, he proved that Habeck could lose a case, big. And get his name in the newspaper every day while he was doing so. What I don't understand is, how come you served only eleven years?"

"That's the point! After all this punishment of my sister in the newspaper, after wreckin' her, one day this Mr. Habeck stands up in court and says, 'Your Honor, my client changes his plea to guilty on all counts.' "

"Wow. And he never told you he was going to do that?"

"Never! He never said a word to me. And I had things to say. I didn't mean to bother the children! I was just lovin' 'em up!"

"You were 'lovin' 'em up' with two dogs on them."

"Sure! They loved the dogs. The children always came to the dogs!"

"You'd corner the children with the dogs."

"Listen! Have you ever seen a schoolyard? The little kids are always in the corners! The dogs didn't put 'em there! The dogs would go see 'em. They'd call the dogs!"

Fletch made a gesture of impatience at himself. "I don't mean to harass you."

"I understand all about it! I had things to say. See, there was this psychiatrist who spend a lot of time with me when I first went to prison. I felt guilty about my sister. When we were little kids I pushed her behind my father's car when he was backing out of the driveway. She got crippled from that. My father got mad. He went away. Never heard from him. See? I was tryin' to make it up to little kids. I was just lovin' 'em up. Tryin' to love 'em up."

"A psychiatrist told you all that?"

"Helped me to realize it, he said. I was sick. I had things

to say at that trial. Habeck just fucked me over, and threw me to the pits.''

Fletch shook his head. ''How did you get so fat in prison?''

''None of the crews wanted me on 'em. None of the work crews. I was sent to the prison farm. I'd go in a corner. They all knew all these terrible things about me, from the newspapers.'' Felix Gabais was sobbing. ''If Mr. Habeck was going to tell the court I was guilty of everything, why did he let the newspapers wreck my sister so long?''

''So you killed Habeck.''

''I didn't kill nobody!'' Felix's angry, reddened eyes blazed at Fletch. ''I needed to be gotten off the streets. The dogs were dead! I had to be wrecked!''

''But not your sister.''

Felix pointed at himself with both hands. ''I'm going to go out in the streets and kill somebody? I'm a wreck!''

''You're pretty angry at Habeck.''

''I don't want to go in the streets for nothin'! The mattress, this chair, I had to have. What day is this?''

''Wednesday.''

''Thursday. Tomorrow. I have to go to the parole office. You'll come with me?''

''What? No.''

''My sister can't come. It's way downtown.''

Fletch stood up. ''I think you'd better check in with your parole officer.''

''You won't come with me?''

''No.''

''What are you going to do about my sister?''

''Have I heard that question somewhere before?''

''Now that you finally show up, you just wanted to sit and hear the story of my life?''

''I wanted to hear you say you murdered Donald Habeck.''

''Who are you?''

"I.M. Fletcher."

"You're not from the public agency?"

"I said I'm from a newspaper." Fletch was standing at the door of the room. "Didn't you hear me?"

Felix Gabais's eyes grew huge. He tried to get up from the big chair.

Fletch said, "The *News-Tribune*."

Felix fell back into the chair. He switched the beer bottle to his right hand.

Fletch ducked through the door. In the dark outer room he bumped into Therese Gabais's wheelchair.

The beer bottle smashed against the doorframe.

Therese Gabais said, "My brother doesn't like the newspapers."

"I understand."

"Blames 'em for everything," Therese Gabais said.

Down Twig Street, Fletch ducked into his car quickly.

Opening the door of his car, Fletch had seen the car Biff Wilson used, lights, antennae, and NEWS-TRIBUNE all over it, stop in front of number 45447.

37

"555-2900."

It was exactly twelve-thirty.

There were many places Fletch felt he ought not be. His apartment was one. The *News-Tribune* was another. Driving around the streets without his driver's license or car registration, both of which had been taken by the police with his wallet and keys, and, with the police prone to recognize him as Alexander Liddicoat, the robber, and probably looking for him as Irwin Maurice Fletcher, angel-dust merchant, also struck him as imprudent.

So, after he watched Biff Wilson lift himself out of his car, button his suit jacket, and lumber into number 45447 Twig Street, Fletch drove into the used-car lot. He parked his Datsun 300 ZX in the front row of used cars, facing the street. All the other cars in the row, bigger than his, nevertheless were newer and cleaner.

No car salesmen were around. Undoubtedly they were off reenergizing their smiles and chatter with soup and sandwiches.

Fletch took a cardboard sign off the windshield of another car and put it on his own. The sign read: SALE! $5,000 AND THIS CAR IS YOURS!

Seated behind the FOR SALE sign in his car, Fletch could make his phone calls. He also could watch number 45447 Twig Street.

Cindy answered immediately. "Fletch?"

"You feel okay?"

"Sure. Why not?"

"Sorry about the pizza last night."

"Isn't that what men do? Negotiate with women and then walk out on them, ignoring their agreements? I mean, even about bringing back pizza? It was no surprise to me. Of course, Barbara mentioned being both hungry and disappointed in you."

"Hey, Cindy. Don't be angry. If you only knew what happened—"

"I don't want to be told. From what I know of men, they're as incapable of telling the truth to women as snakes are of singing four-part harmony."

"You've met a lot of snakes."

"I'm not doing this for you, Fletcher. I'm doing this for Barbara."

"Wedding presents are for brides and grooms, aren't they? Isn't that why, so often, there are rods and reels among the packages?"

"We all have to give men everything their little hearts desire so that a few of the good things of this world will dribble down to their dependent wives. Isn't that the way the world works?"

"You're doing it to screw Marta."

"That, too."

"Where are you?"

"None of your business."

"Cindy, I just want to make sure you're on a safe phone. That no one is listening in."

"No one is listening."

"Good. Who owns the Ben Franklyn Friend Service?"

"Okay. Wood Nymph, Incorporated, as I said. I got into the filing cabinet in Marta's office this morning. She spent most of the morning at the reception desk. Found references to two other corporations. One is called Cungwell Screw—"

"That's funny."

"A riot. The other is called Lingman Toys, Incorporated."

"Someone has a sense of humor. What's the relationship among these three companies?"

"I don't know. I wouldn't expect terribly accurate or complete evidence of ownership to be lying about Marta's office, would you?"

"No. But it's more of a lead than we had, I guess."

"I think Cungwell Screw and Lingman Toys are investors, owners of Wood Nymph."

"Any reference to any of the officers of any of the companies?"

Down Twig Street, Biff Wilson dashed out of number 45447. He slammed the door behind him. Looking back, he stumbled down the steps.

"Marta. President of Wood Nymph, vice-president of both Cungwell Screw and Lingman Toys. President of Cungwell Screw is a Marietta Ramsin."

The door of 45447 Twig Street opened again. Felix Gabais, empty beer bottle in hand like a football, stood on the front stoop. Really, he was a massive person.

Felix threw the empty bottle at the fleeing Biff Wilson.

The bottle hit Biff on the ear. It fell into the gutter and smashed.

"Jokes everywhere," Fletch said.

"And president of Lingman Toys is an Yvonne Heller.

Treasurer of all these companies is a man named Jay Demarest. I know him.''

"You do?"

The ground-floor window of 45447 Twig Street opened. Therese Gabais leaned as far out the window as she could from her wheelchair. She was shaking her arm and shouting at Biff in the street.

"Yeah. Comes in all the time. Uses the place, you know, as if it were all for him. Never gets a bill. Exercises, gets what he wants when he wants it.''

"What's he like?"

Now Felix was bending over as well as he could in the gutter and scooping up broken glass from his beer bottle.

"Actually, over the two years I've known him, he's gotten himself into pretty good shape, one way and another. He's in his thirties, not married.''

"Why would he marry, with the friends he's got?"

"What?"

Head tilted, hands pressed against his wounded ear, Biff turned back to attack Felix.

Felix threw the bits of glass in Biff's face.

"Nothing."

"I've even been out with him on dates, you know, as escort. When he takes friends out for dinner, that sort of thing.''

"What are his friends like?"

Brother and sister Gabais screaming at him from the street and the window, Biff hustled into his car.

"Losers. You know what I mean? People who think that if they ever get their lies properly organized they'll make it big and be as good as other people.''

"Do you think Jay Demarest is a real owner?"

Biff seemed to be having trouble getting his car started.

All the lights on the *News-Tribune* car began to whir and flash.

"I think he keeps the books, and orders the ground elk's horn. The fall guy."

"Being given a few good years and meant to take the fall for the real owners."

Now Felix was beating up the car. He kicked the rear left fender hard enough to rock the car and leave a good-sized dent. Arms joined at the fists, he landed his considerable weight on the car's trunk. That made an impression.

"Yeah. He and Marta better look out below. I think they're both just employees."

Biff's car engine roared.

"When can you have the rest of the stuff for me?"

Twice dented, lights whirring and flashing, rear end skittering, Biff's *News-Tribune* car fled down the street.

A stone Felix had ready in hand caught up to it and broke its rear window.

Skittering around the far corner, Biff almost hit a bus.

"Ah," Fletcher said. "The reportorial life does have its ups and downs, its ins and outs."

"What?"

Retreating slowly, unwillingly, back into their depression, Felix and Therese Gabais intermittently shouted and shook their fists at the corner around which Biff had disappeared.

"When can you have the other stuff?"

"Anytime you want to meet me, I'll be ready. I'm preparing a list of the services and charges. I've got the names and addresses of some of the clients. I've even pinched some of the still photographs and videotapes for you."

"Great! Any of Marta?"

"Sure. She's not beyond takin' a trick now and again. She has her vanity."

"Jay Demarest?"

"You bet. Marta probably took those, to keep Jay in line, should the need ever arise. Nice lady, uh? All in the same cesspool together."

"I don't want you to risk yourself, Cindy."

"Not to worry. You can't make pie without crust."

"What? Right! Sure. I suppose so. Will you be at this number later?"

The window and the door to 45447 Twig Street were now closed. Therese and Felix Gabais were now back inside their own morosity.

"If not, I'll be back. Don't call me at Ben Franklyn."

"Course not. Marta would ask me when I'm coming to work."

In the street in front of Fletch, a police car cruised by slowly.

Alston Chambers said, "Glad you called. I've been trying to get you. Your apartment doesn't answer, the beach house doesn't answer, your car phone hasn't answered. No one at the newspaper seems to know where you are. I've got some news for you. By the way, where are you?"

"At the moment, I'm hiding out in a used-car lot disguised as a satisfied mannequin in a Datsun 300 ZX."

"Why didn't I guess that?"

"I need a couple of favors, old buddy."

"Why should I do you favors? Aren't I already marrying you off, Saturday, or something?"

"Cause I'm trying to find out who murdered your boss, ol' buddy."

"Not even a topic of discussion around here. Bunch of cold-blooded bastards. It won't interest anyone at Habeck, Harrison and Haller who murdered Donald Habeck unless and until they get to defend the accused, always presuming he or she is rich, or, good for publicity. By the way, who did murder Donald Habeck?"

"You're always good for the obvious question."

"That's my legal training."

"I don't know who killed Donald Habeck. So far, I have

spent time with each member of the Habeck family, and I believe any one of them could have and would have done it, if, and that's a big if, any of them knew Habeck was disinheriting them in behalf of a museum and a monastery.''

''Monastery! What in hell are you talking about?''

''I forgot. You and I haven't talked lately. Believe it or not, ol' chum, I believe a liar for once told the truth.''

''And no one believed him?''

''Of course not. I believe Donald Habeck really wanted to give five million dollars to the museum and, knowing how to use the press, by making the announcement through the press, embarrass the museum into accepting the gift and promising to use it to develop a collection of contemporary religious art. Of that Habeck crafty scheme, I and the *News-Tribune* were to be the unwitting tools.''

''Telling the truth once in your life doesn't make you a monk. Does it?''

''I believe Donald Habeck wanted to enter a monastery. If you can believe any of my insane and otherwise unreliable sources, you can believe it. Over the years, he had taken religious instruction. He had not divorced the only wife he ever had. She had been permanently endowed in an institution years before. Maybe Donald was trying to relate thusly to his son, a monk. Maybe they each had the same instinct. Maybe, as sometimes happens, the son, thinking he was rebelling from his father, instinctively and inadvertently perceived and fulfilled his father's innermost ambitions. Also, of course, Habeck was not lying when he said no one cared 'a tin whistle' for him. No one did. Plus, lately Habeck had been reading Russian novels, in which icons abound and the theme of personal withdrawal is very strong, especially as written by Dostoevsky.''

There was a long pause before Alston next spoke. ''Er, Fletch?''

''Yes, Alston?''

"Do you also believe you are following approved, police methods of investigation here?"

"Of course I am. Why not?"

Alston's voice sounded distant from the phone. "I've never known the police to consider the victim's recent reading list as evidence of anything."

"Why not? What better way is there of knowing what a person is thinking?"

"Back to hard facts." Alston's voice became stronger. "You know Habeck and Jasmine never married?"

"Donald and Louise never divorced. I know Jasmine is not Mrs. Habeck. I know she isn't even Jasmine. Which brings up one of the favors I ask, ol' buddy."

"Jasmine isn't what?"

"She thinks she's in the Federal Witness Protection Program. In fact, while she was giving evidence in a trial in Miami, Donald Habeck absconded with her."

"In the middle of her giving testimony?"

"I believe so. Donald apparently gave her the impression she was through testifying, free to go, and that he was some sort of an official. Jasmine has a one-cell brain. She believed him because he was a lawyer, was kind to her, in his fashion, and, I suppose, wore a nice suit."

"He did have nice suits," Alston mused.

"Not from the internal view. Would you please ask a federal officer to call upon her at Palmiera Drive and attempt to straighten out her life for her? She might still have evidence which would interest courts in Miami, as well as points north and west."

"That's a favor? Sure. Always glad to get in good with the feds. My news is that Donald Habeck did indeed have a will, drawn up five years ago, and not altered since."

"And this will stands?"

"Yes. Under its terms, everything goes straight to the

children of Nancy Habeck and Thomas Farliegh, as they come of age.''

"Wow! This shoemaker's children have shoes. Or will have.''

"Nothing remarkable about leaving everything directly to the grandchildren.''

"You haven't seen these grandchildren fight over a noisy toy tank.''

"Brats, uh?''

"Given an inheritance, the violence those kids will be able to raise might astound the Western World, as we know it.''

"Great. Sounds like they'll each need lawyers.''

"Of one sort or another.''

"And you don't think their papa, the poet of violence, bumped off their grandpapa?''

"What Tom Farliegh is best at is engineering mud into his babas' maws.''

"Come again?''

"Violence is not natural to Tom Farliegh. He gets it from his in-laws.''

"I was hoping you'd pin the punk. So none of the family bumped off Habeck?''

"Any one of them could have, including Louise, including Nancy, even including the son, Robert, who is a monk. Each in her or his own way expressed the sentiment, *to hell with Donald Habeck*. Two elements, one big, one small, bother me. The big one is that I can't establish that any of them knew before Donald was murdered that he planned to disinherit them all in behalf of a museum and a monastery. Of course, it's hard to prove what people know and when they know it. But with the wife in an institution, the daughter in squalor, and the son in a monastery, when each says she or he didn't know the change in Donald's life and death plans, how can one not believe them?''

"A lawyer never believes anyone, and that's the truth.''

"The weird thing that bothers me is how these people get around. Would you believe, in this day and age, none has a car? The Farlieghs' car is just one more broken toy in their front weed-patch. Robert's use of vehicles is limited. Louise sits in cars until their owner comes back and takes her where she wants to go, ultimately. None would seem to be able to time things, such as murder, too well. I don't think the murderer drove into the parking lot of the *News-Tribune*, but how did he or she get there without a car?"

"Pardon me for saying so, Fletch, but there are other lines of investigation to be followed. I hope you're leaving something for the police to do. Wash out my mouth, but Habeck's partners, for example."

"You're right. But the family came first. Donald Habeck was about to announce he was disinheriting them. That's a clear motive for murder, isn't it?"

". . . The list of his present and past clients . . ."

"Yeah. I saw Gabais. Habeck used him for publicity; in Gabais's words, wrecked not only him, but his crippled sister. Hates Habeck. But I don't think Gabais could organize himself enough to do murder. I think he pretty well gave up on his life when he saw his dogs' heads bashed in."

". . . Stuart Childers."

"Yeah. Tell me about him. How strong was the evidence that he killed his brother?"

"Very strong, but, unfortunately, all self-admitted. I've got the file somewhere here on my desk. Thought you'd want it. Here it is. Richard was the elder brother, by about two years. A complete playboy. Never worked, never married, sponged off his parents, hung out with the yachty set, wrecked about one sports car a year. In his last car wreck, the girl who was with him was killed. Variously over the years Richard had also been charged with possession of small amounts of controlled substances, paternity twice, vandalism, one case of arson. He tried to burn down a boat shed. His parents always got him off.''

"Using Habeck, Harrison and Haller?"

"Yes. That's how I know."

"Parents are rich?"

"You've heard of Childers Insurance. Biggest, oldest, richest insurance brokerage firm in the city.''

"On City Boulevard, right?"

"That's where their main office is, yes. Stuart, on the other hand, was the good son, dutiful, diligent, all that, never any trouble, graduated college with honors, worked for Childers Insurance every summer since he was sixteen, entered the firm as a qualified broker the November after he graduated."

"Good son, bad son, bleh," Fletch said.

In the street in front of him, another police car cruised by slowly.

"After the last car wreck, in which the girl was killed, Mama and Papa Childers turned Richard off. No more family money for him. He had to prove himself, go get a job, stay out of trouble, et cetera, et cetera."

"There's always an *instead* right about here in this story."

"Instead, Richard proved himself by blackmailing his brother. Or attempting to."

"What had Stuart done wrong?"

"Gotten his honors degree by cheating. Paid some instructor to write his honors thesis for him. Richard, of course, never graduated from college, but had contacts at the old place, knew the instructor, et cetera."

"And the thought of being exposed, especially to his parents, proven to be no better than his brother, drove Stuart crazy."

"So he said."

"Who said?"

"Stuart said. Richard was found dead on the sidewalk

fourteen stories below the terrace of his apartment. There was lots of evidence of a fight having happened in the apartment, turned-over chairs, tables, smashed glass, et cetera. Stuart's fingerprints were found in the apartment. So were others'. Because of Richard's wild acquaintance, the inquest's finding was Death by Person or Persons Unknown.''

"I know Stuart confessed.''

"Loud and clear. He walked into a police station late one afternoon, said he wanted to confess, was read his rights, taken into a room where he confessed into a tape-recorder, waited until the confession was typed up, then signed it.''

"Enter Donald Habeck.''

"Donald Habeck entered immediately, as soon the Childerses knew their son was at the cop house confessing to killing his brother. Habeck ordered an immediate blood-alcohol test. Apparently, Stuart had braced himself with almost a quart of gin that day, before going to confess.''

"So the confession was no good?''

"Not only did the cops know he was drunk while making the confession, they even gave him maintenance drinks, of whiskey, to keep him going during the confession, and before he signed.''

"How could they be so stupid?''

"Listen. Cops try to get what they can get before the lawyer shows up. And that's usually when they make their mistakes.''

"*In vino veritas* is not a tenet of the law, huh?''

"In Habeck's own handwriting, I read you from the file: '*In court, keep Stuart sedated.*' ''

"They drugged him.''

"Right.''

Fletch remembered Felix Gabais saying, *"You know what a defendant feels like at a trial? He's in a daze. . . . What they're sayin' has nothin' to do with what you've always thought about yourself. . . . You're struck dumb. . . .''* "Maybe they needn't have bothered.''

"The confession was found inadmissible by the court. And, even though Richard and Stuart were known not to be friends, Habeck pointed out that a person's fingerprints found in his brother's apartment is insufficient evidence for the charge of murder, especially when there were many unidentifiable fingerprints there.''

"You said everyone has a right to the best defense.''

"Of course.''

"Even involuntarily?''

"I don't know. All Habeck had to do here was raise a question of reasonable doubt, and that's what he did.''

"Stuart Childers confessed!''

"Now, Fletch.''

"What?''

"Now, Fletch . . . Have you always meant absolutely everything you've said after too much to drink?''

"Absolutely!''

"If I believed that, I wouldn't be talking to you. Or you to me.''

"In *vino* a germ of truth?''

"Inadmissible. Especially when the *vino* came out of the cops' locker.''

"I give up.'' At the edge of the used-car lot a man wearing a ready smile and a lavender necktie dropped a lunch bag from a fast-food store into a waste receptacle. "In behalf of leaving no stone unturned, I guess I better go see Stuart Childers. The cops won't listen to him again.''

"Maybe he keeps confessing to every crime in town just hoping for another free drink at the police station.''

"I've listened to every other nut in town. Might as well listen to him.''

"Got a story to tell you.''

"No more stories.''

"You like stories about lawyers."

"No more, I don't."

"I remembered that in the old days, when my grandfather was a lawyer in northern California, lawyers used to charge by the case, rather than by the hour. So in their offices they would saw a few inches off the legs of the front of the chairs their clients would sit in. You know, to make them lean forward, state their case, and get out."

"What's funny about that? The chairs in modern fast-food restaurants are designed that way."

"What's funny is that when lawyers began charging by the hour instead of the case, they all bought new chairs for their clients, and sawed a few inches off the back legs. You know? So the clients would relax and talk about their last vacations?"

On the sidewalk, the car salesman stood, arms akimbo, smile ready, looking for a customer.

Fletch cleared his throat while Alston laughed. "My second favor, ol' buddy . . ."

"Yes?"

"Would be a real favor. Three corporations called Wood Nymph, Cungwell Screw, and Lingman Toys. . . ."

"I don't think they're on the exchange."

"Even the telephone exchange. I need to know their relationship to each other. And, of most importance, who owns them."

"I'll trace them right now."

"No need. Anytime within the next half-hour will do."

"No. Seriously. I'll do it right now."

The salesman spotted Fletch sitting in the Datsun. "Doesn't Habeck, Harrison and Haller give you any other work to do?"

"Not anymore. I resigned from Habeck, Harrison and Haller an hour ago."

"What?"

Alston Chambers had hung up.

*   *   *

"So. How do you like it?" the used-car salesman asked
Fletch through the car window.

"Like what?" Fletch asked.

"The car. Want to buy it?"

"I hate it." Fletch turned the key in the ignition. "Listen
to that! Muffler's no damned good!"

To the amazement of the used-car dealer, Fletch put the
Datsun in gear, roared off the lot into the street, and away.
The FOR SALE sign blew off the windshield and landed on the
sidewalk, not far from the salesman's feet.

38

"You're from the *News-Tribune?*" Stuart Childers looked young and neat in his business suit and necktie behind his wooden desk. He looked basically healthy, as well, except for bags of sleeplessness beneath his eyes. His teeth kept tearing at his lips.

"Yes. Name of Fletcher."

"I take it you're not here to see me about insurance?"

"No. I'm not. The doorman at your apartment house said you were here at your office."

"You may be the answer to a prayer." Stuart Childers took a .22 caliber revolver from the top drawer of his desk. He placed it in the center of the desk blotter in front of him. "If I'm not arrested for murder by five o'clock today, I intend to blow my brains out."

"That's some threat." Fletcher sat in a chair facing the desk. He quoted, "'When the gods wish to punish us, they answer our prayers.'"

The office was small but paneled with real wood. There was a Turkish rug on the floor.

"You want to find out who murdered Donald Habeck, is that right?" Childers asked.

"That's the job of the police and the courts," Fletch answered.

"The police!" Childers scoffed. "The courts! Oh, my God!"

"I want the story," Fletch said. "I'm a journalist. My own purpose is to understand Donald Habeck, as much as possible, and why he was murdered."

"Have you gotten far?"

"Yes. I've gotten some good background."

Childers contemplated the handgun on his desk. "I murdered Donald Habeck."

"The hell you say."

"The police won't listen to me."

"You've confessed to everything that's gone down in this area in the last two months."

"I know," Childers said. "That was a mistake."

Fletch shrugged. "We all make mistakes."

"Don't you think we have a need for punishment?" Teeth tearing at his lips, Childers looked to Fletch for an answer, waited. "If we are being punished for what wrong we did, at least we can live with ourselves, die with ourselves." He waved his fingers at the handgun. "Just going bang is not the better way."

Still Fletch said nothing.

"What do you know of my brother's death?"

"I know you were drunk when you confessed to the police. I know Habeck kept you drugged during the trial."

"Yes. Tranquilizers. Habeck said he always gave them to his clients during a trial. I had no idea how strong they were. The trial went by in a blur, like a fast-moving railroad train." Childers's teeth worried his lips. "I murdered my brother."

Fletch said, "I expect you did."

"How is that forgivable?" Again, he seemed to be asking Fletch a real question. "Richard said he was going to blackmail me, for money to keep up his whacky, careless life. Even if I was paying him, he couldn't be trusted to keep his mouth shut. His need to hurt me, and my parents, was too great. My mistake was that I was horrified at the threat of the college, the world, my parents learning that I had cheated, hired an instructor to write my honors thesis. I went to Richard's apartment. I didn't intend to kill him. We fought like a couple of shouting, screaming, crying, angry kids. Suddenly we were on his little balcony. Suddenly the expression on his face changed. He fell backwards. Fell."

"You confess very convincingly."

"I woke up on the other side of the trial. I was back living in my apartment, coming to work here every day. Everybody was telling me the incident was over, closed, that I had to get on with my life. How could I get on with my life? The so-called incident wasn't over. My parents knew I had cheated on my honors thesis. One son was dead. The other son had murdered him. And my parents knew it. I had destroyed my parents' every dream, every reality. I might as well have killed them, too." From the way he was looking at him, Fletch knew another unanswerable question was coming. "My parents did what they thought was best in hiring Habeck, in getting me off. But wouldn't they feel better in their hearts if their sole remaining son took responsibility for what he had done?"

Fletch said nothing.

"You asked for a story," Childers said.

"So you took to confessing."

"Yeah. I'd read enough about a crime to be able to go into the police and say I committed it. They had to listen, at first. I'd make up evidence against myself. That was my mistake.

The evidence wouldn't check out. So they wouldn't believe me at all."

"You're sure you just didn't want to play a starring role in court again?" Childers gave him the look of a starlet accused of being attractive. "Some people get a kick out of that."

Childers sighed and looked at the gun.

"Stuart, you can't be tried again for murdering your brother."

"I know that. So I murdered Habeck."

"Now the story gets a little hard to swallow."

"Why?"

"Murdering your brother was a crime of passion. Two brothers, very angry with each other, probably never having been able to talk well with each other, finding each other tussling, hitting each other, all kinds of angers at each other since you were in diapers welling up out of your eyes. And one of you got killed. That's very different from the fairly intellectualized crime of killing the person who had prevented your receiving punishment for the first crime."

"Is it? I suppose it is." He looked sharply at Fletch. "Frustration is frustration though, isn't it? Once you've taken a life, it becomes easier to take another life."

"That's a cliché. People who commit crimes of passion seldom do so again. The object of your rage was dead."

"Couldn't I have transferred my rage from my brother to Habeck?"

"Keep trying, Stuart. You'll work it out."

"Who says a person who commits a crime of passion, as you call it, isn't capable of commiting an entirely different, rational murder?"

"What's rational about your murdering Habeck? The son of a bitch got you off!"

"Yes, he got me off!" Leaning forward on his desk, Childers spoke forcefully. "And the son of a bitch knew I was guilty! He obstructed justice!"

"In your behalf! You're the one who is walking around free!"

Childers sat back. "I don't know that much about the law, but I'd call Donald Habeck an accessory to murder, after the fact. Wouldn't that be about right? Think about it."

Fletch thought about it.

"How many times was Donald Habeck an accessory to a crime, after the fact?"

Fletch said, "Before the fact, too, I suspect."

"What?"

Fletch remembered saying to Louise Habeck, about her son, Robert, *"Shooting his father would accomplish two goals, wouldn't it?"* And her answering, *"Splendidly!"*

"Okay, Stuart. If you shot Habeck because you wanted to be punished so much, how come you didn't stay there? How come you weren't found standing over him with the gun?"

Childers smiled. "Would you believe I had to pee?"

"No."

"Go shoot someone, and see what happens to your bladder." Sitting behind his desk, Stuart Childers was then speaking as evenly as someone might discussing a homeowner's fire-and-theft policy. "I did wait there. I had thought someone would hear the gun. I shot Habeck sort of far back in the lot, where he parked. I shot him as he was getting out of the car. No one was around. The guard at the gate was talking to someone entering the parking lot. I could see him. I waited. I had to pee in the worst way. I mean, really bad. I didn't want to have to go through the whole arrest process, you know, having shit my pants. So I went into the lobby of the *News-Tribune* and asked the guard there if I could use the men's room."

"Why didn't you come out again? There were police, reporters, photographers who would have been interested to actually see you at a scene of one of your crimes."

"I felt sick. Jittery."

"That would have been understood."

Stuart Childers said something Fletch didn't hear.

"What?"

"I wanted a drink. A few drinks before I gave myself up."

"You wanted to get drunk before you confessed again, is that it? What did you supposedly want, Stuart?"

"I wanted to get control of myself. I went home, had a few drinks, a bath, a night's sleep. In the morning, I had breakfast. Then I went to the police station to confess." Childers shrugged. "A gentlemanly routine, I suppose. I was brought up that way."

Fletch shook his head. Then he asked, "How did you know Habeck was going to be in the parking lot at the *News-Tribune* a few minutes before ten on Monday morning?"

"I didn't. Murdering Habeck was something I decided over the weekend. So Monday morning, I drove to his house. Got there about seven-thirty. Waited for him. He drove out of his garage in a blue Cadillac Seville. I followed him. He drove to the *News-Tribune*. While he talked to the guard at the gate, I parked outside and walked in. It was the first stop he made. When he opened his car door, I shot him."

"Then you had the irresistible need to pee."

"I had been sitting in my car since before seven o'clock! Then, after I peed, I felt really sick in the stomach. My legs were shaking. I had a terrible neck ache." Childers rubbed the back of his neck. "I wanted time! Isn't that understandable?"

"I don't know. You say you wanted to get caught, but you ran away. There is no evidence at all that you were at the scene of the crime. Everything you've told me so far, that Habeck drove a blue Cadillac Seville, that he was shot at the back of the lot getting out of his car, all that was reported in the press."

"Sorry if my story conforms to the truth."

"You didn't confess until after you'd been able to read the details of the crime in the newspaper."

Childers stared at the gun on his desk.

"Okay, Stuart. What did you do with the murder weapon?"

"You know what?"

"What?"

"I don't know."

"You don't know what you did with the gun?"

"I don't know. When I got home, I didn't have the gun. I've tried to remember. I was upset. . . ."

"You had to pee."

". . . Tried to reconstruct."

"I bet."

"I couldn't have had the gun in my hand when I walked into the lobby of the *News-Tribune*. I must have thrown it into the bushes."

Fletch watched him carefully. "You threw it into the bushes in front of the building?"

"I must have."

"What kind of gun was it?"

"A twenty-two-caliber target pistol."

"Stuart, your twenty-two-caliber target pistol is on your desk in front of you."

"I bought that last night. The one I used on Habeck I've had for years. My father gave it to me on my sixteenth birthday." Childers grinned. "He never gave Richard a gun."

"Oh, my God!"

"What?"

Fletch stood up.

Childers said, "Why didn't the police find the gun?"

Fletch said, "Why didn't you find the gun?"

"I tried to. I went back to look for it. It wasn't there."

Fletch nodded to the gun on the desk. "May I take that?"

Childers put his hand over it. "Not unless you want to get shot trying."

"Oh, no," said Fletch. "That would just put you to the bother of confessing again!"

39

"Hello, hello?" Fletch heard his car phone buzzing while he was unlocking the door.

"This is the *News-Tribune* resource desk. Name and code, please."

"Oh, hi, Mary."

"This is Pilar. Code, please."

"Seventeen ninety dash nine."

"Mr. Fletcher, you're wanted at a meeting in Frank Jaffe's office with Biff Wilson at three o'clock."

"Oh. That's what's happening."

"That's what's happening."

The dashboard clock said two-twenty. "Doubt I can make it."

Pilar said, "The rest of the message from Mr. Jaffe is, 'Either be in my office at three o'clock for this meeting, or don't bother coming back to the *News-Tribune*, period.'"

"Life does offer its choices."

"So does the *News-Tribune*. Any last words?"

"Yeah," Fletch said. " 'And that was all he wrote.' "

Glancing time and again at the clock on his dashboard, Fletch sat in the parked car and thought, for as much time as he had.

When it became too late to make the *News-Tribune* reasonably by three o'clock, he started the car.

Slowly, he pulled into traffic and headed toward his apartment.

"Alston? I know you haven't had the time . . ."

"Sure, I've had the time, ol' buddy." Fletch's car was slouching down the boulevard's slow lane toward home. "As soon as I announced my resignation from Habeck, Harrison and Haller this morning, a woman came by and took all the folders from my desk. Even the case I was working on! What do you think of that?"

"Oh, yeah. You resigned. Tell me about that."

"I didn't become a lawyer to become a crook. I don't think they'd mind right now if I went home and only came in Friday to pick up my final paycheck. Maybe I will. Want to meet at Manolo's for a beer?"

"Alston, I don't think there's going to be anyone at my wedding on Saturday who is employed."

"Don't tell the caterer. By the way, ol' buddy, wedding present from your best man will be forthcoming, never fear, but, obviously, a bit late."

"Aren't I supposed to give you a present, for being best man, or something?"

"Are you?"

"That will be late, too."

"As long as the wedding comes off on time, and it's a rollicking affair."

"Yeah." Fletch stopped the car to let a pigeon investigate a cigar butt in the road. "Rollicking."

"So, for the last hour or so, using the considerable resources of Habeck, Harrison and Haller, I've been working for you. Don't worry: you can't afford it.''

"That's the truth.''

"About those companies you asked me to look into . . . Are you ready?''

"Yeah.''

"Lingman Toys and Cungwell Screw seem to exist for the sole purpose of each owning half of Wood Nymph, Incorporated. In turn, Lingman Toys and Cungwell Screw are owned by one corporate body called Paraska Steamship Company. All this is a typical structuring of corporations designed to discourage curiosity and conceal interests. The purpose of all these corporations seems to be none other than owning a single business called the Ben Franklyn Friend Service, essentially a whorehouse, situated at . . . '' A woman in chartreuse shorts, halter, and high-heeled shoes was walking a poodle on a leash along the sidewalk. The gray of the woman's hair matched the poodle's. The woman's shorts were cut halfway up her ass cheeks. Alston was reciting the names of the officers of the various corporations. Names kept being repeated, Jay Demarest, Yvonne Heller, Marta Holsome, Marietta Ramsin. The woman and the dog turned into a passport-photo shop.

"Alston, okay, stop. Who the hell owns Paraska Steamship, or whatever it is?''

"Four women.'' Alston then began to repeat, recite a mishmash of names.

Fletch stopped at an orange traffic light. The car behind him honked. "Say what? Say again?'' A police car drew alongside Fletch. The cop studied Fletch's features carefully.

Alston repeated the names.

" 'Bye, Alston!'' He dropped the phone in his lap.

Fletch stomped on the accelerator.

He went through the red light, made a U-turn in the middle of the intersection, and went through the red light again.

The police car pursuing him did the same thing.

* * *

"Lieutenant Francisco Gomez, please. Emergency!"

It certainly was an emergency. There were now two police cars pursuing him through city streets. His trying to outdrive them while talking on the car telephone clearly was a traffic hazard.

"Who's calling?"

Fletch hesitated not at all: "Biff Wilson."

He put on his left directional signal and turned right from the left lane. Not a good enough trick to throw off his pursuers, but it did cause noisy confusion at that intersection.

"Yeah?" Gomez sounded as if he were in the middle of a conversation instead of beginning one.

"Gomez, Biff Wilson's in trouble."

"Who is this?"

"Fletcher, a.k.a. Alexander Liddicoat. Remember us?"

"Shit! Where are you?"

"Hell, don't you know?" Fletch spun his wheel mid-block and scurried down an alley. "I thought the police were the eyes and the ears of the city."

"What are you talking about? What's all that noise I hear? Sirens? Screeching tires?"

"Yeah, thanks for the police escort. I am in a hurry. Have you got the forensics report on that gun yet?"

"What gun?"

"The gun I gave you. The gun I told you about."

"Who cares about that? Kid tryin' to make a name for himself . . ."

"You haven't even looked into it?"

"You're as bad as Charles, what's his name, Childers, Stuart Childers. Want to play cops and robbers. You want to be the cop, he wants to be the robber."

"The ballistics report ought to be ready by now, too."

Fletch had a moment of comparative peace as he went wrong-way up a one-way street.

"I've got a warrant out for you, Fletcher. Possession of a seller's quantity of angel dust. I've got the evidence right here on my desk."

"I look forward to seeing it." Three police cars spotted Fletch at the corner. They accelerated after him. "Aren't you hearing me, Gomez? Your pal Biff is in trouble."

"Yeah?"

"At the newspaper. He's in Frank Jaffe's office. On the carpet, you might say. In danger of losing his job."

"No way."

"You know it's possible."

Gomez said nothing.

Fletch turned on his lights and pulled into the middle of a funeral cortege. Demonstrating little respect, the three police cars screamed by the cortege.

"He needs your help," Fletch said. "He needs the ballistics and forensics reports on that gun. Immediately."

"Yeah?"

"Would I lie to you?"

"What is this?"

Fletch turned off his lights and ducked down a side street. "As soon as you've got the reports, call the *News-Tribune*. Ask for Frank Jaffe's office. Biff's in Frank's office."

Two blocks up from the next corner, a police car hesitated in the middle of the intersection. As soon as the police saw Fletch's car, they turned and came after him, lights flashing, sirens screaming.

"Gomez, you want to see Biff out on his rear?"

The line went dead.

Fletch dropped the phone in his lap again. He could see the roof of the *News-Tribune* building. The three police cars were back in V formation pursuing him.

There were only two more corners to skitter around. . . .

40

"Hey! You can't leave your car there!"

The guard in the lobby of the *News-Tribune* was known to get red-faced easily. Fletch had left his car half on the sidewalk at the front door of the *News-Tribune*.

Fletch was on the rising escalator to the city room.

"What?" he asked.

At the bottom of the escalator, the guard looked toward the front door. "What are all those sireens?"

"I can't hear you," Fletch said. "Too many sireens."

He passed Morton Rickmers, the book editor, in the city room.

"Did you see Tom Farliegh?" Morton asked. "Is he worth an interview?"

"Naw," Fletch answered. "He's a little, blue-haired old lady in green tennis shoes."

Morton wrinkled his eyebrows. "Okay."

Through the glass door of Frank's office, Fletch saw Frank, behind the desk, and Biff Wilson, in a side chair. The color of their faces was compatible with the color of the face of the guard downstairs, now doubtlessly talking to six policemen.

Frank's secretary said, "You're late."

"It's all relative." He breezed by her.

Fletch closed Frank's office door behind him. "Good afternoon, Frank. Good of you to ask me to stop by." Frank's watery eyes took in Fletch's T-shirt, jeans, and holey sneakers. "Good afternoon, Biff." Biff's jaw tightened. He looked away. His right ear was swollen and red. Fletch commiserated. "That looks like a real ouch." Biff's face was splotched with little cuts from having glass thrown in it. "Lucky for you none of the glass from that beer bottle got in your eyes." Biff looked at Fletch wondrously. Fletch said to Frank, "That's nothing. You should see the *News-Tribune* car Biff drives. Big dents. Rear window smashed. Doubt you'll be able to get much for it on the used-car market."

"How the hell do you know about it?" Biff demanded.

"I'm a reporter." Fletch sat in a chair. "Well, Frank. I'm glad to report that Mrs. Donald Habeck does not slip vodka into her tea. In fact, the poor thing doesn't get to have any tea at all. I've learned my lesson in humility. Never go out on a story with preconceptions. Right, Biff?"

Frank said to him, "I'm surprised you showed up."

"Frank," Fletch said. "In a moment your phone is going to ring. It will be police lieutenant Francisco Gomez calling Biff. He knows Biff is in your office. I would like you to take the message for Biff, please."

"Jeez!" In his chair, Biff threw one leg over the knee of his other leg. "Now the wise ass is telling you what to do!"

Through the windows of Frank's office, Fletch saw six uniformed policemen milling around the city room.

"What's going on between you two guys?" Although high in color, Frank was trying to sound reasonable. "Fletch, Biff tells me you're screwing up in ways even I can't believe. Everywhere he goes on this Habeck story, you've already been there, screwing up, swimming bare-assed in the Habecks' pool, so upsetting Habeck's son, a monk, he refuses to see Biff, angering another suspect so much that when Biff shows up this thug throws a beer bottle in his face. Twice." Fletch was grinning. "It isn't funny. You know you weren't assigned to the Habeck story. Ann McGarrahan and I made that perfectly clear to you. There are easier ways to get fired."

"No rookie should ever come anywhere near me," Biff said. "Especially no wise-guy punk screw-up."

Frank smiled to himself. "I thought you'd burn off your excess energy over the whorehouse story. Instead, last night I heard you say you can't do that story."

"I can do it."

"You said you needed more time on it. Maybe if you spent your time on the story assigned to you instead of bird-dogging Biff . . ."

Through the window, Fletch saw Morton Rickmers talking to one of the policemen. Morton pointed toward Frank's office.

"Screw it." Biff made a move to get up. "This is a waste of time. Just can the son of a bitch and let me go back to work."

"Do you like bullies, Frank?" Fletch asked. "I don't like bullies."

Frank forced a laugh. "Biff's been with the *News-Tribune* all his adult life. You've been with us what? Three months? He's the best crime reporter around. He's got a right to do his work without being bird-dogged by a screw-up kid."

"He's a bully," Fletch said. "I don't like bullies."

"You went after Biff because he's a bully?" Frank asked. "Like hell. You went after Biff because you thought you could beat him at his own story. Little you know."

"I have beaten him."

"Sure," said Biff. "You're ready to wrap up the story of the Habeck murder? Like hell!"

"Right," said Fletch. "I am."

Frank was watching Fletch closely. "I told you two days ago, Fletch, Monday, that we've had about enough of your crap around here. I thought if I gave you a real assignment, the Ben Franklyn whorehouse story—"

"I've got that about wrapped up, too." Fletch looked at the silent phone on Frank's desk.

"Sure," Biff said. "Tell us who killed Donald Habeck, wise ass. We can hardly wait to hear it from your lips. A member of the family, I bet. Crazy Louise? No-brain Jasmine? Daughter Nancy left her five kids in wet diapers and ran out and shot her pa? How about her husband, the two-bit poet? Or better yet, the monk, Robert? Tell us the monk murdered his old man. That will sell newspapers."

The telephone on Frank's desk wasn't ringing. At that moment, Fletch would have appreciated some factual evidence. He took a deep breath. "Stuart Childers murdered Donald Habeck."

Biff laughed. "Jeez! I'll bet you know that 'cause he confessed to you!"

"Yeah," Fletch said. "He did." Biff laughed louder. "Gotta listen," Fletch said. "Sometimes liars tell the truth."

Frank looked through his office windows at the city room. "What are those cops doing out there?"

Six of them stood around Frank's secretary.

"A criminal is a victim of his own crime," Fletch said to Biff, "as you'll come to understand, I think."

The phone rang. Outside, the secretary was too busy with the police to answer it.

Frank picked up the phone in annoyance. "Hello! . . . Who is this? . . ." He glanced at Biff. "Lieutenant Gomez . . . Yeah, Biff is here. . . . No." Then Frank glanced at Fletch. "You tell me the message, Lieutenant. . . . The gun? Okay . . . Twenty-two-caliber pistol. Registered to Stuart Childers . . ." Biff looked up. "Stuart Childers's fingerprints . . ." Frank glared at Biff. "... Ballistics ... It is the gun used to murder Donald Habeck.... Right. I'll tell him...." Slowly, Frank hung up.

Frank sat back in his chair, hands folded in his lap. He looked from Biff to Fletch and back to Biff.

Biff sat erect, looking as alert as a rabbit.

- Outside the office, the hubbub made by the six policemen was rising noticeably. Clearly, two were arguing with each other. Each was pointing through the window at Fletch.

The secretary, too, had raised her voice.

Irritated, Frank asked, "What's going on out there?"

"Okay." Biff straightened the crease in one trouser leg. "Gomez has been working closely with me on the Habeck murder." He cleared his throat. "That call was for me."

"You didn't even know he was calling," Frank said.

Outside, Hamm Starbuck had arrived. He stood between the police and the door to Frank's office.

Fletch leaned forward in his chair. "Now, Frank, about the Ben Franklyn story ..."

"Fuck off!" Biff shouted.

Frank raised his eyebrows. He said to Fletch, "Tell me."

"The Ben Franklyn Friend Service is owned by Wood Nymph, Incorporated," Fletch said. "Which is owned by two companies, Cungwell Screw and Lingman Toys." Frank, looking from Biff to the ruckus outside his office door to Fletch, nevertheless appeared to be listening. "Cungwell Screw and Lingman Toys are entirely owned by Paraska Steamship Company, which is owned entirely by four women, Yvonne Heller, Anita Gomez, Marietta Ramsin, and Aurora Wilson."

The blood splotches disappeared against the color of Biff's face.

Outside now, even Hamm Starbuck was shouting.

Frank looked at his telephone. He said, "Anita Gomez." Then he looked at Biff. "Aurora Wilson." Frank moved his chair closer to the desk. "Gomez and Wilson. I guess you two did work closely together.'' He reached for his phone. ''And that's how the pictures of those whores got on my sports pages Monday morning.''

Biff exploded. ''Son of a bitch!''

''Matt?'' Frank said into the phone. ''Frank Jaffe. Draw up a severance check for Biff Wilson. I want him out of here by five o'clock. Fired? Yes, fired. Not another minute's protection does he, or his enterprises, get from the *News-Tribune*.''

Biff jumped to his feet. His hands were fists. ''You son of a bitch!''

He took the few steps toward Fletch and swung.

Fletch rolled off his chair, tipping it over onto the floor.

The door opened.

Hamm Starbuck said, ''I'm sorry, Frank, the cops, something about Fletch.'' He looked at Fletch on the floor. ''What are you, a rug fetishist?''

Biff swung a kick at Fletch, but Fletch rolled away from it.

The cops poured into Frank's office. Fat, slim, old, young, they were arguing with each other loudly. They were pointing fingers at each other and, occasionally, pointing fingers at Fletch on the floor.

Biff, feet planted either side of Fletch, bent over. He picked Fletch up by the neck.

''Alexander Liddicoat!'' shouted one cop. ''I recognized him at the stoplight!''

''You didn't check his license plates!'' shouted another cop. ''We did! He's Irwin Fletcher, wanted for selling PCP!''

Fletch gurgled. ''Help! Police!''

''Armed robbery . . .''

''Were you asleep at roll call this morning?''

''Angel dust . . .''

''Listen, Fletch.'' Frank had come around his desk. Hands on knees, he bent over Fletch being strangled on the floor by Biff Wilson. Clearly, Frank was concentrating hard. ''I want the complete story of Habeck's murder, Childers's confession and arrest in the morning edition. Gomez said they're arresting him this afternoon. The other press will have the story of the arrest, but we'll have complete background. Also the news that he confessed to a *News-Tribune* reporter. You'll do a follow-up for the Saturday newspaper.''

"Grrr-uggg!" Fletch was trying to force Biff's arms apart.

"Cut that out!" Frank hit Biff's forearm.

"Every traffic violation in the book!" shouted a cop. "Whoever he is, we got him on all that! Even a broken muffler!"

Frank continued. "We want a complete wrap-up, all the background, on the Habeck story, for the Sunday newspaper. We'll need that by six o'clock Saturday.''

Hamm Starbuck, after wondering awhile what he was witnessing, took action. Fletch's face, having gone from red to white, was turning blue. Putting his arms around Biff's shoulders, he locked his hands under Biff's chest. He lifted.

Not letting go of Fletch's neck, Biff lifted Fletch higher off the floor.

Six policemen argued vehemently.

The phone was ringing.

Frank stood up as Fletch rose. "Now, what about the Ben Franklyn story? I think that ought to be treated as an exposé in Sunday's newspaper. We'll publish teaser-promos on it tomorrow, Friday, and Saturday. That means we'll need that story, complete, by midday Saturday, for pictures.''

Hamm finally wrestled Biff off Fletch.

Biff's grip on Fletch's neck broke.

Fletch fell flat on the floor. His head bounced on the carpet.

"Can you do that?" Frank asked.

Grabbing breath, Fletch said, "I'm getting married Saturday!"

"Ah, the hell with that!" Frank turned away in disgust. "There's no sense of sport in this business anymore!"

He looked around his office.

In one corner, Hamm Starbuck was struggling, restraining Biff Wilson.

Five cops were arguing with each other about Irwin Fletcher, angel dust, Alexander Liddicoat, armed robberies, and traffic violations. Two had their night sticks drawn.

The sixth policeman was bending over, trying to put handcuffs on Fletch.

Fletch's hands were rubbing his throat.

Almost the entire city-room staff was looking through the door and windows into Frank's office.

"What's going on!" Frank yelled. He grabbed the arm of the policeman about to handcuff Fletch. "Cut that out! I need him!" The cop did stop. "Jeez," Frank said. "Whatever happened to the sanctity of the newspaper office!"

"'Just a breath of fresh air,'" Fletch quoted from the floor, "'a young maverick who would shake things up a bit...'"

Frank Jaffe's secretary leaned over him. "Fletcher, there's a woman on the phone who says she must talk with you. She says it's urgent."

"'...See things differently, maybe,'" Fletch quoted as he got to his feet, "'...jerk people out of their ruts.'" On his feet, he swayed. "That was my assignment, wasn't it, Frank? Isn't that why I was hired?" Frank had six policemen talking to him, mostly at once. Fletch muttered, "Some ruts are deeper than others."

Among the people marveling through the office door was Ann McGarrahan. A smile played at the corners of her lips.

Hamm Starbuck was talking into Biff's ear. Biff nodded affirmatively twice. Hamm released him.

Straightening his jacket, then making fists of his hands again, Biff skirted all the arguing policemen. He marched out of the office.

"Biff!" Fletch held his throat as he shouted after him. "I know a good lawyer! He's available!"

The secretary said, "She said her name is Barbara something-or-other."

Frank was saying, loudly, to the assembled police, "Look, guys, he can't go to the police station now. He's needed here." Frank watched Fletch pick the phone up off his desk. "I'll go with you to headquarters. Straighten things out myself."

"Hello, Barbara!" Fletch croaked into the phone. "I won't be able to make it to dinner with your mother tonight. Not tonight. Not tomorrow night. Not Friday night. Absolutely. I've got work to do. Got a job. I'll try to see you Saturday. Wait a minute. Hang on . . ." Fletch put his hand over the receiver. "Frank?"

At the side of the room, Hamm Starbuck was breathing deeply.

Frank, surrounded by policemen, looked at Fletch.

"When I do the story on Ben Franklyn," Fletch asked, rubbing his throat, "you want me to report the full particulars of the involvement of Biff Wilson, late of the *News-Tribune*?"

"Damned right." Frank grinned. "Screw the bully."